OOTBALL
BABYLON

FOOTBALL BABYLON

**ALL THE SCANDAL BEHIND THE
BEAUTIFUL GAME – BY THE MAN WHO
HAS SEEN AND HEARD IT *ALL***

MEL STEIN

Pennant Books

First published in hardback 2008
by Pennant Books

Text copyright © 2008 Mel Stein

The moral right of the author has been asserted.

British Library Cataloguing-in-Publication Data:
A catalogue record for this book is available on request from
The British Library

ISBN 978-1-906015-16-9

Design & Typeset by Envy Design Ltd

Printed and bound in Great Britain by Creative Print & Design,
Blaina, Wales

Pennant Books
A division of Pennant Publishing Ltd
PO Box 5675
London W1A 3FB

www.pennantbooks.com

ABOUT THE AUTHOR

Mel Stein is a prominent sports lawyer and football agent, who has represented many national team players. He qualified as a solicitor in 1969, and cut his teeth in the field of entertainment law. In 1980 he decided to change direction and began representing sportspeople – including the great Geordie trinity of Chris Waddle, Alan Shearer and Paul Gascoigne.

He is also the author of eighteen books, including the official biographies of Gascoigne and Waddle; a guide to becoming a sports agent; a fictional trilogy set in the world of football (*Marked Man*, *White Lines* and *Red Card*) and, most recently, a much acclaimed guide to how to complain – fittingly entitled *How to Complain*.

Mel is also a regular contributor to Talk Sport, Radio 4, Radio Five Live, and frequently provides insider comment on football to the TV networks.

For my wife, Marilyn, who will perhaps now understand that, when I am watching endless football matches, I really am working.

For my sons, Nicky and Paul, who realised from a very early age that football was more important than any matter of life and death.

For Jonno, Cressie, Beatts, Redders, Waddler, JO, PW, AR, and all the players who stayed loyal to me throughout their careers and became my friends.

For AAK, AA and JP, and all the other good guys in football who help to make it a beautiful game.

And finally, to all of those of who shared their stories with me when I was writing this book.

JUNE

"This is a great adventure for us."
The Chairman, 1st June

The promotion party seems a million light years away. Probably just as well, given the way everybody let their hair down. Even I allowed myself a glass of champagne. Mind you, I was the only one sober by the end of the evening.

I like to be in control, like to be able to remember everything. I'm the one person at The Club who can't afford to take his eye off the ball – not like the central defender we just got shot of. He had what we called 'moments' on the pitch, and he certainly had his moments off it, too. Like the time The Chairman had to pay off a girl who claimed that he'd raped her. She was probably right, but she'd had a fair amount to drink and, if you accept an invitation from three red-blooded footballers to go up to their hotel room, you should have a pretty fair idea of what's about to happen.

I suspect we'll see a bit more of that as the season goes on. The remedy will still be the same, the price may just be a bit higher. The Chairman has a slush fund set aside just for things like that. (It has other uses as well.) I try not to get myself involved. But, as The Club Secretary, it's hard to turn a blind eye. And it's getting harder.

I've been at The Club for over twenty years. Nothing goes on here that escapes my notice. Not just here, either: club secretaries have their own jungle telegraph. We gossip amongst ourselves. We know what every tabloid would love to know, but we never sell our stories, never write kiss-and-tell autobiographies. We are the invisible men of football, yet without us clubs would simply not work. Yet some things need to be told, because without that knowledge you would never understand the world of football. It's not just twenty-two men and a ball on a Saturday afternoon. It's worlds within worlds, each darker than the one you have just travelled through. Turning the pages of a season's calendar is like turning the pages of a whodunit.

When I first joined The Club we were playing in the old Gola League, as it then was. And now we're in the Premiership. We all have to pinch ourselves to believe it, but it really is true. I look at some of the teams we were playing back in that 85-86 season: Barnet, Wycombe Wanderers and Cheltenham are the only three who are in the Football League at all – Cheltenham in League One, Barnet and Wycombe in League Two. Of the rest, only a handful are even in the top tier of the Football Conference – or Blue Square Premier, as it calls itself. Some of the others have simply gone into freefall, with Scarborough going into liquidation – just three years after they were narrowly beaten by Chelsea in the FA Cup. Yet here we are about to face Chelsea in the Premiership, with visits to Old Trafford, the Emirates, Anfield and St James's Park thrown in for good measure.

Goodness knows what they are going to make of it when

they come down to the Basin. We've added a few bits and pieces over the years, and we've had to do some work to bring us up to the necessary standard for a Premiership ground, but basically it's still the ground where Thamesmead City have played for years. We've had a running battle with the Local Authority, all of whom – instead of basking in the glory of having a top team in the borough – seem determined to make life as difficult as possible for us.

The showers in the visitors' dressing rooms are inconsistent, to say the least, when it comes to hot water; the pitch has an interesting slope, just within the permitted tolerances; the catering is organised by The Chairman's brother, who also runs a greasy-spoon café in Walworth Market. Personally, I think the food's better at the café.

I listened to a conversation between them the other day.

"We need to cut down on our catering budget," The Chairman said.

"The only way I could do that is to serve cat food," his brother replied.

"Well, the test of a good cook is to make cat food taste like haute cuisine," was The Chairman's parting line.

As a compromise, he's done away with free alcoholic drinks and we now have a pay bar – probably the only club in the Premiership which is going to make visiting directors buy their own drinks. (They're going to love that.) And at the same time as they're asked to buy their own drinks, they're also offered a programme and charged for that as well. Mind you, it's not all bad news: the team sheets that get distributed just before kick-off are free.

We do have a Board of Directors ourselves, but The Chairman appointed them all and, although he technically allows them a vote, if he doesn't like the outcome he either ignores it or, as a gesture to democracy, calls another meeting. By this time, unsurprisingly, all those who previously voted against him have had a change of heart.

"I don't know why he doesn't just change his name to Mugabe and be done with it," one director said to me the other day.

But The Board like the perks that go with the job too much to take the risk of being removed. The meals at home may not be much, but we've had some crackers at some of the clubs we've visited. Delia Smith at Norwich always comes up with something special, while West Bromwich Albion and Leeds United always provide great food and wine. Not sure what's going to happen at Elland Road, now that they've slipped down the league – but maybe they can fry the goldfish that Peter Risdale, their former chairman, had floating around his office at great expense.

It's not just the food that's the bonus, either. There are free tickets for England games, FA junkets, all sorts of expenses that I have to find a way to hide in the books – not to mention the tracksuits and kit, medical equipment and sponsors' products that get stashed away in their cars at regular intervals. People enjoy being the directors of football clubs, particularly if they don't have to put any money in and don't have their names on bank overdrafts as guarantors. All they have to do then is just strut the stage when they travel.

Our lot have been a bit spoiled of late, because we've been on the way up. I know of clubs where the directors don't even leave their cars in the car park because they know they'll be keyed whilst they're watching their team get tonked. Sometimes, the abuse gets so bad that they just stop going to the home matches altogether. It used to get so personal that their own houses weren't even safe from attack, but now that the clubs have websites the abuse just gets posted online. I reckon that anybody who buys a club, for any reason other than to make money from a property development, is out of his tiny mind.

But then it's not for me to say. I just get on with my job.

Other clubs who have risen from lowly origins have promoted their club secretaries to the role of chief executive officer, or finance director. Our Chairman doesn't work that way. He has an accounts department, and he has me. Everything else he does himself. I get to wrap up the sponsorship deals, but he negotiates them. I prepare the players' contracts, but he negotiates them. I pay the agents' fees, but he agrees them. I deal with The Managers on a day to day basis, but The Chairman hires and fires them.

It's a benevolent dictatorship, with the accent on the dictatorial side of things. He gets all the glory but, rest assured that, as soon as we start losing (and that's a given, now that we're playing at the top level and punching above our weight), he'll be looking for someone to blame. Chairmen are like that. There's nothing a manager fears more than a chairman's vote of confidence. It means that he should be putting his house on the market, basically.

I've managed to squeeze in one week's holiday with my kids. I got divorced about ten years ago. A wife would have to be a saint to put up with the sort of hours a club secretary has to work. And my wife wasn't.

On match days I'm here from seven in the morning till eight at night. For an evening match I start at the same time and leave about midnight. As there's always somebody calling me on my walkie-talkie, I never get to see much of the game. Then we have reserve games and youth matches, and the ladies team and events that involve the hiring of our catering suites. That doesn't cover the away matches when I can get back at about three in the morning, or the unexpected trip to Scotland with The Chairman when he decides we need to persuade some player to come and play for us. I had to get the holiday out of the way because, although the season doesn't start until August 11th, we've got the squad back for training from the first week in July and a whole host of trial matches and friendlies.

We've also got players to sign and contracts to renew, which means agents to deal with. I'm very wary of some of the agents. For the most part they come in, negotiate the deal for their player, agree their fee, sign off on the documentation – and then you don't hear from them again, unless they're on the phone for tickets for a big match. It's amazing how many people believe they have an absolute right to free tickets. And woe betide you if you give them ordinary tickets, or even try to charge for them. They want tickets with bells on: directors' lounge; players' lounge; pre-match meals. I've no idea how they (or we) are going to handle the new Football Association football agents' regulations, which were introduced in September of last year. Now we aren't supposed to pay agents any more – that's down to the players. (Some chance.)

So June is a working month for me, even though everybody else seems to be on holiday. It's just me, the groundsman, the ticket office staff and The Marketing Director, we're all here and we're rushed off our feet. We've laid a new pitch and the groundsman is terrified it won't take in time. Everybody is coming out of the woodwork for season tickets. At that last game of the season, when we gained automatic promotion, we could have sold out the stadium six times over. We had a capacity of eighteen thousand, we've managed to build a few more seats and push that up to twenty thousand, but we also have to cater for away fans, and the big boys are not going to be very happy when we only allocate them five thousand tickets.

So that leaves me with about eight thousand season tickets in our main stands that, come hell or high water, are going to be in use for our fans. The other seven thousand we'll put on sale on a month-by-month basis. The Chairman thinks he'll be able to charge more when the big clubs come to town. The odd phone call gets through to me with the caller claiming to be a lifelong fan, and not to have missed a match since our non-league days. I have a few questions I ask then: Who was our reserve keeper in the two seasons we spent in the Conference? Who was our top scorer in the old Nationwide League 3? Who was The Assistant Manager in League 2? If they can answer all of them then I might help them jump the queue – but it's never happened yet.

The Chairman is on his yacht for the first fortnight of the month, but seems to spend most of his time on the phone to me. How he finds the time to run all his other businesses I don't know. He's got a property development company, a car dealership and a ticket agency. At the time I joined he was still selling used cars off The Club's parking lot and offering tickets to hot West End musicals as an incentive to persuade players to join The Club. I'm told that, when we were back in the lower divisions, he made the same offer to a referee. But as we lost the match in question, I doubt the ref got his front circle seats for *The Phantom of the Opera*.

Generally speaking, The Chairman has had to become more respectable. I'm told that, just before I arrived, there was a 'dumb' turnstile at The Club where the takings were only in cash and the spectators that passed through were never added to the official gate. The Chairman's then wife (he's since moved on to a younger model) would turn up at halftime, empty the cash into a wheelie-basket and toddle away with it back to their house, to count it and stash it away. The remnants of that may still form part of the slush fund – though I suspect his other business activities provide him with a fair amount of ready cash.

However, his respectability is hardly complete. He has a son who fancied himself as a goalkeeper, and at least one manager departed after refusing to select him. The Chairman's Son is now an agent. He also happens to be The Agent for our current Manager. And, amazingly, he's been appointed by his dad to supervise all player sales and purchases for The Club.

No nepotism there then. I'm sure he's very good at his job.

I have to say though, I've always found The Chairman rather likeable – indeed, he can be generous. That's not always the case with wealthy men. One chairman I know, who could buy out about fifty percent of the guys he meets at League meetings, still keeps his elderly parents in abject poverty. (Maybe they did something to upset him when he was growing up. Like taking away his table football set.)

It's going to be a hot June, we're told. It's certainly going to be for me. The new administrative centre is not yet complete, so I'm still working from the portacabin with the tin roof. I'm the cat under the hot tin roof, the one who doesn't get the cream. After twenty years though, I may well be the cat with nine lives. But I've used a few of those already, so we'll have to see what this season brings.

The phone rings. It's The Chairman again.

"My boy's coming in a bit later. He's bringing in a new player. I've agreed the terms. Just get the contract drawn up will you?"

He tells me what to say in the press release. I switch on my screen and begin to type.

June. Midsummer. Football never sleeps. And, just lately, it seems that neither do I.

JULY

"I have a number of targets and The Chairman is backing me to the hilt."

The Manager, 1st July

It's that time of year. We're back from our pre-season tour. Didn't go too badly, but it did show we have some dealing to do before we even have a chance of staying up. Fortunately, nobody got injured and nobody got arrested either, both of these being serious risks when you take a bunch of footballers abroad.

Most of them haven't looked after themselves during their summer holidays. Still full of late nights and too many cocktails, they're overweight. One player used to take diuretics as soon as he got back, to get rid of a few pounds before the new season's weigh-in. Another used to run in dustbin bags, so the plastic helped him sweat and reduce weight. But the more drastic, the more artificial the means, the more dangerous they are.

As for arrests, there are so many stories of what goes on in pre-season tours they could fill a book of their own. One of my best friends in the game is secretary at a famous club who took their players off to Cyprus, at a time when there were more British troops there than in either Iraq or Afghanistan. Their manager at the time himself had a reputation for drinking and womanising, and turned a blind eye when the players went off on a tour of the local clubs and bars.

A couple of them got lucky and pulled two English girls, who were pretty much the worse for wear by the time they got back to the hotel – ready and willing, but somewhat incapable. The players took them up to their rooms, where the girls flaked out. But, as the players left them alone, one of their team-mates nipped in and, after a brief moment of awareness from one of the girls, took his chance and had his way. The next day all hell broke loose. It turned out that the girl was the daughter of a high-ranking officer in the British Army, and an immediate panic set in amongst the ranks of the club.

She described the one who'd had sex with her as one of our foreign players. The club needed to avoid what could have turned into an international incident, but it was hardly surprising that there was no confession. The club then decided on another tack. They would aim a charm offensive at the girl; the manager was delegated the task. He and some of the club officials took her out and treated her like royalty. Flowers; champagne; the best restaurant in town. The flowers and the food were fine. The champagne was a mistake.

The manager, the girl and a few of the hardier club officials ended up at a nightclub.

"Okay, she's been with one of our foreign players. Let me show her how the English do it," the manager shouted at the top of his voice, then put his suggestion to the proof in his own hotel room.

This time the girl didn't tell Daddy; she acknowledged she'd been a willing party to the first event, and everybody was able to get on with their lives.

My favourite story of a pre-season tour involves a player who was well-known as a practical joker. He arrived at the hotel with his team, inspected his room and then went down to the reception.

"Do you have anything on the fourth or fifth floors overlooking the street?" he asked.

They found him a room and his roommate reluctantly moved with him. A few minutes later he was back downstairs, this time looking for the kitchen.

"Do you have any fresh eggs?"

"How many do you want?" replied the hotel, which had a reputation for attending to its guests' every need without too many questions.

"Oh, about two dozen."

Without the raising of an eyebrow, the eggs were provided. The player galloped back to his new room, opened the window and then watched the cashpoint immediately opposite. As soon as somebody arrived to take out some money, he let fly. Startled, the person looked around but, seeing nobody, took the yolk-stained notes and left. This continued for hours, the player's accuracy improving until he could even hit the keys of the machine as the customers tapped in their PIN numbers. The eggs finally exhausted, the player returned to the kitchen for a fresh supply.

This continued day after day during his stay. He left behind a foul-smelling cash machine and a perplexed kitchen staff who never did work out what the Englishman was doing with his constant egg supply.

Meanwhile, back in England, we've got players we need to

get out and players we need to get in. For agents, it's a festival time. But we don't pay the wages of the big boys, so we either have to pick up the crumbs from the tables of the rich, or else dig for nuggets in the lower regions of the league – or even the non-league.

The Manager has a good record there. But the problem is that, once we find a decent player and he starts to make a name for himself, everybody gets interested. Rarely do the likes of Manchester United and Chelsea sign anybody from the Football Conference. They have their own youth development schemes (not that many of them come through that anyway), or else they just write out a cheque to buy whoever they fancy from abroad for twenty or thirty million.

That's why the kids don't get their chances. However good the home-grown talent may be, the manager of a big club will never admit he's better than someone for whom he's paid out big bucks. It makes him look stupid, and if there's one thing a football manager hates it's to admit he's made a mistake. When things go wrong they'll blame everybody but themselves. The board didn't give them enough money to spend; a star player was disruptive; they've had the worst string of injuries since the Somme; the referees have got it in for them; the fans didn't get behind them. You can write the scripts of their post-dismissal interviews.

So far as player development is concerned, clubs like us do all the hard work in finding the player, bringing him on, giving him the chance to shine, and then the big birds swoop down and carry him off. You can see their scouts in the stands; you can see the agents they use whispering in our player's ear after matches. All the time you look up and there they are, hovering like bloody birds of prey, just waiting to sink their talons into our emerging talent. And that's how we've stayed alive in the lower divisions, just by selling our best player every year and hoping we can replace him with yet another untried youngster The Manager has found in non-league football or even, in one famous instance, playing in his local park.

Contracts aren't worth the paper they're written on, as far as our players' loyalty is concerned. The way it works is that a top six Premier club identify their targets. They leak a story to a friendly journalist who faithfully mentions their interest in his column. That unsettles the player. He calls his own agent, who says he knows nothing about it but will find out. That unsettles the player too. He wonders if his agent is up to the job. The Premier club then get their favoured agent to 'tap up' the player. The greatest hypocrisy in football lies in the clubs' attitude to agents. They vilify them, but don't hesitate to use them when it suits. Tapping-up is the bane of our lives, and all it takes is a phone call.

"Don't sign a new contract, so-and-so is going to buy you."

And there we are, suddenly up against a brick wall in our contract renegotiations, which had been going really well up to then.

You always know when it's happened. Everything is fine, you're down to the last details, and then suddenly you're back to square one. Sometimes the player's own agent is involved, but at other times he's also out of the loop. The player's been told by the other agent that he, and he alone, can get him a move to the club of his dreams. He's told to dump his long-established agent, and then the scam really starts to kick in.

The new agent begins to act for everybody. He tells the buying club he'll deliver the player . . . for a price. He tells the selling club he'll get them the best price . . . if they give him a chunk of it. And now he's telling the player he'll get him the best deal. I've known an agent take money from all three parties, and I don't think any of them knew they weren't the only ones paying him.

As I mentioned, the Football Association brought in a whole load of regulations to make things more transparent. Clubs, players and agents all have to sign documents setting out who is paid what; nobody can act for more than one party and everybody has to have a contract with everybody else.

And all it does is make life difficult – if not impossible – for the good guys. The bad guys just work their way around it: cash payments; offshore bank accounts to receive monies for offshore services that are never provided; mysterious salaries and retainers to shadowy figures who may, or may not, exist. That's the dark underbelly of the game. All the regulations in the world won't stop a crook being a crook.

Sometimes it's actually the manager of a club who starts the ball rolling. One well-known Premiership manager promised an agent £40,000 as a commission for a particular player. The agent was young and just starting out in the game. He turned up at the club with the player, to find the club's secretary had been told that the fee was to be £20,000.

But worse was to follow. Another agent, who suddenly appeared on the scene, was a good friend of the manager. It soon became apparent that he was about to act for the club, for a fee of £20,000 – exactly the amount by which the young agent's fee had been reduced, coincidentally but not surprisingly. The other agent and the manager left the meeting with broad smiles on their faces, each having pocketed £10,000 for doing precisely nothing.

That's not to say directors are above turning a dishonest

penny. One of my fellow secretaries relayed a conversation he wasn't supposed to have heard between one of his club's directors and an agent.

"Listen, I'm a bit short of cash this month, so if I double your agency fee can you help me out by splitting it with me?"

It seems the agent didn't know which way to turn. He eventually extracted himself by persuading his player to go to another club and then lying to the director.

"I did my best to get him to come to you, it was in my interests wasn't it? But he wasn't having any of it."

Another very high-profile manager was called in by his chairman after an expensive foreign player was sold. The chairman was unhappy because the manager had made £1m out of the deal, pretty much the same amount as the club. The manager just smiled enigmatically, challenging the chairman to prove it. The chairman couldn't, but the manager left the club soon after. Many years later, he's still finding it impossible to get another job in the game. Football is a village, and spreading gossip takes no time at all.

Today, at least, we're not at risk of that. There's a big deal happening – big by our standards, anyway. I've not sat in on the negotiations. There are reasons why The Chairman doesn't like me there. He's happy for me to know enough to do my job, but not so much as to compromise me. (Or him, in the final reckoning.)

I've just been told to draw up the contracts. There's one between us and the player, obviously – that's a standard Premier League agreement, and I just have to insert the particular financial terms that have been agreed. But there's another between us and The Agent, who it seems brought the player to us. All I know is that he's acted for the player in the past, and that The Chairman's Son works for him. (Which is why we're not at risk of the sort of scam I just mentioned.)

I haven't even questioned the fact that the player has signed off on a document that says nobody acted for him. I haven't questioned the size of the fee paid to The Agent, even though it's equivalent to about half of the not inconsiderable transfer fee. Nor have I told the player that, even though The Agent has certified that he's acted for The Club, the Inland Revenue may not accept it and may well assess the player for tax by way of a benefit in kind.

That's what I would have had to do if The Agent had admitted he was really acting for the player, and we'd paid his fees *on behalf* of the player. Mind you, when we've gone down that route, I've had the player in question running in to complain to me about the whopping deductions of tax from his monthly salary. I point out that he signed off on it. He says that he didn't understand. They always say that. They're so keen to get to The Club that, at that stage, they'll sign anything that's put in front of them. But when it comes to paying for the service, well, that's a different story. With professional footballers in general, it's the same when it comes to paying for anything.

We always use one private hospital for treatment for our players. I've forever got their pharmacy on the phone to me, saying they can't let our lads have their prescribed medicines because they're refusing to pay and referring the bill to me. Sometimes it's just a tenner. They earn thousands of pounds a week but they won't pay for their own drugs.

We always pay – just as we pay for their car insurance, their legal fees, their hotel bills . . . once we even paid for a player's girlfriend's abortion, to make sure that his wife never found out. We knock it off their wages. That way it doesn't feel like the player is paying. It's almost like a stealth tax, not that they'd understand the analogy. (Or indeed what an analogy is.)

I've heard the player talking to The Agent. The Agent's assured him that he'll be at the top of our wage scale. (In fact, what he's earning is way off of it.) "Look," he says, "he's The Club Secretary, he'll confirm it."

I just nod and say nothing. I don't lie, but silence can also be deceitful. To be honest (if you'll forgive the phrase), there's not a lot that goes on here that keeps me awake at nights. The player will lie about what he earns anyway. They all lie to each other. That wouldn't be so bad, but it makes for a nightmare when it comes to contract renewals. They all know they're lying, but it suits them to believe it so they can demand more money. It's all a bit like *Alice in Wonderland* – though if Alice were here for any length of time, she'd be fighting to hold onto her virginity.

Everything gets signed off; I fax it all through to the FA and the Premier League. 'The Premier League' has a nice ring to it; I wish I could believe that we'll be here for more than one season. The bookies don't give us a snowball's chance in hell, and The Chairman is already looking ahead to receiving his parachute payments when we go down. (They're the payments a relegated club gets for the first three years after its drop from the upper heights.)

So if you don't use that money wisely and get yourself back up, the odds are you'll have marooned yourself in the Championship for years to come. Or even worse – you might do a Leeds or a Nottingham Forest and tumble into League One; or you might face the ultimate doomsday of Bradford City, who are in League Two with the Conference beckoning if all goes wrong. Oxford United, who played in the old First Division in the Eighties, didn't even manage to get promoted back to the Football League after their fall from grace in 2005-6. It's a fine line between success and the doomsday scenario.

We have a clause in all our contracts saying that, if we get relegated, the players' salaries will drop between twenty-five and fifty percent. I don't point it out; it's not my job. I merely follow orders. And anyway, it's in the same size print as everything else. It's the player's agent's job to tell him what's in the contract. My responsibility ends when it's typed up.

Now we've made our buy we need to do some selling. The Manager went in to see The Chairman.

"The players who got us up won't be good enough to keep us up."

"So sell them," The Chairman replied.

Just like that. I was driving to a match with The Chairman once, sitting in the back whilst his chauffeur took the strain.

"Players. It's no different from selling second-hand cars. If they've got a fault under the bonnet and you know about it, there's no need to point that out to the buyer. "

They both like selling players. In The Chairman's case, it's because he hates overdrafts – though he shouldn't be too worried this year at least, as we've a cheque for over twenty million coming from the television monies, with more to follow. The Manager likes a good sale because he's on ten percent profit of every player he sells. That's why he's always looking for those bargains: the cheaper he buys, the higher he sells, the more there is for him. There's nothing illegal in that.

Other managers have similar deals, but they can lead to arguments. One manager got the sack and was claiming for years after that he was still entitled to his 'sell-ons'. It all got settled out of court, I've no idea how much he finally got. Where it all gets a bit messy is when a manager is also looking for kickbacks from an agent. You won't be surprised to learn that, for most of our sales, we instruct The Agent to find us the clubs and handle the negotiations.

The Chairman has the last word, of course, but as long as he thinks his son is earning out of it he's not going to be too difficult. I've always had this vision of a Dickensian thieves' kitchen where The Chairman, The Agent and The Chairman's Son all sit down and divide up their ill-gotten wealth. Maybe some days as well they have The Manager round for tea, though frankly I think that what goes on between The Manager and The Agent is a bit like what goes on in Vegas. It stays in Vegas.

We've got a striker who scored quite a few goals for us in the lower divisions, and I know The Manager's been calling in some favours. I'm not sure how much thanks he'll get when the club that buys him finds the striker is always injured. We're supposed to send on the medical records, and of course they'll make their own medical checks. But some injuries don't show up on x-rays or scans, and sometimes statistics can be misleading. This particular player looks like he's played most of the games, but we've often had to get him out on the pitch after a cortisone injection, just before kick-off. And I know that not all of those injections are down in his records.

Players don't complain. They want to play. They want the buzz and the bonuses. When they're arthritic at forty, they might look back and ask a few questions – but by then it'll be too late.

It's not the players who are at fault all the time. The clubs too can be pretty ruthless. I know of one player who was on loan at a club. The club told him they wanted to sign him. The manager got him into his office and told him not to bother with an agent who was offering a pretty good deal. The terms did look quite attractive, so the player signed.

The manager then tore the contract from the player's hands before the ink was dry, put it into the top drawer of his desk and turned the key. He shook the player's hand, welcomed him to the club and then – to the astonishment of the player – told him he'd just been sold. The door opened and in walked the chairman and manager of the buying club, with their contract for the player to sign. The terms were just a little bit better, the club just a little bit bigger, and the player was so shell-shocked that he went along with everything, gaining the selling club a chunky fee.

That wasn't quite as bad as the case of a manager who got a player into his office, told him to take a seat and then said, "Look son, I know your agent got you a decent deal when you came to the club, but I have to tell you he could have done better. I'm going to get you a new contract which will be better than anything he can do. So why not dump him, let me handle it with my chairman, and you give me 10k in cash when it's all done and dusted. If you trust me, I'll trust you."

The player called his agent in a panic to ask him what to do, being terrified of upsetting the manager upon whom his whole career depended. In any other business, the agent would have blown the whistle on the fraud. But, this being football, he knew it would make him a pariah as the manager had some powerful friends. He just regretfully told the player to do whatever he thought was best for him. The player used the manager, paid over the cash, and nobody was any the wiser. You shouldn't believe it when you read that they've abolished the slave trade.

That was particularly the case when one former England international, who'd served out more than ten years at one club, was told he could have a free transfer. He found a foreign club who offered a very attractive deal that would ensure him of a more than comfortable retirement. The foreign club arrived to finalise the deal, and then – to the astonishment of everybody – his present club demanded a fee. This was long before the Bosman case meant a player could leave for nothing at twenty-four, still at a time when clubs basically held players to ransom during their contracts, knowing they could still get a fee for them at the end. In fact, the poor player ended up paying the club he'd served faithfully some £80,000 just to get away, a lot of money in those days. So much money, in fact, that I hear he still has to work for a living.

I make no comment. I've been asked to do far worse things for my club. You can't have a conscience about anything in football, or else you would never sleep at night.

As far as our crippled striker is concerned, I get a call from a club secretary in the Championship. I know him well. He's telling me they've agreed terms for our crock. He's asking me if there's anything his club ought to know about the lad. What do I say? Not only do I know that if he were a horse he'd be shot by now, I also know we've had to 'look after' the police a few times after incidents involving him at local bars. I mumble something about him being married with kids. That's true at least – we've had his wife in here a few times, demanding that she gets his salary paid directly into her account before he pisses it away at the bookie's.

And his fitness? Rarely missed a game, I say.

I'm told to call him in, to tell him we've accepted an offer for him. He wants to know how much we will pay him to go. The Chairman tells him to fuck off, and that, if he doesn't go quietly, he'll be telling his wife about certain hotel-room incidents at away matches. He'll take the move, he decides. Within twenty-four hours, the deal is done. How he's passed a medical is a miracle. We've got a sell-on, so that if he's sold for a profit we get a slice. But I'm not holding my breath and nor, I think, is The Chairman, because if the striker gets to the end of the season and is still playing they'll be very lucky. We've got enough problems with the ones he's left behind.

AUGUST

*"This match and this sort of opposition clearly sets out
our ambitions for the season."*

The Chairman, 2nd August

It's our last pre-season friendly today. We've had to guarantee
a lot of money to this top Spanish club to get them to come.
And then we've had to pay The Agent to organise it all.

I've worked out that there's a considerable difference
between what we're paying out to the visitors and what
they're actually getting. It doesn't take a forensic accountant
to work out that the difference is going to The Agent – and
goodness knows where after that. The Agent is licensed by the
FA, but God alone knows how he keeps his licence. In fact he
got his licence in some offshore jurisdiction where football
plays second fiddle to golf, and where they weren't too keen
on his activities. It's not the sort of place that likes to attract
attention, so he was politely but firmly told to take his
activities elsewhere.

And so here he is, back in England and employing The
Chairman's Son. I'm not sure who else ever would. He's lived
off his dad for years and, in the unlikely event that he should
ever find himself in *Who's Who*, he would list his hobbies as

drinking and womanising. Presumably, what The Agent earns from The Club is a price worth paying for employing the equivalent of a village idiot.

For The Chairman's Son is not his father, and never will be. Whatever his failings, The Chairman is a shrewd and successful businessman who, unlike many other football chairmen, did not simultaneously throw good business practices out of the window as he acquired control of a club.

I know of one very successful, very wealthy entrepreneur who was such a big fan of a club that he actually bought it. This is the formula for disaster. He became the target for every agent and every club, who soon realised he would buy any player at any price with a view to impressing the club's supporters. They got relegated, his business went into liquidation and he was declared bankrupt. Amazingly, some years later he actually came back for more.

Then there was the chairman who so loved he club he'd bought that he decided to do everything himself. He designed the club shirts and programmes, even had a hand in writing the club song, and nothing happened unless he personally approved it. Talk about living the dream. I've little doubt that, had he been a few years younger, he'd have put himself on the substitutes' bench every week. Mind you, he at least had the charisma to attract some big players to the club. It was only when he decided to buy one star too many, when he'd run out of personal funds, that it all went pear-shaped. And after this disastrous attempt to live his dreams, he also popped up years later at another club. What is it about men and their toys?

As far as our friendly match now is concerned, I know I'm not going to earn any brownie points by pointing out to The Chairman that The Agent is earning from both sides. It's not perfect, but I've been in this job a long time and I'd quite like to keep it until I can take my pension. Club secretaries are a bit like Vicars of Bray. As long as we don't get political, don't get ambitious for a chief executive role and don't fall out with successive boards, we tend to be left alone to get on with our jobs. After a while you become the fountainhead of all knowledge at the club. Once you know what nobody else knows, once you know where the bodies are buried (assuming you haven't buried them yourself), then your job is pretty safe.

Today has been a day of problems. The Spaniards have contracted to bring their first team. Their office gave me all of their names, photographs, biographies etc for the programme. Then I get a call from the hotel where we've booked them in. They've insisted on first-class travel all along the line.

The receptionist at the hotel is a friend. We use the hotel all the time, so he needs to be. We give him the business and he tips me off whenever there's a player who needs to be collected after drinking the bar dry. Or before he gets some girl into trouble.

We always have problems with girls. Not the WAGs. By the time they get to the status of footballers' wives or girlfriends, they've stopped being a danger to anything other than their partners' credit cards. It's while they're in the *formative* stages that we have issues. Not only is kiss-and-tell every player's nightmare, but it's not great for The Club either to have its name all over the headlines for the wrong reasons. Once a club gets that sort of reputation via its players, then it tends to stick.

It's always the case that players with some value to them get treated differently from those who are worthless.

Particularly so when it comes to drugs or drink. A couple of high-profile players have been sent off for treatment and one, at least, instructed his agent to tell the club they should pay for a protracted stay in an expensive private clinic in the States, rather than him going to a local psychiatric hospital and paying for himself. When the club refused the player asked again, saying that a foreign stay would attract less attention than if he were just around the corner. Astonishingly, this time the club agreed and made him a loan which was never repaid.

All loans are meant to be documented and carry interest at a commercial rate – but there are loans and then there are 'loans'. Meanwhile, young kids who have smoked pot, got tested and been found positive are usually on the first bus out of town, their careers and reputations in ruins. (Unless they're really talented, in which case it's the private clinic for them as well.)

Everybody in the game has heard the story of a very talented seventeen-year-old who made his debut for a league club, then decided within twenty-four hours that the world of football wasn't for him. Some four years later, during which he'd become quite attached to drink and drugs, he was lured back. The night before his first game for his new club, he was out as usual, partying, drinking and smoking his favourite substances. (This was before dope-testing had really got underway.) He lasted half an hour into the game, and then was so violently sick on the pitch that they had to stop play to clear up his mess.

Mind you, this same player nearly made a third comeback a few years later, when a club with a substantial slope on its pitch tried to sign him

"Tell you what I'll do," he said, "I'll play half of each match, the half that's played down the slope. It's less of a strain on my legs," and the manager agreed. But the player then changed his mind, and that was the end of what might have been an illustrious career.

Not that drugs themselves aren't a pretty efficient way to shorten a career. Even with the introduction of drug testing, there are always some prepared to take the risk – particularly midweek, and a good few days before a match. Cocaine isn't endemic amongst footballers, but it's not an unusual substance to be found at parties either. Players like the buzz they get from snorting, and the delusion of grandeur that, although transitory, can be regularly revisited if they have the money. Or sometimes even when they don't, which is often a reason for them falling under the influence of dangerous individuals. We operate a zero tolerance policy here, but I can't say the same for all other clubs.

Mind you, some old-school managers actually encouraged a bit of drinking. Plonking a bottle of brandy on the dressing room table before the first match of the season, one said, "If any of you feel at any time during the year that you need a bit of Dutch courage before you go out onto the pitch, you can take a sip of that."

One of the younger players, going immediately for the bottle, took a huge swig and then felt himself hit on the back of his head so hard that he spat it all out again.

"I meant the older players, lad, not the underage drinkers!"

But back to tonight. Our call from the hotel wasn't about famous Spanish footballers leading underage girls up the stairs to bed. That I could have lived with, as it might have put a few more numbers on the gate. It wasn't to say that there were

Spanish orgies in the corridors either, it was far worse than that. The more famous members of the Spanish team hadn't even come.

My contact had checked the hotel register and, although the names of the guests were undoubtedly Spanish, he didn't recognise a single one of them. And he's a sucker for La Liga on a Saturday night. Some of them, he said, were young enough to have trouble pulling their football shorts up over their nappies.

I had to do some quick thinking. We had to pay most of their fee in advance to get them here, so we can't start threatening that we'll withhold their money. We could go public but our gate would be shot to pieces. If we say nothing then, once we get the crowd in, we'll have had their money; although they may well complain, we haven't made any contractually binding promises to them. We could call off the game completely, but I don't think The Chairman will go for that. We could see if they can fly in at least a few of the names they promised us, but I doubt we'd have time. (When it comes to Spain, things don't tend to move too quickly.) The best bet seems to be that we play the game and sue them for the return of the rest of their money.

We've given them a bank guarantee for the balance, but a quick call to our lawyer tells me we may be able to place an injunction on it. Given the involvement of The Agent and The Chairman's Son, it's not a happy situation. But then, The Chairman can still look after his lad from the money he's no longer paying to the Spaniards.

There's a very fine line between nepotism and downright dishonesty in the world of football. Knowing which side my bread is buttered, I prefer to look on the relationship as pure nepotism. Indeed, given the unemployability of the lad it could be viewed as charitable.

If we go down that route, everybody is happy – except for the poor fans. But they're always the mugs anyway. We'll be inundated with their complaints on the message board of our website, but by the time we kick off for real it'll all be forgotten.

Our Marketing Director has just taken delivery of The Club's new home and away kits. We'd only introduced a new kit at the start of last season, at which point The Chairman had sworn he'd be keeping that for at least two years, slagging off other clubs who chop and change their kits just to make a few quick bucks. And now here we are, just a year later, and last year's kit is as old-fashioned as a virgin in the team.

The Chairman has given his excuses. He should have been a politician really. Promotion has taken everybody – and him in particular – by surprise. He feels The Club and its supporters deserve something really special for our first year in the top flight. And even if we go straight down, he'll stick with these new shirts. But tell that to the poor supporter who's now got to shell out not only for his own replica shirt but for his kids' as well. We sell them for sixty quid a throw. Seventy if you want a player's name or your own embossed on the back. They cost us about twenty quid to have made, and that's offset by the money we get from our sponsors anyway. There's no way any kid wants to be seen dead in a team shirt that's even just one year out of date, so The Chairman can hear the cash registers bleeping even as he turns his Rolls-Royce into The Club car park. He thinks he's pulled off a PR coup by offering a ten percent discount, if the buyer can produce a receipt for the old shirt from last season. I reckon we might be looking to a hundred or so fans taking advantage of that generous offer.

LATER IN AUGUST

*"If you pay peanuts, you get monkeys.
But it's hard to compete with the big boys
when it comes to wages."*

The Manager, August 6th

First game of the season. Just our luck that we have to play host to The Champions. All week I've had their football secretary on the phone. Yes, they have one of those, and he has an assistant and then there's a general administrator, and a chief executive officer, and a director of football, and probably all of them have assistants as well.

And then there's me, and just The Chairman's secretary to help me, alongside the work experience lad who's going back to university in September. The lad's been pretty helpful. He's got the match day programme together virtually on his own, with just a bit of help from an ex-journalist who also happens to be a fan. That's pretty much how we've survived up to now. The Club Doctor doesn't charge, and nor does The Club Lawyer. They get seats in the directors' box, and we're happy to help them out when they want a few extra tickets for friends and relations.

Now we've got this windfall of millions from the television

deal, you would think The Chairman might have loosened the purse strings a bit. But no.

"If and when we go down," he told me, "I want as much money in our hands as possible so we have a soft landing. And what's the point of taking on people if we're only going to keep them for a year? Just not fair," he adds, talking like the most benevolent businessman in the country.

I would sort of agree with him if it didn't mean so much work for me. The last thing a club outside the Big Four needs is to be saddled with a huge wage bill, particularly when it's not absolutely certain of its top-division future. Frankly, nowadays it's only the top four who are certain of the future – I mean, I can't see Manchester United, Chelsea, Arsenal or Liverpool doing a Leeds. But then, nobody in football could ever have foreseen Leeds 'doing a Leeds' either. Or Nottingham Forest, former European Champions, playing in what would have been the old Third Division; or Wolverhampton Wanderers playing in the Fourth Division; or Sheffield Wednesday struggling the way they have. I always smile when I read the hacks writing about the beautiful uncertainty of the game. If you own or run a club, the uncertainty is an absolute nightmare.

We've got some uncertainty already. I've been watching the cars in the players' car park change over the years with much amusement. As soon as they get a bit of money, most of them feel the need to go out and buy a flashy car. Something for their team-mates to see, something that says they earn more money, that they can afford it. Then that need for status symbols spills over to other clubs' players, who have to outdo their rivals not only on the pitch but off it. They have to show off to their mates, their girlfriends and their families, even those they went to school with who may now be working in Tesco or Asda, stacking shelves.

I can't get my head around this obsession with expensive cars. One Premiership player owned eleven of them. He'd paid cash for none and found himself up to his eyes in debt. It wasn't helped when he lent one of the cars to a player at another club, who wrote it off. The mate wasn't insured (actually he was already banned), so he had to make out that somebody else had been driving it. That didn't stop the finance company repossessing it, and the player got into such a mess that, although he was earning well over half a million quid a year, his take-home pay didn't even cover all the interest on the car repayments. He'd had to keep borrowing and borrowing, from ever more dubious sources, and it was only the fact that his legs were his main source of income that kept them attached to his knees. He even thought of making himself bankrupt to bring his problems to an end. That's the thing with footballers: because they can't face any unpleasantness, they just want things to end.

There a few guys around who specialise in selling cars to players. Most of them are fine. They get the players great deals and in return they earn a few bob, and get to hang around their heroes. But there are a few rip-off merchants around too. One Premiership player was absolutely taken to the cleaners on cars. He was persistently overcharged, with second-hand cars sold to him under the guise of brand new vehicles. (*You* tell *me* how he didn't spot it – footballers just don't bother to look at anything remotely resembling paperwork.) Then they finally even tried to palm off a cheaper version of a car as the more expensive top-of-the-range item the player had ordered. The bloke was even charging VAT without being registered for it, just pocketing the extra money which the player couldn't recover. Eventually the player did lose his patience and threaten to sue. But when the car salesman just brazened it out, the player didn't have the stomach for the fight. He just paid the lawyer's fees and moved on.

That's why sharks circle around footballers, smelling blood in the shape of easy cash. It has to be said, they *do* ask for it.

It's not just cars, but jewellery too. Again, there are reputable suppliers who make a very good living because they don't let the players down and provide a personal service, saving the time and trouble of going shopping. That's a good example of the player being willing to pay over the odds, if it saves him effort and doesn't impinge on his quality time at the golf course, in front of the television screen, or at the snooker table.

And then there was the so-called jeweller who was making a fortune, until one of the brighter players took one particularly expensive item he had bought to be valued for insurance purposes, and discovered it was a fake. He still didn't sue, but he put the word out about his former supplier – despite that, players kept buying from him because they thought they knew best, and didn't want to look stupid.

'The Emperor's New Clothes' springs to mind. With these guys it's all about smoke and mirrors.

The car problem we have at the moment is with our Star Striker. The bloke scored twenty-five goals last year in our promotion run, and it was only the fact that he was an absolute pain in the dressing room that gave us the chance to keep him. He does have two more years of his contract to run, but that means nothing to a footballer (or his agent).

The Star Striker was an absolute disruptive influence at The

Club, however, and everybody knew it. Not only was he the worst trainer, but he was late most days and came up with the most remarkable excuses to prevent him being there at all. He told us he didn't have a driving licence or a car, and was dependent upon lifts from other players; nothing unusual in that, all clubs have one or more players banned from driving from time to time, and other players just like to travel in together. They meet up either at one of their houses or at a motorway service station, leave their cars there (if they're not banned!) and have a good old laugh on their way to training. That's better, I suppose, than one English player who went to play abroad and got lost on his first day on the way to the training ground, ending up driving an old motorbike the wrong way up a motorway.

So, given that The Star Striker told us he didn't drive, we were a bit surprised when the police turned up with a warrant for his arrest for driving uninsured whilst banned in three counties. It seems he'd had both a licence and a car at some point. He'd been speeding outside London, was asked to produce his insurance and, naturally, he didn't have any. So he got a six-month ban.

A few weeks later, back behind the wheel of a car (I suspect he never actually left it), he got stopped again by the police. Same story, only this time he panicked, giving the name of a mate who lived abroad, but neither he (nor – surprise, surprise – the mate) turned up at court. They issued a warrant for him, having tracked down the registration number of the car, and the police inefficiently tried to serve it at the address where he'd lived when at his old club.

It gave him the chance to go for a hat-trick, which he duly achieved by getting stopped again. This time it was for chatting on the phone whilst having no hands on the wheel of the car. I'd seen him in the car park before at the wheel of a team-mate's car, demonstrating how to drive with your knees. Although his fellow professionals were impressed, the police were less so.

This time one of the coppers was a fan who recognised him, so there was no giving a false name. But, once again, he thought if he didn't bother to attend court everybody would forget about it and the problem would just go away. If ever there were a team comprised solely of ostriches, they would probably win the Premiership, the FA Cup, the Carling Cup and the European Champions Cup for good measure.

There's no sticking his head in the ground and his arse in the air this time, however. We have a hearing date for him and, although we've got him a decent barrister, we're told that a custodial sentence is inevitable. Given the dates, we'll get a maximum of three games out of him before he gets banged up. Amazingly, he's expecting us to pay for his legal team, and he got very upset when I had to tell him The Chairman said the money would be deducted from his wages.

Still, that's footballers for you. Our last physio walked out, saying he needed to work with normal people! Mind you, he did take about a grand's worth of our equipment with him, not to mention some players' medical records which he'd never bothered to keep up to date.

And still the car park fills with expensive cars. I shudder to think how much it costs for these youngsters to get insured. One player who later became a manager demolished the wall of his own house in a rage when his team manager upset him, so he actually sent the manager the repair bill. That doesn't hold a candle to the player who stole the team bus and tried to take it on a joyride. Unfortunately, he didn't gauge the width of the vehicle and managed to get the bus stuck between the gates of the training ground, causing thousands' worth of damage to both bus and gates.

It's the lack of respect for property that amazes me. They lend each other £50,000 worth of automobile like ordinary folk lend paperback novels. At least one Premiership player specialises in writing off cars belonging to his fellow pros, yet it never seems to cramp his style when it comes to borrowing the next one. One fan suffered at the hands of a high-profile player years ago, when the player borrowed his pride and joy and discovered it was perfect for 'wheelies'. He left it much abused and covered in dust, with words of apology scrawled on the windscreen. Mind you, at least he paid for the damage. (This was the same fan who, after a night staying with the player, woke up to find his eyebrows shaved off and his hair dyed green, and still came back for more!)

To footballers the cost of anything seems an irrelevance, so long as the acquisition is an easy process. One of our players, somewhat more switched on than the rest, was going to buy a car from a guy who supplies loads of footballers. He appeared to be providing a real service, getting the cars they wanted, giving them a discount, delivering the cars to their door and giving them suitable loan vehicles when they were off the road. I say 'suitable' because, when a footballer needs a replacement for a Mercedes convertible, he won't be seen dead driving a borrowed Ford Mondeo. So this supplier gave a Mercedes for a Mercedes, a Porsche for a Porsche.

It was all too good to be true and, as happens so often in football, there was a hidden agenda, a subplot. As part of the service package the dealer also provided finance. It wasn't that the players couldn't pay cash for their cars, they could. But not only did they not want to get their heads around actually paying for something, they were actively encouraged to finance the acquisitions by their friendly car dealer.

This particular player showed me the papers he had been asked to sign; he was bright enough not only to read them and realise that he didn't fully understand them, but also to sense that the monthly payment was high. I had never heard of the finance company in question and, from the look of the documentation, they seemed to be a real Mickey Mouse outfit. I checked it through for him and had to do the arithmetic three times on the repayments, because I didn't believe my calculator was telling me the truth. It looked like he was paying around a forty-five percent rate of interest. It was clear to me what was happening. The car salesman had cut a deal with the finance company to load the repayments, on the basis that footballers never bothered to check what they were paying and would sign anything just to get their cars on time. They were lying about the true rate, banking on nobody checking, and dividing up the 'profit' with the car guy. Everybody was happy, except the poor unsuspecting players.

Did I say 'poor'? Well, you know what I mean. I told the player to get his car elsewhere. I suppose I should have told him to make a complaint to the local Trading Standards Office, or even the police, but I knew he wouldn't do it. I haven't bothered to tell any of the other players who deal with this guy, and I doubt that the player who came to see me will either. In the crazy world of football, the one thing that is sadly lacking is gratitude. Nobody will ever thank you for making them look like a fool . . . particularly footballers.

AUGUST – THE FIRST MATCH

"There are no easy matches in this division."

The Manager, 10th August

I thought we did well in the first match. Like many promoted teams who know they can't match the opposition for class, The Manager told our hard men in midfield to get stuck in early on, and not to worry too much if they picked up bookings, as long as they put a couple of the other side's danger men out of the game. The Manager wasn't too bothered if that was done by way of a physical injury or psychological scars.

He does his research well, does The Manager. Always knows which of the so-called superstars doesn't have the stomach for a battle. It's often the foreign imports who lack the temperament to see it all through. Even if your players don't hurt them, they often get so wound up and overheated that they commit a crazy tackle themselves, and either get booked or sent off. Never believe any manager who says he doesn't like to see players getting hurt. There's at least one out there who not only enjoys it but uses it as a deliberate tactic. He reckons referees rarely send anybody off in the first few minutes, so that gives the window of opportunity to do the maximum damage.

Managers are funny people. Not generally funny ha-ha (although there are one or two who could easily have earned a living as stand-up comedians), but funny peculiar. You can hardly blame them for being slightly mad. Apart from being a kamikaze pilot, I can't think of any other job which offers less promise of a gold watch for long service. I know that, even though The Manager has seen us up through the division, if we have an awful season, if we are tailed off by Christmas, then he'll be getting that famous vote of confidence which is the precursor to getting the boot.

The Manager has always been good on the training ground. He's a great believer in fitness regimes, and even took our lads off to an army camp for a week just before he took them abroad. (You can imagine what a culture shock that was.) Our Manager is very hands on. One now-deceased manager used to look at the older members of his squad before a training session and say, "Right lads, you're the senior players here. What do you fancy doing today?" As you can guess, with that particular team there wasn't a lot of cross-country running. Some managers take fitness to excess though, and the players complain that they hardly ever see a ball in training.

I've seen a change in The Manager already. He's drinking and that's not good. One famous top-division manager drank so much that he had to sleep in his office on Friday nights before home games, just to ensure he got to the ground on time on match days. They even found him asleep at halftime during one match, when he'd nipped back for a quick stiffener at the break. Another had breakfast with the lads at the training ground and surreptitiously pulled out a hip flask filled with whisky, so he could pour it on his cereal in place of milk.

They seem to take on a personality change the minute they swap their training kit for a suit. There was no milder man on or off the field than one ex-England international; yet, when he took over the managerial post at a Northern club, even his wife said that she didn't recognise him anymore. And this about a man of whom she'd previously said if he were any more relaxed he'd be a deckchair.

Yet, one or two of the more fiery personalities on the pitch have moved seamlessly into management, taking all their aggression with them. One actually kicked in a toilet door to get at a player who had taken refuge in there. He regularly caused damage to dressing rooms when the results did not go his way.

Another manager, who is the nicest bloke in the world off the pitch, admits to being a nutter in the dressing room. He would often grab a player around the neck if he thought he hadn't delivered, and wasn't slow to throw china and cutlery around the room either. Mind you, he was sacked on virtually a weekly basis by one of his club's chairmen, so perhaps he was entitled. This man was larger than the club he managed. He actually got questioned by the police one Christmas Day, when they received complaints from neighbours at his club's ground about an intruder. In fact, it was the manager aboard a tractor, desperately trying to get the pitch ready for the Boxing Day fixture.

One manager found his team down two-nil at halftime to a side who were firmly rooted at the foot of the table. He stormed into the changing rooms, red-faced, with veins standing out at the side of his neck. One of the players said, "They're the best team we've played all season."

"Best team? Best team? We are going to be the only fucking team they beat!" screamed the manager, on the verge of a heart attack. With that he picked up the teapot, full not only of scalding tea but also tealeaves, and slung it against the wall. The steaming mess went everywhere, and pieces of china flew into the shower where the players would wash and change at the end of the match. He followed that up by sweeping all the cups off the table, and yelling at the player, "What do you know about football?"

The team lost four-nil, but their opponents didn't lose another game the whole of the season and ended up in mid-table respectability.

There are times when a player thinks he knows more than a manager. We had a player here who stormed in to see The Manager because he'd been told on a Friday that he wouldn't be playing the next day.

"I can't believe you've dropped me," the player said.

"Don't worry about it," The Manager replied, "you'll have another chance."

"But I played well last week," the player persisted.

"Who told you that?" asked The Manager.

"I got an eight out of ten rating in *The Sun*," the player replied, perfectly seriously.

"So because you got an eight out of ten by a journalist who's never played football, I'm supposed to play you? Fuck off."

The player went out on loan shortly after that, and never played for The Club again.

Then, of course, there is the famous Beckham flying boot saga – but only he and Fergie know the real truth about that.

Managers not only want to win, they need to win. They use

any methods to achieve that. They water pitches before matches, turning them into a boggy field. That is their way of creating a level playing field. They get their boys to play loud music in the dressing rooms to annoy the opposition. They make sure that the visitors' dressing room has the minimum of facilities, even to the point of not having hot water.

Without points, their jobs are at stake. Once a manager gets a reputation as a loser it sticks. To get to be a manager in itself is difficult. Even non-league managerial positions, when they fall vacant, get anything up to a hundred applications, many from famous names who have managed (and failed) at the highest level.

Clubs won't give ex-professionals a chance unless they have experience, and they can't get experience unless they get a chance. Managers are reluctant to bring in coaching staff they don't know and, at the lower level, are also hesitant before they bring in an old hand, even as a player, because they know full well that with him on the playing staff that he can easily become a manager in waiting.

Chairmen look around for the easy, cheap option when they sack a manager, and what can be easier or cheaper than appointing one of his players? Managers trust almost nobody, which is why they tend to move around as little teams. The minute a new manager is appointed, you can bet your bottom dollar that his old assistant, first team coach and probably reserve team manager, youth development coach, and even the physio, are likely to be on their way. Managers like to work within their own little comfort zones. If they trail their team around with them, then they know they are unlikely to shaft them. They in turn have their own security to think of, and it doesn't pay to bite the hand that feeds them.

It's when famous management teams break up that all hell can be let loose. Take Cloughie and Peter Taylor, for example. As a combo they were unbeatable, but when Taylor went off on his own then neither of them, individually, was as good as the sum of his parts. Sometimes it's not even about coaching or management skills – a manager just feels comfortable having familiar faces around him, although it's not always immediately apparent what they actually contribute. A very famous manager kept one of his former team-mates around because he was a mate, and was good at running bets and making tea. The manager's argument was that he was good for team morale, and I suppose if that meant going out boozing on a regular basis with senior team members, he was spot on.

But The Champions' manager is a different kettle of fish. He plays mind games of far greater sophistication. He took one look at the changing rooms and said that, if we didn't clean them up, put in fresh towels and wash the floor, he'd be taking his team out to change on the pitch. He got his way. At least he didn't ask for fresh flowers and Perrier.

Nor were The Champions' board of directors the nicest bunch, either. Maybe we do have The Chairman's brother doing the cooking, maybe we don't have a famous chef serving a three-course gourmet meal, maybe our wine would be more at home on the shelves of Tesco than on a table at the Ivy, but nobody complained on our way up. Clearly, at this level it's going to be different. The visitors' board hardly said a word to our people. I could hear their comments about the food from their table even as I stood at the door. Didn't stop them eating it, nor knocking back the wine either. (Mind you, they left at the end of the match rather than paying for their own drinks.)

I didn't have time for lunch, never do on match days. I bring a sandwich from home and perhaps get a chance to eat it once the game starts – provided there's no trouble on the terraces. I don't get a chance to see the match either. I'm always amazed when I see the secretaries of bigger clubs take their seats in the directors' box and relax. I'm forever in motion, walkie-talkie in hand, dealing with each crisis as it arises.

We're not as segregated as some grounds, and there's been a bit of a problem on the north terrace. It's divided down the middle between home and away fans. Our visitors were less than pleased with their ticket allocation for this game and, although the team is from the North, many of their fans live in London and have been able to infiltrate our supporters. Unfortunately, they've chosen where our hardcore sit and it's all kicked off. Although we are all-seated, apart from the two main stands nobody sits down at all. Why you would pay for an expensive seat and then stand for ninety minutes always perplexes me, but there you are. We've tried everything to get them seated, but without success.

This afternoon we've had the two packs of fans braying at each other, with a line of police and stewards in between. It doesn't augur well. We can't afford to have any part of our ground closed down or to be on the receiving end of a huge fine. The police managed to eject the away fans who'd got tickets in our sector, and we *just* managed to avoid a major incident. But I had to be there, and then I had to be with a programme seller who'd been mugged for his takings, and from there it was down to the ladies' loo where they'd had a flood.

Being involved at the sharp end of a football club is not all romance. So I wasn't taking a lot of notice of the clash of the managers, as you can well imagine.

Our Manager, for his part, is a bit of a loner. He has a freelance Sports Psychologist and a Fitness Coach working with him. The Fitness Coach has driven the players through their paces and targeted the ones who put on weight during the close season for special treatment. He's had them on army courses and cross-country runs, but not with the same disastrous results as occurred at one club a few years ago,

The coach there was very keen on cross-country running and, although he had retired as a player a few years earlier, he always led the way. He was taking them through the woods and hurdling over fallen trees with aplomb, when he tripped and fell. The players, being players, thought it was a great joke. Most of them landed on his prone body and then ran on. It was only when they got back to the start that one of them asked, "Where's the coach, by the way? Not like him to finish last."

In fact he was totally finished, as he'd suffered a fatal heart attack and the players had been landing on a corpse.

This season in the Premiership, The Manager has also reluctantly taken on last year's Senior Pro as his assistant. I say reluctantly, as it was that same syndrome that I mentioned: He now has a manager in waiting if things do truly go pear-shaped. I'm amazed he even lets him sit on the bench. There was a lot of noise coming from the pair of them during that first match, and eventually the referee sent the pair of them to the stands, where they simply raised the volume and carried on screaming.

We held The Champions until ten minutes from the end, when one of our defenders who'd already been booked committed one foul too many and got sent off. With ten men we just couldn't hold out, conceding one goal five minutes from the end and another when we tried to chase the equaliser.

Nil-two. No points, no goals. But it was a full house, so neither The Chairman nor the bank will be complaining. It's going to be a long haul to the end of the season.

AUGUST – THE TRANSFER DEADLINE

"How is it nobody wants to sign for us?"

A fan, posting on the fanzine's website, August 14th

Everybody hates transfer windows. Except for FIFA, of course, the governing body of world football that introduced them. Clubs hate them because, once 31st August has passed, they are stuck with the squad they have and can't sign anybody of any note – at least until the beginning of January, by which time it may well be too late.

Players hate them, because they can be stuck in a club from whence they are desperate to depart while an overpriced transfer label or a greedy agent keeps them paralysed. Agents hate them because their earning power is limited to just a few months a year: the end of June to the end of August, and the whole of January. The whole concept of family holidays for most agents no longer exists. I heard of one agent's wife who, when he took one call too many, threw her husband's mobile phone into the sea off the Cape of Good Hope. For club secretaries like me they are a mixed blessing. Yes, we're busy during the windows, but we'd be busy anyway pre-season. But now, once we've got everybody signed up, for a few months that'll be the end of it.

Signing players is nowhere near as simple as it used to be. The player would come in, the manager would tell him what he would be earning, and then the player would agree and sign. End of story. Though there was one manager of a massive club who had a very nice little sideline going: He'd ask the player what he wanted to earn. The player told him and, to the player's delight, the manager then offered him more. The only catch was that the player had to pay him half of the extra money he was getting each week. If the player took the money and tried to renege on the deal, it was no problem: The player found himself out of the team until he coughed up, or, if he was still being awkward, out of the club.

Unless somebody blew the whistle, it was a perfect scam. Although the manager finally left the club under a bit of a cloud, it didn't stop him getting other jobs where I'm sure he found other ways to supplement his income. Everybody thinks it's just the agents who are dodgy, but I've been in this game long enough to know everybody is at it: chairmen, directors, managers, CEO's, agents, family members, Uncle Tom Cobley and all. In one club, even the kit man was getting a slice of the cake for introducing young players to agents. Indeed, I was told that the bloke who made the teas and did a bit of driving for a well-known club up north was earning a fortune by spotting up-and-coming players and obtaining their phone numbers, both for agents and other clubs who wanted to do a bit of tapping up.

The FA have now added even more complications with their new regulations and policing of the old rules. To be able to get a player registered you have to wade through a mound of documentation. Obviously the player has to sign the contract, but the FA and the relevant league also have to approve any unusual clauses in the agreement. Various jobsworths there find it quite hard to think outside the box, and anything slightly outside of the ordinary is treated with great suspicion.

We had some doubts over a player's fitness and ability to see a season through, so we agreed a clause with his agent whereby his salary went down in January if he hadn't played a certain percentage of games. Going by the fuss the FA kicked up, you would have thought we'd submitted the document in Sanskrit.

Then the player has to say whether or not he had an agent acting for him. It may have been in all the papers that the player had an agent, but when it comes to doing the deal then the agent wants to be able to say that he's acted for the club. He may well have had a contract with the player, but unless it's been lodged with the FA there's no proof of that. The FA try to get clever and look at the agent's website to see if the player is described as being represented by the agent. The agent, who is generally more streetwise than the FA, will either have removed the player's name or else say that he simply represents him in relation to commercial matters – although the FA now say that counts on its own as 'acting for the player'.

It's a game of cat and mouse. These new agents' regulations have tried to close off all the loopholes. Whoever is acting for the player has to sign the player's contract, which has to state the fee being paid to the agent, which in turn must be the fee contained in an agency agreement which has to be lodged with the FA. And if the agent has acted for the player (even on outside commercial matters), then he can't act for a club in respect of that player for at least two transfer windows, which is basically a year. I'm sure that agents will find a way around them. There's too much money at stake for them just to walk away.

I can see both sides of the picture, to be honest. I get on well with most agents, who are generally decent guys, trying to earn a living in a very competitive environment. Apart from The Agent, our Chairman and Manager seem to hate the lot of them – probably because they often cost them money without delivering anything in return. The agent knows that, if the player is the one who has to pay, it's very expensive for him. He can't set it off against his earnings like most entertainers, and he can't register for VAT so as to get that piece of the expenditure back, either. Whereas if the club effectively 'retains' the agent then, as far as the club is concerned, it's an allowable expense. It's no more a fiction than most of what goes on in the game, but I suppose our old friends at the Inland Revenue might regard it as a tax fiddle. If the club pays *on behalf* of the player, it not only goes into the contract but also onto his P11D for the purposes of tax. Again, the FA now seem to have sewn that one up by saying that only the player can pay his agent and, if the club does pay on his behalf it has to be done by way of deduction from his salary as he earns it.

We've had a chat about it here. We can see these new regulations are not only going to cost us a fortune, but are also very easily abused and avoided. It's just going to drive the industry back to where it was ten years ago. I can recall how some of my fellow club secretaries have had to meet agents at motorway service stations, with brown envelopes bulging with cash just to ensure a deal happened. It all boils down to how badly a club wants a player. If they really want him then they are going to find a way to get him. If that involves breaking the rules, then the rules are going to be broken. Sometimes it's so blatant that you can't believe all the parties involved really believe they're going to get away with it.

There was a case last season where an agent had run a campaign to get a player out of a club. He'd given interviews whenever and wherever he could, but, when he finally got 'his' player what he wanted, he suddenly found he wasn't acting for the player at all. The player had already muddied the water by refusing to sign a contract with the agent, or indeed, with any of the other half-dozen agents who'd been told to find him a club. (There's nothing like covering every contingency.) But the new club were so desperate to sign the player that, if they'd been asked to, they'd probably have written out a cheque to Hitler or Stalin. So, the agent got a massive payday, as did the player – who showed no interest in what the agent was earning, as long as he got what he wanted and didn't pay any tax on the agent's commission.

This is that time of year when we get impassioned calls from agents acting for foreign players we've never heard of. All they have is a CV and videos (or DVD's, if they are sophisticated), and based on that we're expected to lay out millions. There may be the odd nugget amidst all this, but sometimes it's just not worth the effort of sifting through all the rubbish. The main problem is working out if the guy who phoned us does actually exclusively represent the player, or whether he's just a chancer trying to muscle into somebody else's deal. If the latter is the case, then, the minute he hears there might be a bit of interest the chancer is off like a shot to the agent who really does act for the player, trying to cut a deal on the basis that he knows there is a club who would like to buy him but he alone can deliver the deal, as the club has such faith in him. If the player's real agent buys that story, then suddenly the chancer is in on the deal and in a great position to earn from both sides. The player's agent will cut him in on his commission and the buying club may well pay a fee as well.

The FA have attempted to halt this practice too, by saying that agents have to disclose all the sub-commissions they pay and insisting on agreements being lodged. In their dreams, say I.

It is quite amazing how some of these transfers ever happen, given the number of people involved. It's also hard to understand how some of the fees come about, particularly when the player is patently not worth it. I had a friend on the phone the other day, the secretary at a fairly big club in the Midlands. They've just discovered a wholesale fraud that seemed to have been going on for a while, involving their manager and his agent. It seems that when the manager was appointed he used his agent to negotiate his terms. The club was impressed and grateful. They'd wanted the manager and there was competition for his services. But that was the sting. Once the manager was in place, he persuaded the club chairman to appoint his agent to do all the deals for the club. The arrangement continued for nearly two years and, as the club was doing quite well, nobody asked too many questions.

Then a dispute arose with a foreign club over some instalment payments, and it came out that this particular club had been asking £2m for the player when in fact the English club had ended up paying £4m. The English manager's agent had recommended the player to the club and negotiated the deal. Unfortunately for him, it transpired in discussions that the foreign club had split with him their windfall profit of the extra £2m for the player. As he'd also earned a ten percent commission of the purchase price from the club that retained him, they were somewhat peeved. Having sacked the manager and terminated the relationship with his agent, they were now looking at every deal done and every agent involved. I mildly asked what they were going to do about it. My friend, normally the mildest of men, nearly imploded. The FA had said it wasn't their business, as the transfer involved a foreign player, and the chairman didn't fancy going to the police.

Sometimes I think we get the sort of game that we deserve.

Even if you can persuade the agent that the deal is good for a player, you still have to satisfy the player himself – and very often, more importantly, his wife. You can pay the player all the money in the world, but when the wife asks, "What shops do they have there? Where's the nearest spa? Are there any decent schools?" and you can't come up with all the right answers, then the player simply isn't going to sign, no matter what you do. One player was offered nearly £30,000 per week, but his wife still asked if his agent could squeeze another grand a week out of the deal. When the transfer was finally concluded, she told her husband she didn't think The Agent had done a very good job and persuaded him to terminate the relationship.

Wives continue to be a problem even when the player joins a club. One woman, married to a teetotaller, approached the chairman of a club and asked him to ban alcohol from the players' lounge where they assembled with their families and friends after a match.

The chairman asked, "Why would I do that?"

MEL STEIN

"Well, when all the players have had a drink or two it doesn't look nice," the woman replied.

As you might imagine, she didn't get her way.

At least we, as a club, tend to know exactly what we are buying. As I've said before, if The Club does lose out in any way financially, at least it tends to stay within the family. Many years ago, I remember a well-known English striker going to a foreign club. The club in question had really wanted the current England International centre-forward but had been rebuffed, so they went for the league's top scorer instead. He was sent out by his club with his agent for an initial meeting, to see if he and his wife would like the place. The foreigners arranged to meet the plane and asked how they would recognise him. His agent told them they couldn't miss him, he was well over six feet tall and black. The consternation this caused was great. They'd had no idea he was anything but a white Englishman. As it happened, the deal went through but the transfer was a failure – hopelessly homesick, the player experienced virulent racism and was back in England after just one season.

Another expensive signing arrived at the airport to join his new European club. He was surrounded by journalists pushing microphones under his nose and was rather impressed by the welcome.

"Are you looking forward to playing at the stadium?" he was asked.

"Of course I am," he replied sincerely.

"What number are you going to start with?" the journalist continued.

"Depends on what number the manager gives me," the player said.

The journalist looked puzzled but then he had good reason, as he had mistaken the player for the lead singer of Pink Floyd, who were performing that week at the club's stadium.

Anyway, when I read that an experienced high-profile manager had bought a load of players from videos at the start of his first year in charge of a Premiership club, I wasn't exactly astonished.

It's always a gamble with foreign players as to how they adapt to the English game, and England in general. One player asked for a transfer because he didn't like the traffic and noise in London, and then decided he wanted to go play for a club in a European capital well known for its traffic congestion and pollution.

Another player was due to make his debut for his new club up north, when the manager received a call just a few hours before kick-off to say the player was at Gatwick Airport. He decided to take a chance and put the player's name down on the starting line-up that he handed into the referee. The player arrived with ten minutes to spare, changed in record time and raced onto the pitch without a hint of a warm-up. Neither the fans nor the press got a whiff of potential disaster.

Anyway, closer to home, we've lost our first two games, grabbed a point we didn't deserve from a home fixture, and are now rushing around trying to patch up the holes in our defence and get ourselves a striker who might score a few goals. It's patently obvious now, even to The Chairman, that if we don't do something we'll get relegated with a record low number of points. He can see our crowds melting away and, although our wage bill is peanuts compared to the likes of Chelsea and Manchester United, we do have a number of players who were with us in our promotion year and are reaping the benefits of what, for us, are huge salaries. And quite beyond what they are really worth.

We had a player coming down yesterday for a medical. He has a great pedigree and we were a bit surprised that he wanted to come here. I'm naturally suspicious and, whilst I didn't want to look a gift horse in the mouth, I think I've learned by now that, in football, there's no such thing as a gift horse. As it turned out, I was spot on. We agreed terms with him swiftly. He passed his medical and was about to sign. I turned the television in my office onto Sky Sports News. It gets to you after a while, as the stories run on a continuous loop, but there was one which said that this particular player hadn't signed for one of our rivals because he'd failed a medical – a fact that neither he nor his advisors had bothered to mention. The player, of course, denied it.

"No, it were because I really wanted to come 'ere."

Yeah, right, I thought.

I suppose we would have done the same if we were selling. *Caveat emptor*, and all that. The Chairman went ballistic, but The Manager persuaded him to go ahead with the deal with all sorts of performance-based limitations attached over a shorter guaranteed period.

Gift horses in football fall into the same category as Father Christmas. I don't believe in either of them.

EARLY SEPTEMBER

"We have every confidence in The Manager."
Statement issued on behalf of The Board, 5th September

I have to say it's not going terribly well. On the pitch, or off of it. We finally gave up the ghost with our England Under 21 centre-half and allowed him to go to one of our London rivals, just before the transfer deadline. He'd had an extraordinary conversation with The Manager on the eve of our first game of the season, remarking, "I don't want to play in case I get injured."

"And I don't want to play anybody who doesn't want to wear the shirt," The Manager replied. "So if you don't want to be part of the team you can fucking well train on your own. And bring your own fucking kit, because we ain't washing it for you."

That wasn't quite as bad as the story of a big money signing who joined a new club and, after one day, said he wanted to leave because he was homesick.

"Come on, lad, we're going up to Scotland on tour. Just give it a try."

After three days, the manager found the player alone in his room, sobbing his heart out.

"What's the matter, son?" the manager, who was a kind man, asked.

"I've never been away from home for more than one night before and I miss my mum and dad."

The manager realised he had a hopeless case on his hands, and sold the player to a club a mile or so from his home for about half the fee he'd paid for him.

In fact, unless a player is injured he's supposed to train with at least two other players to avoid this form of solitary confinement, but as long as he was getting paid our player didn't seem to care. An enormous amount of interest had been shown in our recalcitrant lad from at least four Premiership clubs, and his agent had obviously had meetings to try to agree terms. The only thing was that The Chairman was refusing to sell him.

As far as the fans were concerned, the party line was that if we wanted to survive at the top level then we had to keep our best players. The truth was that The Chairman knew he'd let him go before the deadline, but just wanted to achieve the best price. But The Manager was scared to tell The Chairman that the player was refusing to play, and made out that he'd dropped him because he didn't think his head was right. Sometimes it's just best if everybody lies.

In the end we beat the buying club up from £5m to £7.5m, with the possibility of add-ons taking the price up to £10m. So I suppose it was good business. But there was no time later for any of that to be made available to The Manager to buy an adequate replacement, so I suspect most of the money will be used to repay The Chairman's loans. He has said he'll release some funds by Christmas, in time for the January transfer window, but I suspect it will be too late by then. And doesn't The Chairman know it?

Four games into the season and we're still waiting for our first win. We've just been knocked out of the Carling Cup by League Two opposition and the local press are closing in for the kill. Of course, now we are a Premiership club the nationals write about us as well, but if you're a small club like us then the first thing that you reach for is the local rag.

You also tend to develop a relationship with one writer who you use to spin stories. The Journo, as we call him, has been good to us over the years. And we've not only been good to him, but good *for* him as well. He's been able to work as a stringer for nationals and break exclusives, and I suspect he may well have had offers to move on. But he's no youngster, he lives locally and he has a fairly cushy number, so he's stayed where he is. But today, The Chairman is not happy with him.

A couple of our lads were out with their wives at a restaurant which also doubles as a bar. It was midweek and they weren't training the next day, so they had a fair bit to drink. One of the players accidentally knocked over a lamp; one of the restaurant staff, who acts as a kind of bouncer for the bar, got into an argument with our players. Instead of just asking them to leave, he threw them out physically and called the police. Our lads were badly mishandled, got themselves handcuffed, had Mace sprayed in their faces. And then, to their astonishment and the anguish of their wives, they got hauled down to the local nick for an overnight stay. Players being what they are, they didn't actually share the incident with anybody at The Club. The first thing any of us knew about it was when The Journo broke the story. As the story also ran in *The Sun*, we have to assume they got it from him too, for which I presume he was richly rewarded.

Not that these players were particularly troublesome or,

indeed, hard men. I recall one who was a lovely bloke off the pitch but on it he would break somebody in half. And woe betide anybody who riled him at any time, whether he was in football kit or not. After a match he went off to a wine bar, had a few drinks and then decided he was hungry. There was a big, long queue at the chippie, but he didn't pull rank, didn't bully his way to the front of the line by playing Billy Big-Time, and just waited patiently. A local wild boy came along and walked right to the head of the queue. He'd got a bit of a reputation so nobody spoke up. Except the player.

"We've all been waiting a while, lad, so just join the queue."

But the lad stood where he was. "Who the fuck do you think you're talking to?"

Almost before he could finish the sentence he was flat out on the floor. The lad's girlfriend attacked the player with a heavy glass salt cellar, and in a heartbeat she was lying parallel to her bloke. The player decided discretion was the better part of valour, and took off before the police could arrive. At five in the morning Mr Plod caught up with him, and there was no sign of him at training next morning because he was helping the police with their inquiries. The player had some influential friends though, so no charges were ever brought. As I said, except for when he was riled, he was a lovely guy.

Another player, as a youngster, was not averse to wandering into shops, letting innocent team-mates create a diversion and then sticking his hand in the till, pocketing any cash available. On one occasion he bought a more famous team-mate a few drinks, got absolutely hammered and was thrown out of the pub. The team-mate, who'd done nothing wrong, got the fine and the headlines. The manager of the club in question was so frustrated that he forced the young player into his car, drove to the lad's home and sat down to tell his parents their son was a head-case more likely to end up in jail than in his team. As it happens, it did the trick; the player turned himself around and carved out a decent career in the game,

Yet some players are great ones for sticking their heads in the ground and deluding themselves that major problems are simply going to go away. In the past, players haven't told their clubs (or even their own agents) that they've been arrested for offences ranging from motoring incidents and punch-ups in bars to suspected rape. I know of one former international who had an accident on the motorway, and was so panicked that he abandoned his very expensive car on the hard shoulder and legged it across fields, as he didn't fancy the adverse publicity. As he'd borrowed the car, he reckoned he had a chance of getting away with it and, incredibly, he did. His friend the owner was persuaded to take the rap for leaving the scene of the accident.

The Chairman has blown his top, and told The Journo that his entire paper is banned from the ground. Quite how he intends to stop any member of their staff buying a ticket and reporting on the match from the stands, I have no idea. But he has told me to remove their press passes, and that includes their photographer's as well.

I'm not quite sure where this is all going. Clubs generally need the support of the local paper. It may be that, whilst we're higher up the league, we can afford to be independent. But if we go back where we came from, you have to rely on the local press to communicate on your behalf with local residents. A club I know had their development plans scuppered because they'd upset the local press, who ran story after story concerning the dire effect of a bigger stadium in the neighbourhood. Parking, late-night noise, rubbish, pop concerts, undesirables in the area: it wasn't hard to get a local action group really wound up, and they formed such a powerful alliance with the paper that the council refused the club's application.

In local politics, the local club can be a really hot potato. Supporting a club in relation to stadium development is rarely a vote catcher, and local politicians – not unreasonably, from their perspective – are more concerned with appeasing voters who may actually keep them in office. Football fans tend to either live in the poorer part of a ward or else not to live there at all.

Anyway, The Chairman phoned The Journo. "Why the fuck didn't you tell us about this first?"

"I've got my integrity, you know," The Journo replied. "I've got a duty to tell my readers the truth."

"You know what," The Chairman replied, "I don't give a flying fuck about your readers or the truth, and you can stuff your fucking integrity up your arse!"

The Journo asked The Chairman if he could quote him on that, but then told him he was going to regardless. The Chairman got onto the editor and asked him to sack The Journo. The editor told him they were going to report that as well. So, all in all, it looks like we may be in for a rocky ride over the coming season.

The Chairman has now turned his attention to our two players who were mentioned in dispatches. He's told me to charge them with bringing The Club into disrepute, and to fine them two weeks' wages for starters. I did point out to him that we have a disciplinary procedure to follow, to which his response was, "Fuck that too, and if we can let's fine them four weeks' wages."

"We can't," I say, "I've already had the PFA [Professional Footballers Association] onto me, asking for a proper hearing and telling me they're going to appeal."

Meanwhile, it now seems that the police, having been geed up by the article, are going to charge the players with assault, whereas they might have just let it go with a caution. Seems they're saying that, before they handcuffed the players, they were kneed in the groin by them and one of the policemen is now on sick leave, traumatised. My experience of the police is that it takes more than a knee in the groin to traumatise them, but probably quite a bit less for them to grab some sick leave.

The Chairman likes fining players. It saves on wages. There was one league chairman who actually wrote the fines into his budget. He caught the players out on everything: if they were late for training, if they were sent off or just booked, if they didn't wear the right clothing when travelling with the team. He even fined a player once for failing to call him 'Mr Chairman', though that one had to be reversed.

Another chairman, now departed, was also a ticket tout. He went around the dressing room before a match, asking if the players wanted tickets for a touring American superstar. The tickets were like gold dust and the players, thinking the chairman was giving them away, jumped at the chance. At the end of the week the players, as was normal at this club at the time, received their wages in cash in a large envelope. Each and every one of them was short, and when they went in to see the club secretary he explained that the chairman had deducted the price of the tickets from their salaries. He'd even charged them at his normal inflated rate.

On another occasion, the club in question owed a player five hundred quid in back salary. The chairman called the player in to see him and said, "Right, it's a monkey I owe you. One hundred, two hundred, three hundred," he counted out the notes in used fifties. "And there's two tickets for that show you wanted to see on Saturday night. They're going for a hundred quid a time so that's us clear."

"But Mr Chairman," the player said, "we're playing up at Darlington on Saturday and I've no chance of getting back."

"Well, I'll tell you what I'll do. I'll try and sell them for you. I'll let you know."

The player heard nothing more about his missing £200.

This same chairman also had a habit of going into the match officials' dressing room before a game, asking if they had seen whatever the popular musical of the time was, and telling them there might be a couple of good seats made available to them at the end of the game. He didn't actually say it depended upon their performance, but that was clearly the inference. In fact, no official ever got the tickets, which says a lot for the integrity of our referees and linesmen. I suspect it may well have been a different story elsewhere in Europe.

Chairmen in Europe are also a very different breed. Certainly, one French president (as they call them there) of a club had a unique approach. He would generally give the team talk and certainly would never allow the manager to select a player with whom he'd had a difference of opinion. He also once famously turned up before a game in the dressing room with a tray of Rolex watches, and told the players they would each receive one as a bonus if they beat their local rivals. They didn't, and one assumes that, as the Rolexes were never on offer again, he got them on sale or return.

Now The Chairman has turned his wrath on The Manager as well. He's told him that it's his lack of discipline which has allowed recent developments, and that it's also being reflected in our results. At the last board meeting the question of The Manager was on the agenda. On a poll, The Board actually voted to get rid of him. The Chairman then asked to see his contract, worked out how much it would cost to terminate it, and then reversed the decision. He likes the rest of The Board to think they have a say, but thinking is as far as it goes. As I've mentioned, he runs The Club like a benevolent dictatorship – only without the benevolence.

However, having received (at least publicly) the famous vote of confidence, The Manager must now know he's living on borrowed time. It's just possible that things may turn around. I remember how Fergie himself was probably one defeat away from getting the sack at Manchester United, in the early days of his stewardship – the rest is history. The same with Joe Royle, at the start of his successful run at Everton. But in the case of our Manager, I think it's unlikely.

I know The Chairman is already making a few calls to see who he might line up as his replacement. That's the way it works in our industry. The Manager could have left at virtually any time on our way up for one of the bigger clubs, but that fact is now forgotten. You are only as good as your last match in this world. Martin Jol got Spurs into Europe in 2006/7, and then spent huge amounts of money at the start of the 2007/8 season in overpaying for the likes of Darren Bent. Two defeats later that took them to the bottom of the league, and already his job was on the line. Spurs then beat Derby four-nil and all was forgiven. Until they did sack him, a few games later. (His successor delivered the Carling Cup, but their league position was pretty much where Jol would have taken them anyway.) Avram Grant gets Chelsea into the final of the Champions League and loses his job shortly afterwards; Sven does wonders with Manchester City, exceeding all expectations, and reads in the papers about the rumours of his dismissal, which soon became fact. It's not exactly a career for those with high blood pressure, a heart problem, or a desire for security.

I know The Chairman is talking to one of our ex-players who's had a fair amount of success in the Football Conference, with a team that has now been promoted to League Two. They've won all their matches first time around so The Chairman is looking to poach him. He's already discovered that the bloke hasn't yet signed the new contract his club have offered him, so as far as The Chairman is concerned he's fair game.

Again, that's football. If another club had succeeded in tapping up The Manager when we were on the way up, The Chairman would have blown a gasket. But now the boot's on the other foot, well, the Ex-Player is a proper target and all's fair in love and war. He probably owes his whole career to The Manager, but he's spoken not a word to urge The Chairman to stick with him. And why should he, when he has the lure of being a manager in the Premiership himself? He's agreed to hold off signing again with his current club for a few weeks, and I know The Chairman has given him a 'holding deposit' in cash (non-refundable, and certainly non-declarable). Most clubs have a slush fund to be used for occasions like this, and that certainly includes us.

The Chairman tells me what he wants, I just make the arrangements. Invariably, I get to know what's going on and what the funds are for, but, in terms of the public arena, I am the three wise monkeys on a job share: I hear nothing, see nothing, say nothing. It's how club secretaries keep their jobs when all around them are losing theirs. Discretion is by far the better part of valour – as is blind loyalty from time to time, directed toward whoever may own The Club. The new broom introduced by a new owner rarely sweeps away the club secretary, whichever other members of the coaching and administrative staff end up in the waste bin.

So we're only just into September, and already the press (particularly our former friend, The Journo) are billing the weekend's home match against The Club who narrowly missed the drop last season as a make-or-break six-pointer relegation battle. We're on Sky on Sunday, so there's no chance of anybody missing the result or the relentless agony that The Manager will have to endure under the unforgiving eye of the camera. I hate it when we're on the box; The Chairman is none too pleased either. We get more money, but it doesn't compensate for the empty seats. We're not a club which sells out week after week or has a waiting list for our season tickets. All we can do is ensure we have clauses in our sponsorship agreement that guarantees a bonus from the sponsor when we have a televised match, in return for extra perimeter boards at the stadium.

But you can't put cardboard cut-out figures on the empty seats. They tell their own story.

LATE SEPTEMBER

"They've no respect for money. It wasn't like that in my day."

Television football pundit, commenting after a player admits losing £100,000 in one night on a card game

It's all beginning to fall apart. The rumour is that The Manager is losing the dressing room. Mind you, with the amount of refuelling he is doing (in the immortal words of Graham Taylor) it's a wonder he can find it in the first place. 'Losing the dressing room' means he's lost the respect of the players. In some cases, 'respect' is a word that players don't have in their vocabulary anyway – it only takes one disruptive influence, and a manager who hasn't got the bottle to remove that influence from the club (however talented a player he may be), for it to spread and take over.

The disruption can come in all kinds of ways: dumb insolence, downright rudeness, poor displays of commitment in front of the younger players, ambitions for the manager's job, drink, drugs or gambling. There's always one troublemaker in every squad, and he usually has the personality to carry some of the rest of them with him.

Card schools are an everyday part of the life of a football club. The players are travelling long distances in close proximity. They are spending many nights away at hotels. Not many of them take *War and Peace* to while away the hours on the road. But a fair number of them do take a pack of cards. Losing a hundred quid on a coach journey is neither here nor there for most of them, but sometimes the habit gets a real hold.

Players can be real mugs when it comes to gambling. One manager told his team they were absolutely certain to win their next match, and suggested the players back themselves to win. One player took him at his word, placed a bet of £20,000, and then managed to be a part of the squad that lost by the odd goal or three at home. I didn't hear of the manager giving him an indemnity for his investment.

One club won a cup and gave all of its players a free trip to Spain, with a not insubstantial amount of spending money thrown in for good measure. By the time they arrived there, a few of the players had not only lost all of the spending money in a game of brag, but also lost four-figure sums on top for good measure. When it came to paying up there was considerably less enthusiasm than there had been for the game itself.

One of the biggest losers simply gave half of what he owed to a senior pro and said, "That's all you're getting. I spoke to my agent, who's also a lawyer, and he said you can't sue me for it."

And he couldn't.

He left the club, leaving the debt behind him as well. Doubtlessly, if the boot had been on the other foot there would have been more aggressive means of collection.

When a footballer does get deeply into debt there are always people ready to bail him out, for all sorts of reasons. Some of them are the equivalent of the rock world's star-fuckers, whilst others have more sinister aims. Once a loan shark has a player in his sights, then as long as the money is owing (and, with extortionate interest rates, it is always hard to repay), the player is his. If he needs him to assist in fixing the odds on a result, the player can put not only his career but even his life on the line. I've never experienced match fixing myself, but there are all sorts of rumours in the game about players with huge gambling debts, giving away unnecessary penalties which affect the result late in a match, or missing an open goal which could have changed the game. Proving it is impossible, and the players would rather face an angry manager than a gangster about to take a hammer to their knees.

Some players get so hooked that they even miss training to get to the betting shop. One player was so addicted that he spent £10,000 a week on lottery tickets. (And was probably surprised that he never won the jackpot.) Another would take routes around the town that meant he never needed to pass a betting shop, because he knew he couldn't withstand the lure. Yet another had all of his wages paid into an account for which only his agent was a signatory, so that he couldn't use his own money.

None of which stops Vegas from being a fatal attraction for players' stag weekends or birthdays. Although the trips are generally out of season, one hardened gambler managed to fit in a twenty-four-hour gaming session in Vegas, when his club thought he was at a family member's funeral. It would have been cheaper for him to have had his relative killed and to pay for the funeral and the flowers, as he returned not only a heavy loser but also so jetlagged that he was dropped from the next match.

Footballers never think they are going to be caught out. When they are they invariably lie, but to be a good liar you also need to be consistent and to have a good memory – not traits associated with most players of my acquaintance.

I've had a player in today. He's on five grand a week. That's peanuts to a lot of Premiership clubs, but very good money as far as we are concerned. We generally pay five or six thousand a week basic and make up the rest with four or five thousand of appearance money, so the squad that takes the field on a Saturday is generally getting £10,000 per man. It means we don't have to pay huge sums to a player who is injured or out of favour, and also that if we go down we will not be lumbered with a huge wages bill. As I said, we have an automatic reduction on relegation so we can make sure our housekeeping is in order.

But this particular player is in deep shit. He owes almost all the rest of the team money that he's lost on cards; he's bounced a cheque at a casino; he's into the bookies at the local dog track; and, for reasons quite beyond me, he has five loan agreements on five different cars, a couple with secondary lenders who are threatening to do more than just repossess the vehicles.

It's all about to come on top for this young man, but he's only just told me about it and asked if I can give him an advance on his wages. I've promised to talk to The Chairman, but the fact is that we have to charge him interest, otherwise clubs would be granting interest-free loans all the time to circumvent the terms of playing contracts. He's not been playing well lately and now the reason is pretty damn obvious.

That's another problem with footballers. Things that ordinary folk like you and I would just shrug off get blown out of all proportion. One very famous player couldn't train at all one day. His manager realised something was wrong.

"What's the problem?" he asked.

"My fucking plumber has put my bath in the wrong way round. I can't stand to look at it. I can't even bear to have a bath."

The manager had to call his agent, who had to drop everything to go to an onsite meeting with the contractors. The bath was turned around and all was well.

Footballers, generally speaking, are so spoon-fed that, once they retire and leave the cocoon, the world can be a very scary place. One ex-player was complaining about a toothache in our press box the other day. I suggested he might want to make an appointment with his dentist.

"I haven't got a dentist," he replied, "how do you go about getting one? Do you think you could do it for me?"

I did, and then he phoned me to ask how to make an appointment. This was a player who'd been quite ferocious on the pitch, and yet here he was, totally reliant on others off of it.

Many a player has had to request a transfer just so he can pay off his gambling debts. He's gone as far as he can financially at his club, his credit both on and off the pitch has expired and he needs a new payday. That's when domestic pressures come into play too. The fact that he might want a move doesn't necessarily mean that his wife does too. So he'll make some kind of arrangement where he rents a property near his new club and just goes home at weekends.

Boys will be boys and that arrangement gives him a degree of licence he's not had since his bachelor days. Mind you, girls will be girls as well, and footballers' wives are not immune from temptation either. Some players are better looking than others. One particular heartthrob had most of the other wives and girlfriends throwing themselves at him. Many years later, he bumped into one of the wives with whom he'd had a brief fling.

"How are you?" he asked.

"Divorced," she replied.

"Any kids?" he asked.

"Just the one daughter of twenty-one," she replied, then added hopefully, "Don't suppose you're free this evening?"

The player looked her up and down and then replied, "To be honest, love, I'd be more interested in your daughter."

Dressing rooms have come to blows over one player shagging another's wife or girlfriend – which means one or both of the players also have to leave the club. So when you next read in the papers about a player wanting a move down south, or up north, or away from a club where he appeared to be perfectly settled, you need to try to guess the subplot. It's rare that it actually has anything to do with football.

Some players have a reputation for being ladies' men, and others just see it as a challenge to work their way through every available (or unavailable) female associated with the club. This doesn't just mean other players' wives and girlfriends, but also female staff or even the wives of directors or other officials.

A very famous manager who appeared happily married for many years had a tempestuous affair with the club's attractive marketing director, which included romps in the dressing room and even, on one doubtlessly erotic occasion, on the boardroom table. Another manager's wife became so possessive after his much-publicised affair that he was not even allowed overnight stays with the team, or scouting missions, unless she accompanied him. His club didn't make a lot of new signings for a while, but at least she was determined enough to save their marriage.

It's always the unlikely ones as far as the public are concerned. A highly respected English international, part of a long and seemingly stable relationship, had too much to drink at an after-match party and gave in to temptation. Luckily, the girl in question was the sister of another player, understood the rules and realised it was no more than a one-night stand. Yet another established England player had a penchant for young girls. Not underage, but certainly much younger than his very pretty wife. He managed to sneak a regular stream of young women into his hotel rooms, and whoever shared with him had enough sense to make himself scarce when required.

Kiss-and-tell is a big attraction when the tabloids have so much money to throw around. Young men combined with well-toned bodies, big empty houses, fast expensive cars and luxury hotel rooms create the perfect circumstances for transitory sex. And when it's offered to them, they just can't refuse it. Sometimes an offer isn't even necessary. One striker was quite happy to score with total strangers in car parks, whilst three young men from a top club were even happier to pay for a bevy of hookers to attend a party at one of their homes. Mind you, they were less than happy when one of their visitors sold the story to a Sunday paper. It must be hard for these lads to pick potential wives and mothers from the gold-diggers who are just out for a good time. Even some of the respectable wife-and-mother types are not going to turn down the chance of a life of luxury. As my mother used to say, it's just as easy to fall in love with a rich partner as a poor one.

The agents don't always help. Some think that a part of their job is to provide women in much the same way they supply football boots. One agent even owns a flat in London which he uses just to entertain his players with girls. And sometimes I'm sure he'd like to become his players. I suppose it beats the old system of treating mums and dads to a week in Spain to try to persuade their sons to sign for the agency. I can't say I approve – but then, if it came to my disapproval meaning anything, the whole of the Football League would have to shut up shop and go home.

I've no reason to believe that our young lad has woman problems as well as financial ones, but we're going to have to do something with him. He's no good to man or beast in this state of mind, and so much of football is actually played *in the mind*. We're past the transfer window now, so we can't even sell him for a decent payday. In the old days you could just lob a few bob to a player in trouble, whatever his contract may have said. Interest free loans were a good way of getting players into The Club. Even better were interest free loans to the players' parents, which somehow or other managed to get written off. It's all a bit more sophisticated now.

However, The Chairman is pretty good at finding his way around problems like this. He also has his reliable old slush fund to arrange consultancy agreements for the families of players we need to keep happy, or need to bring in. But he has stopped appointing players' dads as scouts and giving them cars, supposedly to drive them around the country on their scouting missions. The FA seem to have got wise to that little ruse and, having got into the Premier League, he's not looking for a points deduction to help him on his way back down again.

Wouldn't the FA would love to pin something on us? We've not made ourselves particularly popular on our way up. We're also a much easier target than the big boys, with their abilities to hire equally big-shot lawyers. Fines mean nothing to them, but they would hurt us. Sometimes it seems to me that, when the game's administrators want to fire a warning shot to clubs, players or agents, they'll always aim at the soft targets.

Meanwhile, the player has told The Manager that he doesn't think he's in the right frame of mind to play the next match. I'd like to suggest that we're not in the right frame of mind to pay him either, but I don't think I'd be thanked for my opinion. Indeed, it's easier not to have opinions, or to keep those that I do have to myself.

EARLY OCTOBER

*"It was a game of two halves and we didn't
win either of them."*

The Assistant Manager to BBC1's *Match of the Day*,

after The Manager had refused a post-match interview, October 4th

Eight matches played and we've just suffered our sixth defeat. We've yet to win our first game in the Premiership, and with only two points we're already nearly twenty behind the leaders.

This weekend was the last before a break for Internationals, and the bookmakers are no longer taking bets on The Manager being sacked before Christmas. We've been up to Anfield and lost six-nil; we were fortunate to be able to 'score nil', as one of the journalists unkindly said. The Manager couldn't face the barrage of TV cameras after the game and left the interview to the Assistant. Never a good sign. Even worse was how The Chairman left after the fourth goal, with ten minutes to go.

I had to stay behind to sort out a few things with my opposite number and to make the call, at The Chairman's request, to tell him the final score. He was not a happy man. His driver told me later that he'd effed and blinded all the way down the motorway. When they'd stopped at a service station they'd been surrounded by fans giving him their opinions, in no uncertain terms. These would have been the same fans who'd cheered him to the echo during our promotion year, who'd chanted his name alongside that of The Manager:

"We've got the best chairman in the land," was the song, just a few short months ago – followed by, "Chairman, Chairman, give us a wave."

But there's none of that now. Fans have shorter memories than goldfish. You have to have just a bit of sympathy with the club director who landed a punch on a fan and ended up in court. He was convicted and sentenced to community service, at which point he paid somebody else to do the service for him and was rumbled. I suppose it's at that point that the sympathy runs out. I can't see our Chairman getting down and dirty like that though. He'd pay somebody to land the punch *and* take the punishment. If our results keep on like this, he might be hard pushed by the end of the season to find a fan to punch.

"Sack the board, sack the board, sack the board!" came the chant from the terraces – which is a bit unfair, considering they don't pick the team or kick the ball. But then nobody said football supporters were fair-minded. They have their favourites and then they have their hate targets. It doesn't take much to become a target. A player can be the most talented footballer in the world, but if he tries a trick or two in his first match which doesn't come off he can be branded a Flash Harry and jeered every time he touches the ball. It doesn't take long before the player starts to hide himself, and the fans aren't slow to spot that either.

On the other hand, they love the less talented bloke who gets stuck in and 'gives one hundred and ten percent' in every game. I've never quite understood the mathematics of that, but the lads on television always use the phrase. Mind you, they couldn't tell an adverb from an adjective if both came up and bit them. There's a whole generation of kids who think it's perfectly acceptable to say, "He done great," or, "He hit that ball lovely," or, "He scored that goal superb." It all sits nicely alongside such annoying phrases as, "You can't win the lottery if you don't buy a ticket," or, "It was a game of two halves." (A game of three halves presumably exists in the same parallel universe as one hundred and ten percent.)

The pundits are a bit like the fans. They decide who they like and who they don't before the first ball has been kicked in anger, and then try and justify their selections in their commentary. Yet at a club, it's the fans that have more influence. One permanently suntanned pro, who was famous for choosing to play most of the match on the sunny side of the pitch early in the season, actually refused to go near one group of fans who took a deep dislike to his laidback style of play. Another, who'd been barracked non-stop for the previous few matches, was relieved to find himself on the bench. When told to warm up in readiness to come on as a sub, he feigned an injury instead.

It's not just the players who get the bird from the crowd. The managers also have to cope with up to fifty thousand would-be's who believe they could have picked a better formation. A top manager who started in the lower reaches of the league remembers his first game at a big club, when one old boy seated in the front row just behind him urged him incessantly to bring on one particular player as a substitute. When he came on, the same fan screamed for him to be played wide rather than in midfield. The next game the manager started the player on the wing. Within minutes the same fan was screaming abuse, telling the player he was useless before turning wrathfully on the manager. That manager never paid any attention to the fans again.

In another pre-season friendly, one particular fan made his views about the performance of his team very clear as the manager walked by on his way to the dressing room at halftime. The manager beckoned him over and then grabbed him by the scruff of his neck.

"Do you want to come into the dressing room with me and give the halftime team talk?"

The fan decided it might be a bit of a laugh. He went with the manager down the tunnel, and found himself facing eleven disheartened players who knew they'd been awful for the first forty-five minutes.

"Okay," the manager said, "why don't you tell them how fucking useless they are?"

The fan looked at the manager in astonishment, but he wasn't joking. So the fan proceeded to tell the equally astonished players, one by one, where they had gone wrong.

"Right," said the manager, "you think you could have done better?"

"Well, I couldn't have done any worse."

"What size shoes do you take then?" When the fan told him, the manager ordered his striker to take off his boots.

"And the shirt as well," said the manager. The fan then proceeded to play the second half, to enormous encouragement from his mates.

That's not to say the fans don't have their darker side. Visitors crossing the River Trent on their way to Forest matches might well have been prudent to leave their team colours in the car. But the Forest fans were wise to that ruse, and would ask the odd fan for the time. If they answered in an accent that could only come from the visitors' locality, there was a good chance of them ending up in the Trent rather than on the terraces. The Forest fans always had a reputation, so it wasn't easy to understand the design of their stadium before it became all-seated. Visiting fans were in a stand with its front row just a few inches above the heads of the home fans in front. Somebody said it was a bit like being at the Alamo; when the home fans got riled and wanted to get at the visitors, they would attempt to clamber over the 'ramparts'.

Cardiff fans are always a difficult mob to handle. When we were making our way up the various divisions, they virtually took over one area from our season-ticket holders. I went down to try and sort it out, but the police just shrugged and suggested I seat our fans elsewhere. It was always the Millwall fans who had the reputation, but I never found them that difficult. They definitely looked the part and were certainly partisan, but their bark seemed worse than their bite. They also had a sense of humour.

Once, when there was a Jewish player in the opposing team, the chanting was incessant: "Jew boy, Jew boy!"

The player went to a corner flag, uprooted it, and stood in front of them conducting their choir. The chants soon turned to cheers, and whenever he played there he always got a great reception. You take as you find in this game.

But Leeds supporters were the real thing when it came to thuggery. We had the temerity to win at their ground, so they surrounded one of our supporters' cars and just rocked it from side to side, before pushing it over – not too worried that some fans were actually inside it.

Generally, fans who have experienced the most success are the worst losers. Some of their chanting, if taking place outside a football stadium, would put you in jail. Spurs, with their large Jewish following, tend to ask for trouble when they unfurl the Israeli flag behind a goal and chant, "Yiddos!", but it doesn't justify the anti-Semitic rants I've heard which wouldn't have been out of place at Nuremburg. Six million dead and gas chambers are unlikely themes for football chants, but those who hate Tottenham always seem to embrace them. As, sometimes, do other supporters who aren't even playing Spurs.

Take Chelsea – notwithstanding a Jewish owner who has made them what they are, and a Jewish manager who did what the Special One couldn't do and got them to a Champions' League Final – a section of whose fans have a repertoire of songs that would not be out of place at a Nazi rally. They were even singing them in Moscow before the Champions League Final. It's also quite extraordinary that, when Manchester United visit, you can still hear chants of, "Munich" and, "One slippery runway". The Munich tragedy was nearly fifty years ago, well before most of these mindless idiots who sing along were even born.

There can be amusing moments as well. I rather liked it when Arsenal fans sang about Emmanuel Petit: "He's fast, he's quick, his name's a porno flick, Emmanuel, Emanuel." And, going some way back, when Newcastle had their first black player (albeit on loan), the Toon Army sang, "He's black, he's brown, he's playing for the town." After the somewhat unsuccessful loan period came to an end and he turned up in opposition colours, it was, "He's brown, he's black, we sent the bugger back."

The Toon also take delight, on their rare wins in London, in seeing the spoiled Southern fans leaving well before the end. Their favourite song on these occasions is, "They're here, they're there, they're fucking everywhere, empty seats, empty seats!"

Staying with Newcastle, it's a well-known fact that Alan Shearer turned down the chance of joining one United, in the shape of Manchester, with another in the less successful Newcastle variant. It's not so well-known that he'd turned Newcastle down when he chose to join Blackburn Rovers from Southampton. The Toon Army loved to taunt the Red Army with, "Fergie says to Shearer, 'Will you come to Manchester?', Fergie says to Shearer, 'Will you come to Manchester?', Fergie says to Shearer, 'Will you come to Manchester?' and Shearer says, 'Fuck off, you cunt!'"

There was a rather lyrical response to that, name-checking their hero on the pitch: "Oh Alan Shearer, he may be dearer, but please don't take our Solskjaer away," all to the tune of 'You Are My Sunshine'. And now both Shearer and Solskjaer are gone. It's a lot harder to make up songs about the expensive new foreign imports.

We had a situation, before we started our ascent to the top, when it looked like we were going to go bust. That was before The Chairman got involved, and for a while a Supporters' Trust were threatening – or promising, depending on which way you look at it – to take The Club over. I'm no great fan of Supporters' Trusts, though I can see that any ownership is going to be better than a situation where there's no club to own. But to me it just seems to smack of the lunatics taking over the asylum. Since all the really successful businessmen who acquire football clubs tend to throw good business practices to the wind as soon as they're seated in the directors' box, why should we want fans to run clubs *as fans* when we criticise management for doing just that? The real issue, as far as I can see, is that these trusts don't want to inject any real money into a club, and *certainly* don't want to put their own money in. Or maybe that's just me being cynical?

Of course, fan power depends on the size of the club. Manchester United fans hated the idea of the Glazers taking over so much that, not only were there death threats, but they actually formed a breakaway club. Meanwhile, life went on . . . and although Malcolm Glazer himself didn't grace the directors' box, his sons did, and United won the title. Those fans who'd been saying the Glazers would destroy the club went very quiet.

When Wimbledon relocated to Milton Keynes though, the fans did get themselves well organised and formed AFC Wimbledon, which attracts decent crowds and is a well-run little club with ambitions of its own. But MK Dons still came into existence and are not only a part of the league, despite all the protests, but also won promotion alongside the cup for teams outside the top two divisions, all within the same season.

Yet, down in the lower reaches of the league and outside the league, the fans *can* have a say, though it very often comes too late to stop a club being run into the ground. One healthy former league club finally gave up the ghost with an extraordinary debt of millions of pounds. The chairman and the board who'd been trying to asset strip for a property deal finally succumbed to local pressure and resigned, but by then the club had to go into liquidation and start working its way up all over again. Mind you, that's not as bad as the club where, for a while, the only two people running it were an undischarged bankrupt and the aforementioned director who laid one on a fan.

Fanzines, the unofficial magazines of the club, can be powerful tools in a campaign for change of control. We used to let them be sold outside the ground, until The Chairman got a bit upset with some cartoon caricatures of himself and banned it. It still survives, they just position their sellers around the corner from the ground. They also run a very active website, the officials of most clubs tending to read the unofficial websites to see what's really going on. A fair amount of what's posted on these, either in the form of blogs or commentary, is probably defamatory, but if any chairman brought an action he'd look really stupid.

As a breed, chairmen are even more reluctant to look stupid than the players themselves – though sometimes their behaviour can be just as dumb. When you see a grownup businessman squeezing his paunch into a replica shirt, wearing it in the directors' box or, even worse, standing with the fans and pretending to be one of them, you have to take a deep breath. Sam Hammam at Wimbledon would stand with the fans wearing a scarf, but he was genuinely interested in hearing what they had to say and they loved him for it. These loaded guys who have just bought a club aren't fooling anybody by pretending to be dyed-in-the-wool supporters. I've always felt that you start supporting a club as a small child, and that's it for life.

Some fans are even prepared to go to jail for their clubs. Football hooligans of the seventies and eighties ran riot, until Maggie clamped down on them with dawn raids as part of her zero-tolerance policy. At some clubs the lines between fans and hooligans became blurred. One club's stewards found it impossible to maintain the life ban imposed on some of its more enthusiastic and violent supporters. They continued to let them in simply because the hooligans knew where the stewards lived.

The chairman of another club decided to take a different approach, being invited to a party thrown by the leader of one notorious gang. They struck a kind of deal to keep the fighting away from the stadium, and ultimately the chairman appointed one of the gang leaders as his minder – which worked well until a tabloid took some photos of them together and ran a massive story. It didn't help much when the minder was arrested and sent to jail, not for violent crimes but for a fairly sophisticated fraud. I suppose you can never tell a book by its cover, or a football hooligan by his tattoos.

Another club was the victim of a clever act of revenge by diehard fans who'd become outcasts over the years. They'd been the victims of Mrs T's clampdown on hooliganism, and had all been subjected to highly-publicised early-morning arrests. Only on this particular occasion the charges failed to stick, and the fans were left fighting (metaphorically this time) for reinstatement at the club, so they could watch the beloved team for which so much blood had been shed over the years. The police officer in charge of the embarrassingly unsuccessful operation to put them behind bars had retired from the force, and was now head of security at the very same club.

One of the leading lights of the fan base had written a book about his adventures, and it was decided that the club itself would be a perfect venue for the book's launch. The club's commercial team were new, bright-eyed and bushy-tailed, but knew little about football generally and less about the club's history of violence – particularly relating to the infamous gang whose member had now written his memoirs. When the club received an enquiry as to the availability of their conference facilities, they almost bit the hands off the football agent who had been designated to front for the publisher. The contracts were signed and the date fixed. Players and celebrities were invited and sent their acceptance.

Just under a week before the event was due to take place, the board finally woke up. Instead of smelling roses, they caught a whiff of kippers. All hell broke loose, letters flew between the parties and eventually, much to the embarrassment of the club and amidst huge publicity for the book, the launch was moved to a backup venue. One-nil to the fans.

The publishers then had the *chutzpah* to ask the club for signed shirts and footballs for the charity raffle to be held at the event. The club, despite threatening any of its staff who attended with instant dismissal, actually came up with the goods. Two-nil to the fans.

Two of the club's iconic star players attended, as did hundreds of season ticket holders and a fair number of the club's staff who simply didn't want to miss the occasion. The ex-police officer stayed away, as did the board. The book became a bestseller. Three-nil to the fans, and I suppose to the ex-hooligan as well.

It's just amazing how people try to make capital out of supporting a football club. Tony Blair always claimed to be a Newcastle United fan, but when he had to name his all-time top team for the fanzine, he couldn't even muster up eleven names. Then there are the Johnny-come-lately's who switch allegiance just to latch onto a successful team. Although I don't support anybody myself (not even The Club), I can't see how you can ever change your allegiance. Still, I suppose when you're a young kid you do tend to support a team which is more likely to win something. And if it becomes apparent that this simply isn't going to happen, the peer pressure may just prove too much.

Most chairmen and directors are pretty thick-skinned, their perks more than making up for the ninety minutes of abuse they have to suffer every other week at home. And, as I've said, there are a lot of old boys around the country who you couldn't shift with dynamite from their seats in the directors' box. There's the car-parking space a few yards from the entrance to the ground, the drinks before the game, the free four-course meal (with yet more alcohol), the reserved seat with an uninterrupted view, the free programme and the up-to-date team sheet, the blanket to keep you warm on cold days, or the large television screen back in the boardroom to follow the match on even colder days. Then there's the hot soup/tea/cake/coffee/sandwiches/biscuits at halftime, the chance to sit alongside various celebrities who long to be associated with football, and then the post-match drinks and food as part of the wind-down. Then you watch out of the boardroom window until the traffic clears, and stagger down the stairs to be driven home – as you're way over the limit by then.

And you know what? You can still have the benefits of all that and know fuck-all about football. I remember the old-time Sunderland player who wrote his autobiography with a chapter about the average director's knowledge of football, which consisted of one blank page. He wrote that over fifty years ago, but he'd probably do the same today.

The fans and the board of directors – I'm not sure I really like any of them. But then I don't need to. I just need to do my job.

LATE OCTOBER

*"It is with regret that The Club has to announce that
its contract with its Manager has been terminated with
immediate effect. A decision as to his replacement will
be made shortly, but meanwhile team affairs have been
placed in the hands of The Assistant Manager."*

Statement from The Club's press officer, 24th October

The ink's not yet dry on the compromise agreement between
The Club and The Manager, and already we've received
over fifty applications for the job. It was like that when we
were non-league as well, before The Manager joined us. You
wouldn't think anybody would have wanted to work for the
peanuts we were paying back then, but still we had over a
hundred applicants before we whittled it down to a shortlist
of six. Everybody thinks managers earn fortunes, but there are
guys outside the Football League, even today, who are getting
as little as £30,000 a year and are grateful for it. I suppose
when you've been picked out of all those fighting for a foot on
the managerial ladder, you're going to be satisfied with
whatever's on offer. And don't the clubs just know it?

Management is a Catch-22 situation. You can't get a job
unless you have some experience, and you may not be
astonished to know that you can't get experience without a job.

One of the big problems with managerial contracts is
getting the right balance. If the bloke's successful you want

both him and the club to have some security. But if he's rubbish, and you need to get rid of him, then you don't want to pay out so much money that you can't afford a decent replacement. Some clubs try to insert a 'golden handcuffs' clause. This means that, if the manager wants to leave, he has to pay the club exactly the same compensation they have to pay him if they give him the sack. Given the long pockets of some clubs, they are also happy to stump up that sum to get him out of a contract elsewhere, if he's that good. I've discovered that you can put all the clauses into a contract you like to try to stop your manager talking to other clubs. They are all a total waste of time. Poaching takes place in the public arena, and all the manager's agent has to do is to plant a story in the paper that this or that club is interested in him.

Inserting a 'gardening leave' clause is equally ineffective. Basically, as long as the manager's present club is prepared to keep on paying him just to sit at home, they can, in principle, delay his joining a rival. However, in the real world, it is just delay rather than prevention, as all it does is push up the compensation payment from the acquiring club. Everybody knows that it's impossible to make somebody work for a club he doesn't want to work for. It's no different from players, so you would think managers would be a bit more understanding. But the football industry doesn't run on understanding.

There are some managers who always seem to be able to get a job, however badly they've done in their previous position. They have had some success at some stage in their career, and the hope always lingers that they might just be able to rekindle the flame. But I find it's a bit like racehorses. Just because they've won a chase as a seven- or eight-year-old, you can't expect them to be romping home over the fences at fourteen. A football season is a bit like a steeplechase. It goes on for a very long time, you need luck and stamina and, even with both, you can still fall at the final fence.

Somebody will pick up our Manager, no doubt. There are all sorts of reasons why managers don't make it at the very top, if they are given the chance. They may well be able to judge raw talent, find bargains and polish them until they turn into diamonds, but when they are given an open chequebook (not that one was available to our Manager) they become like kids in a sweetshop, happily overpaying for any piece of confectionary they can lay their hands on.

The real experts are only too happy to have them around, because the other managers know they can get rid of players who are surplus to requirements and appear to be better than they are, just because they've had a few meaningless matches for top teams. They'll give them a couple of games, knowing full well they have no future at the club, just to push up the price when they come to sell by describing them as having top-level first-team experience.

The agents can also make themselves busy filling the shelves at a club where there's a rookie manager, or indeed a rookie owner. Everybody in the game remembers the poor bloke who spent the fortune he'd made buying the club of his dreams, and then buying everything that moved at crazy prices. Not only were the transfer fees mad, but the salaries and agents' commissions were equally off-the-wall. He was just ill equipped to play with the big boys, putting himself at an even greater disadvantage by acting as a quasi-manager and buying the players.

Other managers with a modicum of success at the lower levels may be shrewd judges of players, but they also throw caution to the wind when they get a bit of money. One manager, in charge for the first time of a club at the highest level, ended up with over sixty players in his squad and found himself struggling against relegation. It's only possible to play a rotation system at a really big club where the huge salaries compensate for the fact that even the biggest names are not necessarily automatic choices. An ordinary club with a huge squad will just have a bunch of discontented players, who will speedily turn into bad apples that turn the whole tree rotten.

Then there are the managers who just go rogue when they realise they can virtually buy whomsoever they want at any price. One manager who returned to the club where he'd played quickly surrounded himself with a veritable rogues' gallery of agents, assistants and even support staff, who all, in one way or another, were hell-bent on squeezing as much money as they possibly could out of the club before getting rumbled. The manager was prepared to buy practically anybody, provided that there was some illicit profit in the deal that he could spread around his cronies. The profit could be made in all sorts of ways: the selling clubs paid him a commission to buy players at inflated prices; agents gave him a kickback from an inflated agency fee; other managers were paid by agents to sell a player (so that the agent could earn out of it), and then the manager tossed a piece of the action their way. It's extraordinary how many ways there are to cut a cake, particularly when the cake has so many layers of cream.

As ever, it's a case of who can tell the most effective porkies: the manager denying he's been tapped up; the club denying they are already lining up a replacement; or the replacement saying there's no way he wants to step into a dead man's shoes. The whole saga of managerial appointments sometimes reads as surreal. One manager went on to the field of play at the end of a match after a defeat, shook hands with one or two members of the opposition, went up to the player who'd scored the winning goal, gave him a weak handshake and then head-butted him in full view of the fans. Others just shout themselves hoarse in their technical areas, as if anything they scream out can actually be heard or followed.

As far as our guy is concerned, the straw that broke the camel's back (or in this case, tore the camel coat) was that The Chairman didn't like how The Manager was becoming paranoid about the media, and his not talking to the TV crew after the last match. Mind you, I suppose it was preferable to one very famous manager telling a charming and attractive female interviewer to "fuck off", when she put a mike in front of him after a rare poor performance by his team. Unfortunately for him, the mike was live and, although the TV station did not air the confrontation, everybody knows about it.

As for our poor bloke, well, we were playing away in the Northeast so we booked a hotel on the Friday night. The Chairman used to hate the expense of an overnight stay and insisted we travelled on the day, when we were in the lower divisions. This meant the team generally arrived tired and stiff; looking back, it was a miracle that we did as well as we did. He can't get away with that anymore, though he still makes me negotiate to get the best discounted rates. We were booked into a very nice hotel on the banks of the Tyne, and the night before the game the team decided to play a few tricks. Now, generally speaking, footballers' tricks are neither subtle nor inventive. One leading Premiership team's squad used to delight in trashing hotel rooms. Maybe they had delusions of being a rock band. One night they thought they'd destroyed the room of their least favourite director, only to discover it was occupied by a total stranger.

Another team targeted their chairman on a plane travelling abroad to a pre-season friendly. One by one, the players tapped the chairman on the back of his shoulders and disappeared before he could turn around. This happened a dozen times or more, and the chairman was getting cross.

Then they got the thickest player in the squad to repeat the exercise. As he went to do so, they all called out in unison, "Mr Chairman, he's behind you."

The chairman swung around, saw the player and said, "So, it's you. That's just cost you a week's wages."

To be fair, all the other players did chip in with their share.

Our squad were slightly cruder. They managed to set off a fire alarm and have everybody down outside the hotel at one in the morning. They then took the opportunity to get a rather large turd and put it under the bed in The Manager's room, leaving him to work out from whence the foul smell emanated. When he finally discovered the cause, he did not say a word. But at halftime in the match, with us three-nil down, he lost the plot and began throwing crockery at the players. Now this was real china, not like the plastic stuff that one manager aimed at players when he was in charge at one of the Sheffield clubs. The players were ducking and diving and the centre half, never the quickest at the best of times, took a saucer right between his eyes and had to be substituted. We went on to lose by six without response. The Chairman got a letter from the centre half's agent (who also happened to be a lawyer) and a cleaning bill from the hotel, and that was the finish.

So here we are, just a couple of months into the season, rooted to the bottom. Somebody new needs to come in and perform a miracle. They do happen in football, but somehow I just don't see us as water about to be turned into wine.

EARLY NOVEMBER

"A Club with as much potential as ours should be able to attract any manager it wants."

The Chairman, 3rd November

It's not exactly been encouraging for The Assistant Manager – now Acting Manager – that every day the newspapers link us with another unlikely candidate for New Manager. It would be even less encouraging for him if he knew what I know – that it's The Chairman leaking the information to the press. Basically, the way it works is that he thinks of a name, tells a favoured journalist that this name is very keen to leave wherever he is, and then the rumour factory gets to work.

It was bad enough that The Manager came to be known as 'Dead Man Walking', but now we have the man who passes for his successor in exactly the same position. It's not helpful in instilling confidence in the team, let alone the training staff who can see their jobs on the line as well, once The Assistant Manager gets the chop. It's all a bit unfair really. He was taken on to do a particular job, and now he's going to get the sack because he can't do a totally different one. We're in between transfer windows so he can't even sign any new players, he can only hope to pick up a few bits and pieces on loan.

It's always a temptation when a managerial post gets offered to somebody already on the staff. I've heard of situations when the bloke is in charge of the youth team, has the big one handed to him on a plate and is told not to worry, if it doesn't work out he'll just get his old job back. But, this being football, the chairman in question was lying through his teeth.

It didn't work out, and when a new manager was appointed from outside the club, the guy who'd been promoted from within found himself without. (Without a job, that is.) Mind you, if you had known the chairman in question you'd have known he was a ruthless bastard who would promise anything to anyone, and then not only break the promise but deny it had even been made. I suspect the fellow who took the job knew that, and also knew it would end in tears. Nothing less than the treble, and a couple of European trophies, would have satisfied his chairman. Yet still the temptation was too great, and the youth team manager lived to regret it.

Our Acting Manager is just tiptoeing around the job. He doesn't want to upset anybody, so his selections and formations are as predictable as his post-match interviews. It's a fine line to draw, between arrogance and timidity, but it's not just successful managers who can be arrogant. One manager, who had won absolutely nothing, somehow found himself in charge of a club where the chairman was throwing money at a promotion bid. He began to equate himself with the chairman, and sent an email to all players and staff, saying, "If you see me around the club I don't want to be approached. If you have any matters you want to raise with me, tell my PA who will arrange an appointment to see me if it is thought necessary."

A couple of defeats later he was gone, and the chairman of the club had no hesitation in sacking the manager directly rather than asking his PA to deliver the message.

Some clubs get through managers like packets of Maltesers. They come looking tasty, they get consumed and they're gone. And even if they don't get swallowed up, they still have a sell-by date. Everybody knows the high-risk clubs and the high-risk chairmen. Doug Ellis at Aston Villa was not nicknamed 'Deadly Doug' for nothing. Simon Jordan at Crystal Palace is another scary chairman who has little or no patience with unsuccessful managers. Neither of them are unpleasant people. But if you invest a lot of money in your club then you have the right to demand results. It's just that some chairmen demand more than others.

You have to feel sorry for some managers when they're clearly living on borrowed time. Claudio Ranieri at Chelsea didn't do a lot wrong, but was always going to be replaced by Mourinho. Martin Jol at Spurs saw almost every available manager linked to his job (and some that weren't available too). The rumour was, only the fact that Bill Nicholson was dead prevented him being summoned back by the chairman for interview. And even then, I think Spurs' chairman had to be presented with a copy of the death certificate before he took him off his shortlist.

At least one manager went to see his chairman at the club, and found him having tea with his successor. The only problem was that he had no idea that he was being succeeded. the chairman actually had the gall to invite the incumbent in and introduce him. The rumour is that the manager told the chairman exactly where to put his cuppa. He was doubtless tempted to resign, as so many of them must be. Yet there's the golden handshake to protect and so genuine resignations amongst managers are few and far between. Doing the honourable deed is one thing, committing financial suicide is quite another.

The late Stan Flashman at Barnet used to sack Barry Fry on a weekly basis, but Barry never resigned. You can bet your bottom dollar that, if you do hear of a manager resigning, it's because he's agreed a deal with the club that makes it worth his while. It's lucky we are outside of a transfer window at the moment, so The Acting Manager can't sign anybody new. That offers him a perfect excuse, because he can say the squad, which is letting him down, isn't the squad he would have chosen. Even if he gets the push – which, in my opinion, is pretty inevitable – he'll be able to claim he never had a fair chance to work with players of his choice. That way, his brief period of tenure won't be a real blot on his CV.

Some are known in this business as 'talking managers'. They're the ones who talk a good game and, somehow or other, get job after job on the basis of one or two successes in the distant past. Then there are the fellows who fail on their first real break, and are never heard of again. There's no rhyme or reason to it, other than the fact it's an unforgiving industry. The good guys generally lose, both on and off the pitch. Management needs a mean and ruthless streak. An up-and-coming manager in the lower leagues once brought in a mate as an experienced face about the club, and then gave him a few coaching opportunities. Next thing he knew, he was getting his P45 and his mate had been named as player-manager. Much cheaper for the club.

The really tough ones are often as unforgiving as the game itself. A very high-profile manager had as his number two the man who'd not only played alongside him, but had also been the best man at his wedding. Number two was offered a managerial post at another club, tried to discuss it with his friend and was told that, if he took it, that was the end of the friendship. In fact they didn't even speak for over ten years. Everybody knows how Brian Clough treated Peter Taylor when he wanted to be his own man, and that break-up signalled the end of the success story for both of them in many ways.

Yet some managers are astonishingly loyal. One man has taken his own team from club to club and, even though he'd been out of a job for over a year when he was offered a high-profile club, he immediately reassembled his team, who'd been patiently waiting and turning down everything that came their way, having been ensured they were part of the package.

And some managers are very dodgy. The reputation of one particular manager precedes him, and yet he is never out of work. His agent seems to have established an understanding at certain clubs, which becomes more understanding if his manager is in charge. Eventually, he will run out of road (or understanding clubs), but for the moment both he and his agent – not to mention one or two individuals at the clubs in question – are all making money.

I don't know how some managers get away with it. If an agent gives a manager a holiday, or a share in a racehorse, or even a property, everybody knows about it – yet the FA seem unable or unwilling to deal with it. It seems that the rougher and the tougher you are as an agent, the dirtier you play, the more likely you are to get away with it. We're looking for a new manager, not a new agent – but, given the chosen occupation of The Chairman's Son, I am not all sure that the two are inseparable.

We've started interviewing our shortlist and I've been sitting in to take notes. Some of the candidates have astonishing CV's, but so much is historical that I doubt they have the up-to-date network necessary to take The Club any further. A manager needs his contacts, needs his little black book. That's how a club like ours can pick up the bits-and-pieces players that other clubs don't need. A year's loan from the likes of Chelsea, Arsenal, Liverpool or Manchester United can be a lifeline for a small club such as ours. We are unlikely to be able to keep them if they work out, but we can return them as much better and more experienced players. At least with us they get the chance to play. To get the pick of those loans, your manager needs to know the managers and/or the coaching staff of the big clubs. There's a sort of informal cabal in the game: the managers who are outside the inner circle have to build their teams either from the non-league clubs or from abroad.

One of our interviewees actually ended up interviewing *us*. He produced a whole sheaf of papers, gave us a long motivational speech, set out his aims and told us exactly what he would need from us if he were to take the job. I could see The Chairman's eyes glazing over. I know exactly what he's looking for. A bit of a name to keep the fans happy, but not so big a name or personality that he'll prevent The Chairman getting his own way. I've glanced down the list and, if I were a betting person, I think I'd know exactly which one he would choose. Not that betting doesn't go on when it comes to managerial appointments, and not that they aren't placed by those who already know the outcome. It happens all the time. The secret is not to be too greedy, and not to put on such large amounts of money as to attract the attention of the authorities. In a way, that just about sums up the footballing industry. You can get away with most things as long as you don't get too greedy.

Some of the applicants are rather sad. Out of work for so long that they're almost begging for a chance to get back into the game, they're like addicts – not getting their daily fix of football is killing them. Yet we are a Premier League side and, though we're by far the smallest club in the division, it's a great opportunity for somebody.

The know-alls are saying we may be relegated by Easter, but the chocolate eggs seem a long way off, and everybody who's applying truly believes he can deliver the goods. But if they think that The Chairman is going to open his purse, or that dealing with him is going to be a doddle, then good luck to them.

EARLY DECEMBER

"I feel I am leaving this club in the best health it has enjoyed in its whole history. It has been a pleasure and a privilege to have been involved in our exciting rise to the Premiership, and I am confident that my successor will be able to take us to even greater heights."

The Chairman, December 1st

I can't believe it, but The Chairman has actually agreed to sell The Club. I've seen his statement, but what it fails to say is that he is cashing out with a profit which must have been beyond his wildest dreams when he first bought in. I was going to say when he 'first bought into the dream'. But The Chairman doesn't have dreams. He has business plans and this one has worked out very nicely, thank you.

I suppose I should have guessed when The Chairman asked me to prepare management accounts before the end of the month. But with him one just does what he asks, when he asks it. He doesn't encourage questions and club secretaries have to be an obedient breed. We aren't necessarily paid to think for ourselves, but to carry the thoughts of others through to fruition.

Club owners are strange creatures. I've already given you my opinion that, though they usually run very successful businesses, the minute they buy a football club they throw all their good practices to the wind. Some, the minority, are sensible and leave the running of the club to those who understand football. Others, the majority, go to the other extreme. One wealthy chairman not only chose the players to be signed, but also told the manager who he should play from week to week. Then, when the manager failed to get results, he quickly went public, blamed him for everything and gave him the sack.

I'm not even quite sure where the new chairman comes from. Not England, that's for sure. It's hard to programme myself to call him The Chairman, so I'm going to think of him as The Newcomer. He has no connection with The Club, or the region, or even the country, but he has pledged to ring a lot of changes – none of which involve me, fortunately. As I've said before, I'm a survivor because I have the knack of becoming invisible. I just do my job and, as long as The Club's administration runs smoothly, nobody even notices me enough to fire me.

The Newcomer has brought in a whole new team of advisors, moneymen for the most part. We have a new Chief Executive, a new Marketing Director, a new head of Public Relations and a new Finance Director. For the first time since I've been involved with The Club there is actually an infrastructure. The Chairman has become a Life President with the use of the board room on match days, but all the old directors have gone, none of them willingly. However, since there are all sorts of rumours as to how The Newcomer made his money, I get the impression they would have been ill advised to argue. The Newcomer seems to be a man who always gets what he wants, and does not appreciate anybody getting in his way. He says he is going to make us another Manchester United, but our fans would be grateful if only our back four became united. He's also talking about a new fifty thousand-seater stadium, although he hasn't yet said where he intends finding fifty thousand fans to fill it.

There are all sorts of rumours concerning the source of his wealth. Some say he received huge rewards from his own country for his silence. (It's suggested that he not only knows where the bodies are buried, he actually put some of them there himself.) What is certain is that he has remunerative state contracts for the supply of zinc and copper in South America and Africa. Whatever the truth of it, he is seriously rich and, if he puts his money where his advisors' mouths have been, then The Club is in for an enormous sea change in its fortunes. I'll take as I find. It seems that, under the new regime, I'll be reporting to The Chief Executive.

Just as interesting as the arrivals are the departures. I've been told that The Chairman's Son is no longer welcome at The Club, and nor is The Agent. I assume The Newcomer's accountants must have found some interesting payments listed which sent out a whole barrage of warning signals. Mind you, since The Manager left, the whole relationship between The Club and The Chairman's Son (not to mention The Agent) has been on the wane. I can't say I'm upset. I don't have to like the people with whom I have to work, though it might help.

To be a director of a football club, you need to satisfy the FA that you are a 'fit and proper person'. I can't see anybody having the courage to suggest that The Newcomer is not. I know he intends to establish a holding company (which will be controlled by his offshore trustees, who doubtless take instructions from him) and that it will own and control The Club – of whose board The Newcomer will not actually be a member. But he will be filling The Board with his own people, and it seems I'll be the only survivor from the old regime.

I did tell you that most club secretaries double up as the Vicar of Bray, and in my case that appears to be about right. As always, I will do as I'm told, run The Club's administration, and hope I'm not directed to do anything that might land me in jail. One of my pals told me how he was regularly instructed to change details on contracts after everybody had signed, but before they went off to the FA. Sometimes an alteration to a date of payment can make the world of difference to a club's finances. Players and their agents are often in such a rush to sign and get their money that they don't read what they're signing, and forget to ask for a copy of the contract. That's where the fun starts. The FA rules are quite simple: If it's not in the contract, then it simply doesn't exist. So arguing that it doesn't truly reflect what was agreed at the time gets you absolutely nowhere.

The Newcomer scares me a little. He did ask me to visit him at his office, which is about the size of my house. He was very polite, very professional and invited me to take a seat, offering me tea and biscuits served on very expensive china.

"Everybody tells me you are the heartbeat of The Club," he said in his foreign tones, but with surprising fluency.

"That's very kind of them," I reply, wondering if I'm going to get a raise.

"So, I will expect you to be my eyes and my ears. I think that very little will happen at The Club which does not come to your attention, so I will expect it to come to my attention as well. For the most part all you will need to do is tell my Chief Executive. Unless it is about The Chief Executive, in which case you will tell me."

I had just enough time to finish my tea and eat one biscuit before I was out of there. And I have to tell you, I let out a huge sigh of relief. Mainly because I reckon I'd been holding my breath the whole time I'd been in there.

Don't get me wrong. The Newcomer certainly won't be the first person to own a football club without anybody having the faintest idea as to how he made his money. Certainly, one really well-known chairman 'vanished' for years of his life, and when he reappeared he'd reinvented himself as a self-made millionaire. He bought a club for a song, sold it for a fortune, and happily rolled along without ever revealing anything about his missing years.

There are several kinds of owners. The fan who buys the club he has always supported, and then tells everybody who interviews him how he was driven to make money because he'd wanted to own the club since he was a kid. Then there's the successful businessman who claims to have supported the club all his life, but, when asked how many games he has seen, replies by saying he's been too busy. (Presumably busy making the money to buy the club.) There's the man who sees the whole process as a business opportunity, particularly where there's a property deal involved. He's never going to become a favourite of the fans who, generally speaking, seem to have a better grasp of club owners than the Football Association itself.

Some who take that last route do end up in the poorhouse themselves. A very successful property developer thought he'd spotted an opportunity to buy what was then a club in the top division. It had a relatively small ground with an equally small following. I'm not sure he'd even seen them play before he bought them; what drove him was the belief that he could get planning permission to build a supermarket at one end of the stadium, relocate the club, sell it and move on. But it didn't quite work out that way. The fans pressurised him to put more money into the club for buying players; the planning permission failed because the local authority didn't like the cut of his jib; as the club tumbled down division after division, neither did the fans. The investor eventually had to take a huge loss to get out of the club, and it took many years of property dealing to get himself back to the point where he'd come in. Football is a very seductive mistress, but she can be very cruel – particularly when she finds out you were only after her money in the first place.

For some chairmen, owning a football club is a little like playing the three-card trick where the punter has to find the lady. They know where the lady lies, but so long as nobody else can find her they can continue with the game. It's far more difficult now, but in the past there have been many acquisitions carried out with smoke and mirrors to conceal the buyer's lack of substance. The individual concerned may have a little money of his own, but certainly not enough to buy his target club. He'll either have leveraged his money using the assets of the club he doesn't yet own, or else brought in a strategic partner who has the property assets of the club firmly in his sights.

For some, just making a bid for the club is enough to get them the publicity they crave. They know they've no chance of ever completing the transaction, but the offer has been enough to ensure that for a few months they've been wined and dined at the club, photographed in the directors' box, or – on one memorable occasion – paraded as a saviour on the pitch before a crowd of thousands, in the club's replica kit. It's rumoured that one potential acquirer actually entered into a back-to-back contract to 'flip' the club and make a juicy profit. It was only the hesitancy of one or two key share-holders to sign up to the deal that scuppered his plans.

What most people outside the inner circle of football don't appreciate is that so many clubs are built like a house of cards. A club is sold and money goes in via a loan from a parent company. In theory, those loans can be called in at any time. If a rich and devious investor acquires a club through loans and then flogs off the assets to repay himself, the investor can then sell off whatever is left (often less the freehold of the stadium) to make himself yet another profit. What's most significant for the future of the club (or, if the club is big enough, for football itself) is the scenario where repayment of the loans is demanded, the club can't pay, and the new owner just sends the club into oblivion. If a club becomes the plaything of a multi-billionaire with no roots in the game, then anything can happen.

Chairmen are often all too willing to pawn a club's family silver – either to avoid putting in the money themselves, or else for a quick fix to raise money to buy players. Unless they achieve success, i.e. a decent run in Europe, then that way only disaster lies. The 'family silver' can be the stadium itself, the training ground, or future revenue by way of advanced season ticket sales, advertising, sponsorship, television money or stadium naming rights. If the club in question doesn't achieve the sort of success that the level of investment demands, then administration or bankruptcy are sure to follow.

The FA got wise to clubs going into strategic administrations a few years ago. Any club undergoing an 'insolvency event' suffered an automatic ten-point deduction by way of a sanction. But if the club was going to be relegated anyway (which was often the case, as disasters off the field generally led to disasters on it) then that sort of penalty was meaningless. So now the FA have got even cannier: depending on the timing of the administration, that penalty may now really bite if it's applied at the start of the following season.

I think the cynicism of one chairman, who sat at the last match of the season with an administrator waiting by the side of the phone in his office, was one step too far. If the team in question won they would stay up. If they lost, well, they were going down anyway and any point deduction was academic. The chairman waited and waited. Then, a few minutes from the end, when all hope was lost for his team, he made the call and the club plunged into administration. The fact that they went down with ten less points was irrelevant. And it was all within the rules that existed at that time.

Our club has always had quite a few shareholders who own just one or two shares. A few diehards turn up to the AGM for a cup of tea and a slice of cake, ask a few harmless questions and are not seen again until the following year. But generally we have a whole group of people out there that we just don't know. In some cases we don't even have an up-to-date address for them, and they may be dead anyway. What's often happened is that an original shareholder has died, a widow has inherited, who's also died, a daughter with no interest in football has inherited, and her kids don't even know she held any shares when she shuffles off to the great stadium in the sky.

How are the shareholders going to take to The Newcomer? I have no idea. But you know what? I don't think he really gives a damn.

SECOND WEEK IN DECEMBER

"It is our intention to make this Club a bigger brand name than Manchester United and Arsenal combined. As for Chelsea, well, we believe that our oligarch is better than their oligarch."

A spokesman for The Newcomer, December 8th

So, that's finally it. The King is dead. Long live the King. The Newcomer is well and truly here and is determined to erase all memories of the old regime. It seems that, in the legal contract to acquire The Club, it was agreed with The Chairman that he could use the directors' lounge on match days for as long as he liked. Just before our most recent league match, I was given instructions to rename all the rooms on the executive floor. What was the 'Directors' Lounge' became the 'Board Lounge'. What was the 'Executive Lounge' became the 'Directors' Lounge'. The only thing is that you won't see any directors in there – unless they happen to be a director of the local plumbing company that advertises in our match-day programme. Or unless one of our directors has a meeting with somebody who doesn't rate an invite into the inner sanctum of the board lounge.

All that the re-branded directors' lounge now does for you (much as the old executive lounge did) is give you somewhere warm before kick-off. You have to buy your own drinks, and the only food supplied consists of nuts and crisps (plain, not flavoured) and a few cheap biscuits from Makro. You do get to watch the television for free, though I'm not so sure The Chairman would see that as any kind of perk. If he went to use the facility, he'd be rubbing shoulders with just the sort of person he'd never have invited into the old directors' lounge, let alone the directors' box. Then, just to add insult to injury, there is no direct access to his seat so he would have to go downstairs, out into the cold and into another entrance to get back into the ground. With the time that takes, it would almost be impossible for him to get back into the lounge for a halftime drink and back into his seat for the second half.

The Chairman has instructed his solicitors to write a letter before action. I know, because I opened it when it came. I was also there when The Chief Executive ripped it in half and threw it in the bin. I was going to ask if he intended telling The Newcomer about it, but had second thoughts. I can't see myself winning brownie points by showing any sympathy for The Chairman.

The Chief Executive just laughed and said, "The Chairman should sue his own lawyers for not making the agreement watertight."

I did notice that the letter was not from the firm The Chairman used to instruct, so perhaps he's doing exactly that.

The Chief Executive gave me more time than I'd had with The Newcomer, and clearly knows a lot more about football. "You know your job," he said to me, "and I'm not going to interfere with the administration. It's just that your job description is going to change a bit. So you won't be doing anything I don't ask you to do, is that understood?"

I nodded. This is going to be fun. I've been appointed a spy by the new owner and threatened by his man on the ground. Let's see which of the three of us lasts the longest.

Everything is changing, and the journalists are loving it. The Newcomer has everything, even a trophy wife. Not that anybody has heard much from him directly. Everything comes from The Chief Executive, who was headhunted from one of the bigger clubs. Upon first inspection he seems to have a great record in making clubs profitable, both on and off the pitch. But he also has a colourful background, although recent successes have caused it to fade a little. He has presided over at least one club that went into administration and made himself a lot of enemies in the process. Mind you, he also saved that club's owners a lot of money.

The Chief Executive also has associations with some of the bigger foreign agents doing business in this country, an association that might not withstand the closest scrutiny. One foreign agent in particular seems to have taken up an almost permanent residency at The Club, alongside his English associate. It seems that he brokered the deal for the purchase of The Club and, apart from receiving a substantial finder's fee, has now got himself appointed as The Club's exclusive buying agent. What that means is that, come the January transfer window, he is going to clean up. Since we didn't appoint any of the applicants for The Manager's job, The Acting Manager is still notionally in charge. The Foreign Agent will buy anybody that The Acting Manager identifies as a target and, along the way, he'll also negotiate the fee, whilst selling anybody that The Acting Manager wants out of The Club. This assumes that The Acting Manager will stay in his post long enough to be a part of the process. It won't take long for all the other agents to realise that, if they want to bring a player into The Club, then they have to make this duo their first port of call.

I can see the duo's coffers filling up from all sorts of directions. The Newcomer has already paid the pair of them to find The Club. The Club will pay commissions on transfers in and out. I can see them asking agents who bring players in to split their commissions with them. And who is to say what they'll get from clubs selling to, or buying from, The Club?

The Chief Executive is going to have to be either a very honest man who rises above it all, a very stupid man who doesn't realise what is going on, or a thoroughly dishonest man who will take a big slice of the cake in return for pretending to be either honest or stupid. The Football Association have now introduced fairly draconian rules, not only to get foreign agents to register with them if they are conducting business in the UK, but also for agents to file details of all payments they make to or receive from third parties. But these rules are unlikely to make any great impact on that particular part of the money machine. It's going to be hard, if not well-nigh impossible, to monitor the route of monies once they leave The Club.

It's odd how clubs can treat agents well when they feel they have something to offer, and then turn on them when they seem of no further use or are making too much money out of the relationship. It's not like any normal business where a contract regulates the relationship. There's always something of the Wild West about the situation. I know one agent who knew a club was being wildly overcharged for a player. He phoned the club's chairman and asked to meet him for lunch.

"I can get that fee down from two mil to one," he said.

"And what would you want out of it?" the chairman asked.

"Well, if I'm saving you a million quid then a fifty-fifty split wouldn't be unreasonable, would it?" proposed the agent confidently, adding, "so everybody wins. Except the sellers, that is."

"No," the chairman said.

"Why not?" asked the astonished agent.

"Because I'd rather pay the full price than let a little shit like you earn that amount of money for doing fuck-all," the chairman said, and with that he walked out and left the agent to pay the bill.

Then there was the struggling club who, when threatened by relegation, had an agent help them appoint a new manager and promised him £100,000 on the next deal he did at the club, when that new manager was actually in. They also offered him £50,000 if they stayed up. The agent did bring a player in, and sent an invoice for what he thought was the agreed amount. The club told him they'd decided that £50,000 was enough of a cut, and if they stayed up he'd get £25,000. Take it or leave it. The agent then had a dilemma. Did he burn his boats and take the club on in the courts, when he had very little proof of the deal, or did he just take what was offered and live to fight another day? Inevitably, he decided discretion was the better part of valour and took the money: exactly what the unscrupulous chairman had banked on. Some chairmen don't leave their best business practices behind when they buy a club. They just use them to play the game in the sharpest way possible.

There are some very odd things happening around here. The Acting Manager has been limping along from week to week. He's actually achieved a few half-decent results and, although we're still bottom, we are no longer adrift at the foot of the table. In fact, if the results go our way this weekend, we may even have two clubs below us.

However, he's no big name and I've been told to calculate what it will cost to pay up his whole contract. So keen was he to get the job that he just stayed on his old salary, so he's earning a quarter of what any other manager in the Premiership does. But that's not really the point. There he was, nice and secure before The Manager left; since then he's come to the aid of The Club in its time of crisis, and helped to steady the ship. For The Newcomer though, that counts for exactly nothing. Money is no object; he can do exactly what he likes with The Club, and anybody in it. A very scary prospect. Where he comes from life is cheap, but we used to have different values at this particular Club – even under the benevolent despotism of The Chairman. Should I be thinking of my own future? For now, I'll just keep my head below the parapet and do what I'm told.

How the journalists continue to lap it up! Suddenly we are at the forefront of media attention. They know that The Acting Manager is on his way out. There's a herd instinct amongst the newspapermen: one of them gets a whisper, and it's as if all their heads automatically turn in the direction of the wind that's blown it along. If one of the herd has totally fabricated the story on a bad news day, it doesn't even matter. Within twenty-four hours it's gospel, and they're all writing about it as if it was brought down from Mount Sinai on a stone tablet.

There are now all sorts of names being linked with The Club, and I've no doubt that some wannabe applicants are throwing their hats into the ring. That's easier than it sounds – just a call from a manager's agent (yes, they too have agents) to a friendly journalist. He'll drop it into the conversation that his client had an informal approach from a club, and the next day it's headline news. The manager concerned may be out of work, he may be with a club, it simply doesn't matter. There's no contract written in football that can't be broken. There just has to be enough money spread around to ease the pain.

Most of today I've spent fielding phone calls. We are getting, so I'm told, a full-time Director of Communications (he'll still be The Press Officer as far as I'm concerned), but he's not arriving for another week or so. Meanwhile I'm left to do what I can, along with all my other duties. The problem with journalists is their bloody persistence. Yes I know they have a job to do, but it would be so much easier for all concerned if they would just write the facts rather than an entry for the Booker Prize. They even have a way of phrasing questions to justify the fiction they're about to write.

"Would I be wrong to write that so-and-so is in the frame for the job?"

You respond by saying, "I'm not commenting on so-and-so or any other individual."

By the next morning this will have translated into, "The Club's reluctance to confirm or deny so-and-so as a target can only lead to one conclusion. He is their prime target."

Or, worse still, "SO-AND-SO is their target," all beneath an 'exclusive' by-line.

You couldn't make it up. But they do. And the astonishing thing is that the public continue to lap it up. They only need to look back at the stories the papers wrote the previous month to know that the great majority of their predictions never come to pass, yet there's still a market for this kind of pulp fiction.

Even I've had calls from the odd manager I know, asking if

there's a chance of a formal interview. All I can do is ask them to send in their CV's, and then I'll pass them up the line. It's a bit rich asking somebody who has actually managed the national team (or *a* national team) to send in a summary of what he's done, but that's the way of it. As I've said before, clubs outside the Football League actually get the highest level of applicants when a job falls vacant. It does take a while for somebody whose previous jobs have been top drawer to come around to realising they have to get back on the job ladder. But, eventually, they nearly always do.

There are still one or two former managers so arrogant that they can't bring themselves to apply for a job. They're so sure that somebody will come knocking on their doors, but after a year or two in the wilderness with their CV's becoming evermore historical, they come around. By then it can be too late. Some managers are regarded as too dangerous to employ. They've made the fatal mistake of writing their memoirs early, and apportioning the blame for their own failings to the board of a club they either got relegated or steered into administration. Any club will wonder whether or not he'll do the same thing to them once he's been dismissed, despite any confidentiality clauses they may try to entangle him in.

There's a familiar scenario where a manager tries to put the blame on his chairman by going public, saying he couldn't compete in the transfer market when it came to buying players. The chairman can't lose face with the fans so he has to cough up the money. The manager rushes to spend it and buys foolishly. Results go against him, he gets the sack. He sells his exclusive story to a tabloid and his version is, "Too little, too late." Or he claims the team wasn't of his making, that he was told he had to sell before he could buy.

No matter if it's a lie. Very few people involved in the world of football allow truth to get in the way of their plans. Here the paper pays for the story, the journalist acts as a sort of ghost-writer and the public gobbles it up, globules of fat and all. Nobody wants to hear from the chairman of the club – and, for the most part, he doesn't make any great effort to tell his side of the story.

A photogenic manager who's got a strong personality, who has been a player himself and who appears regularly on television, is just the sort who appeals to the fans. Even when a manager is subject to all sorts of rumours and allegations about his propriety and integrity, once he's gone to another club and won a few matches it's all forgotten. Managers are loved because they win matches not because of how they live off the pitch. They can be all over the tabloids the whole week and, come Saturday afternoon, have fifty thousand chanting their names as if they're homecoming war heroes. And as they raise their own hands in a salute to their admiring fans, it almost appears as if they believe the myth themselves. I've always thought that, if Hitler had possessed the acumen to manage a successful team, its fans may well have forgiven him for bombing their local chippie.

Mind you, if there are unemployable managers then there are also unmanageable clubs . . . Or at least they're unmanageable so long as a particular chairman is in charge. Everybody knows which clubs they are, and the managers (and players) who have any choice simply steer well clear of them. Agents don't bring players there because the chairman either flatly refuses to pay fees, or else is virtually impossible to deal with when negotiating a contract. They'll nickel and dime until all the goodwill that came with the arrival of the player and his agent is dissipated.

One chairman sits in silence as the agent sets out his terms. Then he produces his own contract, which he has prepared before the meeting. The agent tries to argue his corner. He makes point after point regarding the attributes of his player. The chairman still says nothing and gives no real indication that he is even listening. Eventually, he'll look at his watch, rise and say, "I've got to go now," and make as if to leave.

The agent now has a choice. Does he take what's on offer and spin his client a line as to how he beat the chairman up from his original figure Or does he call his bluff and go? Anybody taking the latter course with this particular chairman soon discovers he's not bluffing. He never budges from his offer as a matter of principle. It is what it is – so is whatever he offers in respect of fees.

I've mentioned them before, but we all have to learn to live with the new FA agents' regulations that came into force on 1st January 2007. Now only the player can pay the agent and we, as The Club, are trying to think of ways around it. We need to be on some kind of level playing field with the big boys, who are going to drive coach and horses through the rules with impunity.

Until now, clubs were able to make payments to agents whether or not the agent had acted for the player. Everything was rather cosy. The Club paid the whole fee and, with the acceptance of the Inland Revenue, we would put about half of the amount actually paid to the agent on the player's P11D at the end of the year so he'd pay tax on it. The problem that the agent had was that, if the payment was less than the percentage to which he was contractually entitled from the player, he couldn't ask the player for a 'top-up'. Well, at least not legally.

I certainly know of a few agents who'd have the player come into their office with readies for the top-up payment. I've had players come into my office asking for cash for that very purpose. Indeed, sometimes the agent won't even tell the player they'd had anything from the club at all. Yes, there were forms to be signed, but so few of the players ever read anything that's put before them. There might be an awakening when they get a big tax deduction from a monthly salary someway down the line, but by then the agent has moved on to other matters and if the client walks, then the client walks.

If the agent and the club are playing it strictly by the rules then only one party can pay. So, if the club just pays, say, two percent of the value of the contract instead of the five percent that the agent is due, then if the agent is going to play it straight he has a dilemma. Does he say no to the two percent and insist his client pays him? If he does he'll probably lose the player. Or does he take the two percent and lose himself money, all with the chance that the player will still dump him for some reason or other? It's particularly risky now, because the FA insist on a clause in the representation contract stipulating that the player can act for himself if he wants to, without involving his agent in any way.

(Heads you lose, tails you lose. Still, not a lot of people in the game shed tears for an agent's loss.)

You see, up till now everybody in The Club has come to me and told me everything about everybody else. That's how I'm aware of it all. But I can't see the same confidences continuing under the new regime. In fact, I've just been told after the event that The Newcomer and The Chief Executive have decided on the appointment of the new manager. I can't say I'm really surprised to learn he's of the same nationality as The

Newcomer. He's managed their national team and lifted them into the world's top thirty. He even got them to the quarter-final of the World Cup, and I suppose that's a better qualification than most of the home-grown managers who've been linked with this job.

He had a less successful time in Italy, where it's rumoured he didn't bother to learn a word of the language. It's going to be the same problem here, I suppose. I've been told he speaks no English whatsoever, and so I've been asked to secure the services of an interpreter. That's what we've come to at The Club. I'm The Club Secretary and I've no means of communicating with The Manager. The Newcomer and his new agent had better succeed, or else I can see the fans taking the trouble to learn a few words in their native language which are unlikely to be too welcoming.

As for The Acting Manager . . . well, I was asked to tell him what he was going to get by way of compensation, to thank him for his contribution to The Club over the years, and then, if he asked for more money, to gently explain to him that he was already being made an offer he could not refuse.

As you can imagine, I didn't take kindly to my new role as an enforcer. So I sold it to him in a gentler, subtler way, and he accepted graciously. But then, he's a football person and they are not. I like to think of myself as a football person too – but I'm beginning to have my doubts.

SECOND WEEK IN DECEMBER

*"I do not know this team. But then I do not know
my own team either."*

The Foreign Manager (through his interpreter), on hearing the draw
for the Third Round of the FA Cup, December 10th

We have the new manager in place. There have been so many changes happening so fast that I can only think of the new arrival as The Foreign Manager (or The FM, for short), to distinguish him from his two unfortunate predecessors. It's not often I get to the training ground, but I've heard that he just stands there in a designer tracksuit, hands deep in his pockets, shaking his head a lot.

We're fast running out of staff who know anything about the squad, and the actual training is more or less under the aegis of our Academy Director. He was very reluctant to take on the responsibility himself; having had a good record with our youngsters, he can see himself losing his old job if he gets too involved with first-team affairs.

I love the story of the non-league club who go through managers at about the same rate as its chairman changes girlfriends. The experienced ex-pro in charge was not getting the results, which was hardly surprising given the budget he was forced to work within. The old maxim of paying peanuts and getting monkeys is never truer than in football.

Eventually, in desperation, he brought in an experienced player to try to get some semblance of order into the team. The player made one appearance, the team lost, and the manager promptly got the sack. The chairman decided that the cheapest way forward was to give the player-manager position to the experienced player who'd just been signed, though he had no experience of management at any level.

The player was in charge for two matches (one of which his team actually managed to win) and was then offered the job on a permanent basis. The player-manager not unreasonably asked for some money to buy decent players and get the club out of its desperate situation. The chairman listened attentively and then told him that, not only could he not have any new players, but also that some of the players he did have were so bad that he needed to get rid of them to reduce the budget. The player-manager told him where he could stick his team and walked, leaving the chairman to appoint his third manager in ten days.

The FM is a bit bemused. He could not understand why the players were coming in at ten in the morning to train, and then going off home at lunchtime . . . all of that with a full day off a week. He's now got them staying on and doing double sessions. One of our players, who hadn't quite got the hang of it, promptly got into his car and drove off. The FM has told me, through The Chief Executive, to fine him a week's wages.

I hate it when The Club disciplines a player. I have the agent on the phone, telling me his boy has done nothing wrong. Then I have the player coming in with a letter of appeal (clearly drafted by the agent or his lawyer – players never reduce anything to paper, unless it's a note to the girl in the canteen, telling her to meet them after training), and then the PFA get involved.

The Professional Footballers Association is the players' trade union. Some of them don't even realise they are paying subscriptions, but they're all members. The PFA always seem prepared to defend the indefensible, but then isn't that what a union is supposed to do? The players have paid enough to them over the years, but there's this terrible suspicion amongst the agents that the PFA will use any opportunity to try to steal the players away, and represent them in their contractual negotiations as well.

I don't care who I deal with. Some agents are really professional and some just come in with their demands scribbled on an Asda receipt. The PFA are fairly consistent but, in my opinion, don't have the flair or imagination of the better agents. Even though I am on the other side, I can still admire somebody doing his job well and coming up with new ideas.

The PFA say that agents are only interested in the money. Agents claim that the PFA just want to use the contractual stuff as a loss leader, to help them grab hold of the players' financial investments and earn commissions that way.

They also say that, as a trade union, the PFA is trying too hard to be all things to all men. They may well be right. The Lord Stevens Report said the PFA should dismantle its agency department, but I don't see any real sign of that. It's a bit like any other report into football: the people involved go out on a jolly and get paid a lot of money; forests are chopped down to print the report, and all the column inches that the newspapers devote to it.

And afterwards? Life goes on very much as it has before. Task forces, governmental 'white papers', the Quest investigation – you name it, at the end of the day none of them have made any real difference. But, as I said, I really don't care. If we, or any other club, are desperate to sign a player then we'll simply buy a long spoon and sup with the devil. Principles and morality are fine, but taken together in the world of football they rarely lead to promotion and more often than not to relegation. Good guys rarely win.

Some clubs have actually banned certain agents from their environs. Even if they buy a ticket through a friend, they still risk being refused admission at the turnstiles if they are recognised, or forced ejection if they get picked up on the security cameras that scour the crowd. We've never done that, as we've always needed all the help we can get. Until now, that is.

The FM has banned all agents from the training ground, even the agent who clinched his deal for the purchase of The Club. He's also banned them from the players' lounge on match days, which has not gone down very well. Formerly they would prowl the corridors and the lounges in their distinctive long black cashmere coats, smoking cigars (when smoking was permitted) and giving out their cards to all and sundry. I know some clubs where the bar staff are on their payroll, texting the whereabouts of certain players or supplying their phone numbers. It's a cheaper method of scouting than paying a full-time employee to actually watch matches.

All these old tricks The FM may or may not know, but he is very much his own man. We now have a Dietician, a Fitness Coach, a Sports Psychologist, a Statistician, and even, to analyse matches, an IT Specialist. For the most part, the players simply don't know what to make of it.

I stood at the back for a while when The Psychologist was giving them his first talk. It was like the fourth year at a secondary school, when some of the pupils can't wait to get away: lots of nudging and giggling, a few scribbles on the paper he'd distributed (doubtless obscene). One or two of the senior pros seemed to be getting the hang of it, but the kids just see it as an intrusion into their Sky Sports/video game/snooker table time. But time has always been something that professional footballers have had in spades. I would guess that 'roastings', 'dogging' and compulsive gambling wouldn't happen if they had to be at a desk from nine to five every day.

Meanwhile, The FM is having a hard time getting his head around the concept of our Third Round FA Cup match, which is due to be played at the beginning of January. We're drawn at home to one of the two non-league teams to get through. They view the game as a money-spinner that – win, lose or draw – will help them fund their new stadium. Their manager has said a few things about us being the Premier League team they least wanted to meet, and it's not meant as a compliment.

Basically what he's saying is that a trouncing at Old Trafford, or Stamford Bridge, in front of forty, fifty or even sixty thousand would have been a whole lot more palatable than playing in front of our comparatively meagre twenty thousand. That's a bit of a liberty, considering their average home gate is about twelve hundred. However, for us to even get close to our capacity we have to reduce our prices, a fact about which I've had some heated debates with my opposite number.

But there are always arguments when it comes to cup competitions. League matches are all very clear cut. The home team gets all the gate receipts, the away team bears all its own expenses, that's that. It's a swings and roundabout situation. Except that for us it's not, given that our ground is about a third of the size of those of our rivals. Some pretty speeches were made by The Newcomer about finding us a new stadium, but he has to get the Local Authority on board first. Speaking from past experience, that won't necessarily be easy.

We've been used as a political pawn for so long that any chance of us taking the queen's position on the board has long since receded. Any majority party in local authority is scared to lose votes by supporting us, either by making our stadium bigger or finding a new green field site. As I mentioned before, when talking about our Local Authority, residents vote, football clubs don't. And football fans *rarely* do – even if they live inside the borough, which many of them don't. If a party is in opposition it can make all sorts of promises to curtail our activities or even, if it suits them in a particular ward, to actually help us. Then they'll get into power and all the promises are forgotten.

The old Chairman spent fortunes on having plans prepared, feasibility studies, planning applications, planning appeals even unto the end of time – all of which achieved absolutely nothing. He even threatened to move out of the borough, and The Newcomer has already made some similar noises too. One of the problems is that the FA won't let a club move too far from its heartland – or 'conurbation', as they call it. MK Dons was a special case, but go tell that to the couple of thousand Wimbledon fans who choose to watch

AFC Wimbledon rather than trekking out to the wilds of Milton Keynes.

The secretary of our cup opponents has been on the phone to me several times a day, despite the match still being a few weeks off. He wants to know about the ticket allocation, the number of complimentaries they'll get, the numbers for the directors' box, the executive lounges, the parking for the directors and the team coach, access to the ground before the game, how long their players will have on the pitch to get acclimatised, which hotel to stay in the night before, how long it will take to reach the ground on match day, etc, etc. He'll be up all night, every night, trying to think of things that might go wrong and all the different ways we devious big boys are plotting to con their brave little minnow of a club out of every last penny due.

Today he called again. "Just thought I'd ask what you thought would be the best day for the replay."

The *replay*? I think he's being a bit optimistic, but I can't really say that without appearing arrogant. We're struggling at the foot of the table, I know, but they're also nearer to the bottom of their league than the top, and we're in the Premier League whilst they are in the Blue Square Football Conference – over seventy places below us.

" . . . I reckon that if we grab a draw then the replay will be televised, and my chairman is asking how the television money will be shared."

Don't you just love the optimism of chairmen everywhere?

He's also checking up on our advance sales for the first match at our ground. He's terrified that we're only going to account to him for the ticket revenue for the match, and his chairman is trying to be one jump ahead – he reckons we need to account to him for their share of the executive boxes, the hospitality boxes and the season ticket sales. If The Chairman were still around, then I'm sure he would have been trying to collar all that income; I'm not so sure about The Newcomer, though The Chief Executive and The Finance Director seem pretty switched on. Although they may feel that arguing over a mere few thousand quid is beneath their dignity. I'll put it to them and await their instructions.

Fortunes can be made in the Third Round of the Cup by the tiddlers. If they get a big team at home and the media sense some chance of a giant-killing, then the match is pretty sure to be shown on television. If they draw somebody like us away, then their big hope is to stick eleven men behind the ball and cling on for a lucrative replay. Either way, their players are suddenly accelerated into celebrity status. Agents will wrangle with each other over organising a players' pool, and they'll be taking bids from tabloids for exclusive stories. Now, if they actually get a replay and make it to the Fourth Round, then they've hit the jackpot. But even without that, a draw and a replay may well earn the pool in excess of six figures; with the agent running the pool, taking twenty percent of everything, then he's going to be doing very nicely thank you.

But still, for the moment our own media circus has descended upon us, which has nothing to do with the FA Cup. We've got our first home match on Saturday under The FM, and I've been pestered all week with requests for press passes, photographers' access and interviews for the weekend's television programmes that build up to the game. As journalists they are just waiting, like vultures, for The FM to fail.

Is he the messiah who is going to ensure we stay at the exalted heights of the Premiership? Or is he just another false prophet who's about to take us back to the Championship – or even the lower depths? We'll just have to wait and see.

Me, I have a sneaking feeling that I'll be here long after he has departed for home.

MID-DECEMBER

"Jesus himself could not raise this lot from the dead."

Headline in a tabloid newspaper, December 15th

I think the honeymoon period is over. We've played three matches under The FM and lost them all. Last Saturday's home defeat followed an away defeat the previous week and now, in midweek, we've lost away again. The best anybody has to say about The FM is that he wears a very nice suit on match days. I know he's flown to Italy and back in a day just to buy them. He said he was looking at players, but I'm not sure where you look when you go on a day that no matches are taking place.

Standing on the touchlines, shaking his head as if he has never seen anything quite so bad in his life, The FM seems to be wondering what on earth possessed him to sign up in the first place. I have to say that it's quite awful, and at this club I've seen *really* awful before. It's hard to start a fight when you don't speak the language, but he's managed to it with The Club Captain. He told him (through an interpreter, not the best form of communication) that he didn't think he'd given one hundred percent in the first of the losses, so he'd be turning out for the reserves midweek.

143

The Club Captain promptly replied, "I'm washing my hair that night."

Once this was translated, The FM at once slapped him with a two-week fine.

The Club Captain shrugged, but later dropped into my office to comment, "If that foreign cunt thinks I give a flying fuck, then he's very much mistaken. Oh, and by the way, here's my transfer request." And with that he dropped an envelope on my desk.

His agent sent a contemporaneous copy of that to the newspapers and also fed them the reason. The FM then decided that The Club Captain wasn't going anywhere unless he himself decided he was going to sell him. And so World War III has broken out. The home-grown players we've got are all siding with The Club Captain, while the foreigners, who have a greater awareness of which side their bread is buttered, are all behind The FM.

All of which makes for a happy and settled dressing room, and gives the press a real added bonus.

It's not a great idea to upset a manager, whatever his nationality or his grasp of the language. Managers can be very spiteful people and are in a position of power to make that spite really count for something. One manager, on discovering one of his players was using an agent he particularly disliked, called the player in to see him.

"Change your agent from that crook and conman, or I'm going to ruin your career. You'll never play for this club again and I'll make bloody sure you don't play for anybody else decent either."

The player's agent had upset him years before, and he'd never forgotten or forgiven.

"Who would you rather I used, gaffer?" the player asked. He wasn't surprised when the manager suggested an agency with whom his own son was closely connected. Nothing like doing your best for your children, I always say.

Then there was the equally high-profile manager who told one of his more disruptive players he'd be picking splinters from his backside for the rest of his career on the subs' bench. Eventually, the player in question gave up the unequal struggle and put in a written transfer request, thus giving up the right to the substantial signing-on fees the club would have had to pay him had it instigated the sale.

Amazingly, there are still a few people in this game who don't know that if a club *decides* to sell a player then he's still entitled to the rest of his signing-on fees. But if the player asks to leave then, in the words of Anne Robinson, "You leave with nothing." Mind you, one club refused to give a player the money to which he thought he was entitled after a concentrated campaign conducted by an agent through the tabloids, calculated to persuade the club to sell him. (I touched on this story back in August, but it's worth relating here in full.) The buying club's manager vehemently denied through the papers that he was in any way interested – although everybody involved knew he'd already met with the player's agent and agreed terms for the new contract. The current club maintained that he'd effectively asked for a transfer even though he'd never submitted a written or verbal request. So the chairman held firm, and said that the player could only leave if he acknowledged that there was nothing due to him from the club.

At that point, the player's agent turned around to the suitor-club and told them that, if they wanted his boy, they'd have to give him a signing-on fee equal to that he'd been forced to give up. That presented a problem, because the old signing-on fee was due in one lump sum and the compensatory signing-on fee at the new club would have to be paid over the period of the whole four-year contract, in equal instalments. To combat this, the agent suggested a dodgy side-letter: the player would get all the money upfront; though the club would theoretically agree to pay the same amount each year, the player would give them a post-dated letter waiving the sums due to him.

Then the player's accountant got involved and reckoned that, even if he waived the sums, he might be taxed on them. So, finally, the club and the agent agreed that the balance of the old signing-on fee would be paid as a 'loyalty' payment at the end of the player's first twelve months. That seemed to cover all bases, unless the player left before that point – but as everybody was starting to lose the will to live, the deal was struck.

But the saga was still not over. The agent then decided it suited him (and his client) better to say he had been acting for the new club when it came to payment of his fees. On that basis, he could charge what he wanted (certainly more than the player would have had to pay him) and the player would not be taxed on the sum as a benefit in kind. Given that he'd been trumpeting his representation of the player through the papers, threatening all sorts of GBH to any other agent who tried to muscle in, and had conducted all the negotiations for the player with both his old and new club, it was a bit rich.

But he'd never registered any kind of contract with the player at the FA, and the buying club were so desperate that they just gave in, on the basis that they'd worry about the

Inland Revenue later. That could be the motto of quite a few clubs: *Worry About It Later*. I'm not quite sure how it'd translate into Latin, or look on the club badge, but it's a hell of a sight more appropriate than, for example, things like *Nil Satis, Nisi Optimum* at Everton.

Apart from a one-off situation like this, clubs prefer loyalty payments to signing-on fees. The former can only be made after a player has been with a club for more than a year (football has a different definition of 'loyalty' to the rest of the business world), and if a player leaves before the end of his contract (assuming the payment is being made at the end), even if it's by just a few days, then once again he leaves with nothing. Most loyalty payments fall due at the end of a season; some of the shrewder agents insist on them being paid once the player has stayed until the last competitive league game. That will be in early May for most clubs, which gives him a couple of months to find his client a new club before the start of the following season, which is officially the first of July.

The Chairman was always quite shrewd about the timing of loyalty payments. He tried to arrange for them to fall due on 30th June, so that they acted as golden handcuffs. Some players were so desperate to get away before the summer rush that they just walked away. Others tried to get the money from the new club, and a few just stuck it out and took the risk of not being able to find a new club for the following season. So much depended on the marketability of the player. The better ones knew they were in a sellers' market and could practically dictate their own terms. But with several thousand players available each year, the great majority were not so fortunate and either took the security of what was on offer elsewhere, to ensure they were in work for the following year, or else took a sum substantially reduced from what would otherwise have been due by way of a loyalty payment.

It's very hard for players to come to terms with the fact that their careers are on the decline, or even in freefall. One of our very experienced pros, who retired recently, said that his legs just went almost overnight. Another high-profile ex-player said his body suddenly told him it was time and, because he couldn't perform to the previously high standard he'd attained, he didn't want to do it anymore. Other ex-England internationals are happy to plough a muddy furrow on a Saturday afternoon in the Conference, because they just can't hang up their boots.

We had a player a few years ago who was on a very high salary (for us at least), but was always getting injured. The Chairman grew tired of paying the bloke a few thousand quid a week for lying on a treatment table. Mind you, he wasn't a great one for paying anybody, even for services rendered. One month we had a cash-flow shortage and he just didn't pay the players. As you can imagine, they were up in arms. But at that time we were in League Two, and nobody was banging our doors down to sign our lads – except for one, and he just told us that under the league rules we were in breach of his contract; even if we paid him up we couldn't keep him, so he was off. His agent quickly (*too* quickly, I reckon) agreed terms with another club, and it was goodnight sweetheart. We took it to a tribunal and lost, so that was at least one lesson The Chairman learned about false economy.

But back to our injured player. When he was fit he was really good, so, not wanting to lose him entirely, The Chairman offered him a 'pay-as-you-play' deal, whereby the lad would be on a much reduced basic salary but would receive very high appearance monies when he actually played. So high, in fact, that they would once again have made him the highest-paid player at The Club. The player told him to stick his offer where the sun don't shine, and couldn't understand when The Chairman didn't try to improve it but simply smiled, and wished him well for the future.

See, The Chairman was a wily old fox, and he knew pretty well that there wasn't going to be a future for this particular player and that, in those circumstances, his offer was pretty generous. Everybody knew about the player's injury record, and The Chairman (philanthropist that he was) made damn sure that those who didn't were informed quickly enough. If it's not a good thing to upset a manager, then pissing off a chairman is not a brilliant career move either. When you work in football you're living in a village; everybody knows everybody else's business, and both good and bad news spread like wildfire. The player in question drifted around the lower leagues for a while, then ended up outside of the league system, earning in hundreds per week instead of thousands. Chairmen and managers wield power out of all proportion to their abilities, but generally I find it's best just to do what they want – however irrational it may appear. That's the advice I give to players when I'm asked, and you'd be surprised just how often I am.

Players can be quite unbelievable at times. They listen to everybody and anybody, but, in particular, they listen to the last person they've spoken to. I was once in the middle of dealing with a player's new contract. The Chairman and the player's agent had agreed the terms, and I was just doing the paperwork. The player came in, supposedly to sign, and then promptly refused to put pen to paper:

"I ain't signing."

"But it's all agreed," I replied.

"My man" (meaning his agent) "told me that this deal would make me the top earner at The Club."

"And it will," I said, quite truthfully. He'd got a terrific deal.

"That's not what I've been told," the player muttered sullenly.

"And who told you that?"

He was hesitant about answering, but I continued to press him until he reluctantly replied, "The kit-man." He said this with a totally straight face and no sense of irony whatsoever.

When The Chairman called the kit-man in and fired him (he was never one for taking prisoners, or respecting employment legislation), it transpired that the kit-man had nurtured aspirations to get into the agency business. He'd been winding up the player on instructions from a potential employer, who was looking to cause a rift between the player and his agent.

The phone rings. It's the secretary of our FA Cup opponents again. He wants to discuss the dietary requirements of some of their people who are eating with us. I transfer him to our Catering Manager. He's also new; our old guy did his best, but it was always haphazard. Now we've actually got a proper menu with a choice of main dish, hot soup and French bread at halftime, and smoked salmon and cream cheese bagels after the game in case anybody's still hungry. The rumour is that the wine list had been personally selected by The Newcomer himself, and it's even been suggested he has the food tasted before he samples it. When you're that rich you can make a lot of enemies. You make a lot of enemies in football anyway without being a multimillionaire, but they're unlikely to go to the extremes of poisoning your food.

I wouldn't put that past some of the players, though. One very famous England international actually cooked pies containing human and canine excrement, and served them up to his 'friends' – one of whom doubled him up with laughter when, after a few drinks (or probably more than a few), he asked for a second helping. That he didn't kill any of his house guests with his peculiar culinary skills is a minor miracle.

Speaking of poisoning and footballers' unspeakable pranks, I've just had to pay the balance of the booking fee for The Club's Christmas party. The Chairman had previously decided it wasn't going to happen this year, but The Newcomer had other ideas, and clearly The FM has no previous experience of English club players' idea of seasonal festivities. He's given me a budget (through The Finance Director, of course) and it looks generous – very generous. I'm trying to see how much of it I can use up on food, because giving professional footballers a party with limitless alcohol is a little like inviting al-Qaeda into your nuclear armoury and telling them to take their pick. Someone, somewhere along the line, is going to get hurt – but The Newcomer and The FM will just have to learn the hard way.

I've just noticed that my voicemail light is flashing. Our Cup opponent's secretary is calling yet again. Maybe I should offer him an invite to our Christmas party.

LATE DECEMBER

*"It was as if they had bought us for the night. And we
never even got the money we were promised."*

Trainee beautician, nineteen, speaking to
The News of the World, December 20th

Why do we do it? Why on earth does any football club
permit its players to have an unsupervised Christmas
party? Time after time we ask the same questions, yet once
we've had a few quiet years we tend to forget the memorably
infamous ones.

This year it's been up with the best of them though. The
party paid for by The Club wasn't the problem. Little did we
know that, to the players, it was an aperitif for the real bash.
They'd put in money themselves, hired a local hotel and really
gone for broke. This was a boys' night out. They'd all agreed
not to bring the WAGs – although I heard that one of the more
persistent ones, who had more cause to doubt her husband
than most, *did* turn up and was promptly told she wasn't
welcome. I gather her husband made himself very scarce
during that exchange, and oh, to have been a fly on the wall
when he finally rolled back home in the wee small hours of
that morning.

I wouldn't even have minded being a fly on the wall when

The FM got his much bedraggled squad together the following day – or at least that section of them who were either fit or amongst the walking wounded. Or indeed, those who weren't helping the police with their enquiries.

They'd got themselves a party organiser, our bright lads, whose idea of suitable entertainment for young athletes already tanked up at our expense was to hire a posse of lap dancers, trawl the local shops for attractive young things who liked the idea of being shagged by a famous footballer (or not quite so famous, with our boys), an inexhaustible supply of champagne and loud music. It was the worst chemical recipe for disaster this side of a suicide bombing.

We'd already had a bit of trouble at our own party. One of our loan players drank much too much, much too quickly, and then took a fancy to The Chief Executive's secretary. Sadly for him, that feeling was not reciprocated, but he was too drunk to take no for an answer. He stumbled up to her, knocking over the table where The Newcomer was seated on his way. She was sitting on a counter and, as the drunken player reached her and pushed her backwards, she toppled like a free-range Humpty Dumpty with flimsy underwear. The whole room had an excellent view.

I've already sent him back to his club and, as they wanted rid of him anyway (hence the loan), they've wasted no time in suspending him and starting disciplinary proceedings, with a view to terminating his contract. Nothing like expediency in our line of business. A superstar can do virtually what he wants, short of genocide, and still be welcomed back into the fold (after suitable treatment). But, as I've said before, where young trainees are concerned, unless they're something special then it's one strike and you're out. Even if they're simply caught with recreational drugs, if the club doesn't think they have a future then they're on their bikes. In some ways it's hardly surprising that, when it comes to club loyalty, the players think only of themselves.

Naturally, I've been asked to prepare a report on our seasonal fiasco for The Chief Executive, so that he, The Newcomer and The FM can decide what action should be taken against whom. We finished our do soon after eleven, and The FM magnanimously told his players they needn't come for training until lunchtime. Big mistake, give a player an inch and he'll take a mile.

The party organiser must have done a good job. It seems that, when they arrived at the hotel, the girls were already fed and watered and ready for action. The Club Captain, who we might usually have expected to be a restraining influence, led from the front after his run-in with The FM. He's admitted to me (on my undertaking not to tell his wife) that he didn't see a lot of what was going on, as he went upstairs with a couple of girls to one of the rooms the organiser booked in anticipation of what was now taking place.

Neither girl seems to have complained; neither was so drunk as to not know what she was doing. If things had not got out of hand downstairs then that would have been the end of it. The girls would have left with their 'I shagged a footballer' T-shirts, and a nice little present of a couple of hundred quid each in their purses. (The Club Captain owned up to that too – but he did say it was to buy their silence.) Everybody would have been happy – including, I expect, the wife of The Club Captain, blissfully unaware of her husband's infidelities. Indeed, I suspect he wouldn't even have seen them as such. It's almost as if for one day of the year, the day of the

Christmas party, the players in marital and long-term relationships have a day off.

It seems that a few of the younger players thought Christmas had come a few days early, when a couple of the girls led them by the hand towards the ladies' toilets. Their story is that the girls were willing participants, and that they just gave them oral sex. But the girls say they were dragged into the cubicles and raped. I'm not sure that their stories stack up. They didn't rush out of the party and into the long arms of the law. Instead, they stayed and carried on drinking; it was only when they got home that they both made calls to the local constabulary. It seems they're saying they'd been forced to drink so much that they were incapable of realising the enormity of what had happened, or of being able to act on it, until the morning.

I may be getting old and cynical, but you can't tell me these girls didn't know exactly the sort of party they were going to. I'm not condoning what our players may have done, nor am I suggesting they should be awarded good behaviour medals, but I do think this story has two sides to it. The press, of course, only want to hear one side and that's the girls'. Our players have been released on bail and haven't yet been charged. I've heard a whisper that The Newcomer is going to sort it all out via the girls' parents and is confident the allegations will be withdrawn. I don't think he's actually *heard* of the offence of perverting the course of justice; even if he has, he may well be thinking it doesn't actually apply to people with as much money as him.

There have been some other incidents to deal with. One of our up-and-coming youngsters had a cigar stuck in his eye by one of our expensive signings. Fortunately, they got him quickly to A&E at the local hospital, and although he'll wear a patch for a few days there's no permanent damage. The senior player said he was about to stub the cigar out on the back of the youngster's head, when he turned round suddenly and got it in the eye. So that's all right then. He clearly didn't mean to blind him.

We've got a couple of sprained ankles too, as it seems the players decided to have a race around the hotel courtyard at two in the morning when one of them threw out a challenge to his team-mates. Racing around an icy courtyard early on a December morning was not the best idea in the world. It seems the corners proved a bit of a challenge.

We've one case of food poisoning. The player in question hadn't eaten caviar before, and thought he could shovel it down like liver pate. Combined with a few oysters and stirred nicely with champagne and some flaming cocktails, it's surprising that he's only going to miss one day's training.

I'm not counting the headaches and hangovers as even worth reporting. The fines this time are serious, and I can't see even the PFA finding any grounds for protest on their players' behalves. The FM has said he'll fine them another week's wages if they don't win their match on Boxing Day. I don't *think* he'll be able to get away with that, particularly as we're playing the league leaders away, but in their present state the players are not up to questioning his decision. That's the thing about footballers. They can be genuinely contrite after the event. The problem is they will never, ever anticipate the aftermath at the time the event is planned, or is actually in the process of happening.

One particular club had a reputation for throwing the best parties ever, so much so that players from other clubs would sneak in, helped by the fact that everybody had to wear fancy dress. Another club allowed the players to use its team bus to take them into the centre of London. Some fifty players and staff piled on board, and the driver arranged to meet them all at 3am to take them home. By 4am only six of them had shown up, so the driver gave up and drove the survivors back.

Another club with a very laddish reputation always moved from the club premises to a local pub, where the party invariably climaxed in a free for all. The local police had to be bribed with tickets to avoid the club being unable to field a team in their next match.

The FM has also told them that he's cancelled all holiday leave. They were to have Christmas Day with their families, then travel by coach in the afternoon up north, to stay over in a hotel in preparation for the Boxing Day game. Now he's told them he wants them in training on Christmas Eve, and ready to travel at 8am on Christmas Day morning. It's a bit hard on the families, but then I suppose the players should have thought of that before incurring the wrath of the powers that be.

Christmas at a football club is always a difficult time of year. Everybody is out there, eating and drinking, while the players are cosseted and wrapped in cotton wool to ensure they do their best for the Boxing Day faithful. Me, I can remember the old days when teams played on Christmas Day and then played the return fixture on Boxing Day. And nobody seemed to care what they ate or drank or when they did it, so long as they were able to tie up their heavy, clogger-style boots and head the leather ball, laces and all. There seemed to be far less injuries when their feet had that far more substantial protection than the stream-lined designer boots of today. But on the other hand, heading the mud-soaked balls gave more than one player serious brain damage.

Not that taking the players away and keeping them in a hotel is any kind of guarantee they won't get up to mischief. I know of one club where the manager did his rounds to ensure his charges were tucked up in bed, and then went off to sleep himself. After a suitable interval the players gathered in the bar downstairs, where they'd bribed the barman to open up for an after-hours party, managed to gather a few girls together that they'd spotted earlier and, by careful exchanging of rooms, also managed to get the girls upstairs and ensure that all of those who wanted to partake of their charms had the opportunity. Not surprisingly, the next day they lost heavily.

Perhaps you were surprised when I said that one of our players had been smoking a cigar. Not the greatest for the lungs, but then neither are cigarettes, and at almost every club there's one committed smoker. The thing about players is they think they are invincible, normal rules simply don't apply to them. They'll never have breathing problems, just like they'll never have arthritis or alcohol-fuelled liver or kidney problems. There's always a quick fix. You put on weight in the close season so you take diuretics to lose it, never believing for a moment that it'll weaken you. You get nervous on the morning of a match day, so you light up a fag. Unlike other drugs, nicotine and alcohol don't show up on random drug tests, but they can have much the same effect. It should not be any great surprise when you spot managers and coaching staff lighting up, it's hardly a newly acquired vice. It's just been well-concealed whilst their playing careers were in full swing.

To everybody's surprise we grab a point on Boxing Day.

Players always retain the possibility to surprise. Somehow or other, when they're really up against it, when there are reputations to salvage or, most importantly, when money is at stake, they manage to come up with something. The FM has been full of praise. The corner has been turned. He has big plans for the transfer window, he is confident The Club can stay up. This despite being told that only one club has ever been bottom of the Premiership at Christmas, and still managed to stay up.

"So," he says in broken English, "now we will have two." Maybe he seems overconfident. But his confidence may yet prove infectious. Winning is a habit, just as is losing. It's amazing how a club can play badly, yet still string a few results together, and then start playing well. That's what makes football special. It's the hope factor. For this is the season of goodwill to all men, and of hope springing eternal.

JANUARY

"I would not say I have been given an open cheque book, but it does contain many blank cheques."

The FM, January 2nd

I can't believe what is going on here. The FM has drawn up a shopping list, the agent who brokered the deal to get The Club for The Newcomer is out of favour, and now we have a completely New Agent on board to do all the deals. It seems The Newcomer met him through some of his more dubious business associates and has taken a shine to him. Rich men are subject to sudden mood changes, so I'm told, and as I'm discovering for myself.

The New Agent has been told to source the players The FM wants, and to use whomsoever he needs to deliver them. The only problem is the new FA agents' regulations. I know I've mentioned them several times before, but they are becoming the bane of my life. I'm the person responsible for ensuring we comply, but The FM does not seem to understand this – or is pretending not to understand. Before these new regulations came into force everything was pretty simple. There were rules, but everybody bent them and nobody got badly hurt. But a few dodgy agents pushed it a little further and, as is always the case in this country, people got jealous of the amounts of money they were making. (Well, not just making, but flaunting really.)

What used to happen is that we'd agree terms with a club to buy a player. Somewhere along the line, the player's agent got involved – either to broker the deal or else to negotiate terms for the player, or sometimes both. I've already mentioned the situation where an agent would act for every party in the transaction and get paid by them all. When terms were agreed with the player, his agent would then agree the fee.

Or sometimes it would happen the other way around, particularly if the agent was more concerned about his own financial arrangements than those of the player. I know of at least one instance when the agent walked into a room at the buying club and said, "My commission is one million pounds. Either you agree that or I'm taking the player somewhere else."

The club wanted the player and agreed. That the fee bore no relationship to that which the agent was contractually entitled made no difference to anybody. The player only read about the fee when a newspaper got hold of it; instead of being angry that the agent had been overpaid, grabbing hold of a large proportion of the monies that had gone into the pot for the deal, the player merely shrugged and said that he'd got what he wanted out of it, so why should he care?

Not all players are so relaxed when money has effectively been stolen from them. One player's father threatened the agent with a lawsuit unless he accounted to them for the excess fee he'd received. As the agent was desperate to keep the player, he agreed to repay it. Mind you, he had the *chutzpah* to make it a condition of repayment that the player signed an extension to his contract. Astonishingly, the player did so.

There seem to be no long-term grudges in the world of the agents. It's all about expediency. Nobody is prepared to burn their bridges to somebody who can make them money. You hear about clubs who go public and say that they will never deal with this or that agent again. Meanwhile, if he acts for a player they want desperately then, rather than lose the opportunity to get that player, they'll swallow their pride and principles and deal with the agent.

The agents who deal with their affairs properly would still, in times past, have expected the club to pay their fees. It was an odd situation. On the one hand the FA rules were very clear. An agent could only represent one party in a transaction. On the other hand, even the Inland Revenue accepted that part of the fee paid to the agent in a deal that took a player to a club was for services effectively rendered *to the club*. Basically, the bigger the player's name, the larger the proportion of the fee they would recognise as being for the club – presumably on the basis that the agent could have taken his high-profile player anywhere, and therefore was doing the club a favour by delivering him. The end result was that the proportion of the fee that didn't relate to services to the club was put down on the player's returns, and he would pay tax on it at year's end.

That was the honest scenario. But as I've said before, players hate paying, so agents persuaded them to let them do the deal by pretending it wouldn't cost anything. If the agent just demanded his huge fee before anything else happened, it may well have led a player to believe he wasn't paying. Agents quite often gloss over the end result of the club's payments, and I've often had players in here demanding to know why their wage packets are so slim after I've deducted tax on that part of the payment that's been apportioned to them, our friends at the Inland Revenue treating it as a benefit in kind. I have listened in to one end of a conversation between the player and his agent, and wouldn't have been surprised to see the agent's nose appear through the receiver as he told lie after lie to dig himself out of the hole his short-term expediency had led him into.

I was often asked to agree that the agent had really only acted for The Club. It was one of those little white lies that didn't really hurt anybody. The way it would work was that, although the agent had a contract with the player to represent him, it never appeared in the public domain. The agent would not have lodged it with the FA. Before these new regulations came into force, the FA seemed to have better things to do than play detective as to which player was really signed to which agent.

A little while before the negotiations took place with us, the player in question would mysteriously vanish from the agent's website, as I mentioned back in August. The player would sign the documents to say that he'd had nobody acting for him. The Club would say it had employed the agent, and the agent received his fee from The Club. End of story. The player would not be taxed on the fee, and everybody was happy. Except, it seemed, the Inland Revenue, who began to look at all the transactions with a jaundiced eye.

I never felt particularly comfortable with that approach, but, if The Chairman agreed to go down that route with the agent, then it wasn't for me to raise questions. It always struck me as totally illogical though. We'd all sat down with the agent, and he'd done his best to squeeze as much money out of us as possible. He'd told every Tom, Dick and Harry in the media that he was the player's agent, and then suddenly we found ourselves paying him and saying he'd been acting for us all along. Welcome to *Alice in Football Land*.

But that's all changed now. Or at least the FA would have us believe so. They keep banging on about transparency. They claim that everybody (by which they mean themselves) should know exactly who is acting for whom all along, exactly who is being paid, and exactly who is sharing in that payment. They also claim that the players never knew exactly what was being paid out of the pot to their agents. It's a fair point.

There's only one trough of gold in a transaction, and the more people that feed from it, the less there is for the player. I have to say though that, when we were paying the agent effectively on the player's behalf, it was totally transparent. All the players had to do was to read what they were signing, and then they would have seen what those fees actually were. Mind you, if you expect a player not only to read his contracts but also to understand the tax implications for him, and at the same time to check whether he's been charged the correct amount, then maybe you're travelling with Alice through the looking glass.

The Chief Executive has actually called in a sports lawyer to take us through the new FA agents' regs, as they are just so complicated. Basically it now means that the only person who can pay the agent is the person (or club) that he's representing. We can't even deal with him unless there's an agreement lodged with the FA, and it has to be in a form that the FA has approved. So if an agent is saying he represents a player we're entitled to ask to see the contract, or else we should be phoning the FA to make sure that they've got a contract logged there. And the agent can't switch horses in midstream. So, if he's done anything for a player in the last two transfer windows, even commercial stuff, he can't just drop the player and say he's acting for us now.

I don't think anybody has thought this through particularly well. The PFA, it seems, actually voted for this method of payment, though the players I've spoken to here seemed dumbfounded when I told them they'd be paying their agents' gross fees (plus VAT they can't recover), all out of their net income.

Just today, I've been negotiating with an agent who definitely acts for the player in question. Very pragmatically, he said, "If you want to sign my client and he's going to have to pay me, then you have to pay him a gross sum that nets down to what I am due. Oh, and by the way, I'm registered for VAT, my boy can't claim that back either, so that's another seventeen and a half percent that needs to be grossed up."

Well I've just done the arithmetic. A payment that would have cost us a hundred thousand will *now* cost us nearly two hundred thousand. And the agent is saying that if we don't want to pay then there are clubs who will, or else he'll just take his player abroad to a country where he won't have this sort of problem. I can see quite a bit of a talent draining away from the Premiership if this goes on, or if the rules don't change.

One of the major issues is that players aren't regarded by the Revenue like other entertainers. Musicians and the like can set their agents' commissions off against their tax, or register for VAT. But players are employed under PAYE and can't do likewise. Doesn't seem fair at all. It might have been more sensible for the FA to get the Inland Revenue on board before they started this latest clean-up, but they seemed determined to crack on. Again, it's not my problem, but it does seem to me that there's a bit of jealousy in all this: the pen-pushers and suits at the FA just didn't like all the money taken out of the game to reward what seemed like very little effort on the part of the agents.

The Newcomer isn't sitting back though. He's being wound up by The FM, who's telling him that other clubs are finding ways around all this. I've been summoned to see him again.

"Just remember that if we need to sign a player then we will, and if there are any commercial agreements needed to make it happen then I have offshore companies we can use. I rely on your discretion."

From the day he arrived, it's struck me how The Newcomer – who, I was initially told, could barely speak English – has always understood much more than he's let on. But I'm not too happy about being brought into this particular inner circle. I'll have to be very careful to make sure there's nothing in writing that can be traced back to me.

I can remember the old dark ages of the relationship between clubs, players and agents. The problem with these new regulations is that they may have the opposite effect to that intended by the FA, and drive everything back underground. Everybody in football remembers the club who came up with many and various explanations for a large sum of unaccounted cash in their safe. We've always found it hard to deal with cash in a big way, although, as you'll know by now, The Chairman used to have slush funds both inside The Club and his own company.

The Newcomer may have other ideas though. Some of the agents have already come up with the notion of acting for each others' players, which requires a bit of basic trust between them and may be a bridge too far. But in such an uneasy alliance the agent would deliberately have no contract with the player. The deal gets done and he gets another agent to act for the club. The club pays the other agent the fee, and he keeps it because, if he's going to share it with the player's agent, he has to declare that to the FA. Then, in the next deal that happens, one of the other agent's players just reverses the process. As long as the club involved doesn't go blabbing to the FA, then there doesn't seem to be an awful lot they can do about it. They've got a wide definition of 'connected parties' in these new rules, but it doesn't seem to cover this sort of arrangement. Even if it does, how are they going to find out about it?

It seems to me that the FA is getting us clubs involved as its policemen. Quite frankly, I've never had so much paperwork to complete for the fairly simple matter of signing a footballer on terms already agreed, when the player wants to join and his old club are happy to take the money and run.

It seems that the new form of player representation contract allows the player to represent himself in a transaction, and as soon as he instructs us to that effect we have to deal with him, not his agent.

I've already had one such request. The player went to a meeting the PFA held to explain the new regulations, and was told all about it. I think they were hoping he would ask for their help, but instead he really seemed to be doing it for himself. Now, from The Club's point of view, we're quite happy about that. The Chairman always reckoned he'd make a deal for at least twenty-five percent less when he dealt directly with a player, and, until his son got involved with The Agent, he always tried to persuade the players that they didn't need an agent. I sat in at meetings and marvelled at his approach. Here he was, about to negotiate with a future or existing employee, persuading the player that The Club had his interests at heart, that we'd do right by him and he shouldn't worry about whatever he'd signed – because, as soon as he'd made himself indispensable to The Club, then The Chairman would rip up the document, start all over again and make the player wealthy beyond his wildest dreams.

All these young kids bought into that dream big-time, but would have a rude awakening if they tried to renegotiate a contract that was almost entirely in The Club's favour. Talk about level playing fields! I can tell you that The Chairman was almost at the top of a ski-run, with the poor player floundering on the nursery slopes.

It now transpires that the player isn't really doing his own negotiations at all, but has a 'shadow' agent behind him. The shadow is the one who's wound him up to the point where he'll dump his own agent. He's agreed to help him on this deal on the understanding that he won't charge, but that the player will sign with him in time for the next transaction and will also let him handle all his marketing. I found that out when the player got out of his depth whilst talking to me, and asked if he could use the phone. (Rather than use his mobile, he made a 'free' call from the office in my presence.) I doubt if the shadow had told him that, even if he doesn't use his personal agent, he's still going to have to pay him what he would have been obliged to under the terms of the contract anyway.

The player eventually became quite open with me about how he's dumped his agent. It was an incredible insight into the mind of a footballer. This agent had acted for him for years, and had taken him from earning a few hundred quid a week to being one of the highest paid players at our club. We actually quite liked the agent. He was always straight with us, and we'd even used him ourselves to sound out players we wanted to join us. The player, though, has rather overblown views of his own value. Having seen his agent fail to deliver (or rather, fail to persuade *us* to deliver) the ridiculous sums he was seeking, he'd asked around the dressing room.

Now, the second player who introduced him to his agent wasn't doing it out of love or loyalty, but because agents are quite happy to pay their players commissions for introductions. The agent promptly told the first player that his current agent was too close to the club, and wasn't as prepared to go for the jugular as he would be. He then told the player exactly what to do.

First off, the player sent a letter saying he didn't want the agent to act for him anymore. The letter basically ignored the fact that there was a contract between them with quite a few months still to run, which certainly went beyond the next transfer window. The agent was mortified, and tried to contact his erstwhile client. The player went missing, and resorted to sending text messages telling the agent that it wasn't personal, he still wanted to be friends, but he just thought it was time that he looked after himself. If he didn't do it now then when would he?

Nobody else was involved, the player assured the agent, even giving him false hope that, if he ever needed an agent again, he'd certainly come back. The agent stayed firm, at which point the player was advised to change his tone. Now it was a case of, why would the agent want to keep an unhappy player? As a club official, I've heard that one before!

The agent by this stage didn't care if the player was euphoric or bipolar. He was determined to keep him to his contract. Again, the player assured the agent there was nobody else involved. It was a bit like a wife leaving her husband and telling him the only reason was that they'd grown apart – before he finds out she's had a string of affairs, and her latest conquest now wants to settle down with her.

At this point the player went for broke, and wrote a letter to us to say he was acting for himself. The original agent was forgotten, out of sight, out of mind. Players have an enormous talent for burying their heads in the sand and convincing themselves that, when it's time to surface, somebody else will have sorted everything out for them.

But the agent was still determined to cling on in there. He decided to create a paper trail and tell the player he was still willing to act for him in his contractual negotiations. The player ploughed on with his 'self-representation', naively asking us not to tell the agent what the deal was. (If he didn't know about it, then he couldn't have a go at him.)

The agent wasted no time, issuing a writ for breach of contract. The player was horrified, telling the whole dressing room what was going on, how terrible it was that his agent was trying to get money out of him when he hadn't even done the deal. He'd conveniently forgotten that the agent was contractually entitled to strike the deal, and had spent a good few years helping the player develop his career, which in turn had led to the biggest contract the player would ever see.

If this becomes the norm, then the agent (I was going to say 'poor agent', but managed to resist) is faced with a huge dilemma. Does he go on with his action against the player, taking the risk of the player slagging him off not just at his club but at the international level at which he mixes, or to his mates at other clubs? Or does he take it on the chin, wish the player well for the future and buy his silence, on the basis that, pursuant to the swings and roundabout theory, his chance will come with another agent's disillusioned player? He's damned if he does and damned if he doesn't. It's a brave (or foolish) agent who sues his clients.

The press doesn't like agents, and the way they write about them ensures the public don't like them either. But, as in every profession, there are good ones and bad ones. I can assure you that the clubs and the players are no angels either. Sometimes I'm just happy to go and visit my kids, and feel as if I need a good shower before I can sit down to dinner with them. Football is a dirty world, it's hard to avoid the dirt rubbing off and sticking.

Agents' commission payments for further introductions are not the only payments they'll make. To get a player into their stable, when they know a lucrative deal is in the offing, they will pay anything to anybody. Very often, the parents of a young player see him as their meal ticket for life, and sometimes they deserve to be kept clothed and fed (and sometimes not). I know of one player who'd been brought up by his mother almost entirely on her own. The father was a real wastrel who, when he wasn't inside, was spending the family's income support money. But when he realised the son had some real talent, he was suddenly all over him like a rash. He was at every game and soon made it clear to all and sundry that, if they wanted to represent his son, they had to deal with him first.

Basically, he put his son's agency agreement up for auction – but none of the proceeds were going to find their way to the lad. Eventually the father negotiated himself a new car, a substantial down payment on a new house, a 'scouting' contract with the agency that guaranteed him income for the next few years, and a share of whatever the agent earned from the boy.

And what was the player thinking all the time? Well, the answer is not very much. He was grateful to have his father back, and at his age he wasn't too bothered about the old man's motives. Having expended all this money to get his client, you can well imagine the sort of deal that the agent negotiated with the buying club by way of commission. At the end of the day, if the player had really thought about it, he would have realised he was being taken for a ride both by his father and the agent.

All the monies that went from the club (and it was a very big club indeed) to the agent could just as easily have gone to the player as part of his financial package. Yet he still got a deal that would have been a fortune to a normal working boy, so he wasn't complaining. When salaries get to a certain size, then the odd hundred thousand or so that goes missing becomes pretty irrelevant.

Cynical, me? I don't think so. I've just seen it all, and eventually it becomes like playing Monopoly. I don't even get jealous. They have a talent that I don't have, so good luck to them. I'm well past thirty-five and I still have a job – more than can be said for most of them when they reach that age.

At least, in that case, the son knew what his father was getting. He just didn't care. The father of one high-profile player went to meetings on his behalf and told the agent concerned that, unless he got a specific payment (in cash), he'd just put the boot in (a talent shared with his son) and ensure the boy never signed with the agent. The agent agreed, the deal was struck, and negotiations were conducted for the player's move. The player knew absolutely nothing about it, and was just grateful to his dad for looking after his interests so prudently. It was only when another agent decided to make a pitch for the player, with a view to enticing him away from his old agency, that the player, older and a bit more streetwise, understood how his father had deceived him. The boy never spoke to his father again. Mind you, he never got the money back either. The FA allows parents to represent their kids, but have now stipulated in the new regulations that they can't be paid for doing so. Again, I'll be interested to see how they put an end to *that* practice.

It's not just fathers who get involved. Mothers can get very busy as well and, although less likely to put themselves forward as representing their sons, they'll certainly still try to make some mileage out of their talents. To be fair, the great majority of players are very close to both their parents – even if the parents are separated – and tend to put on rose-coloured glasses when it comes to their failings. I've had players come in here with their agents and, whilst the agent has done most of the negotiating, the player interrupts and asks what can be done to help his parents. When the club really want the player, the answer is quite a lot.

One big club specialises in buying houses for parents of talented young players, so that they can move them to the local vicinity and get round the rules of a club only being able to take on very young players from within a certain distance of its training ground. I like it when a player looks at the contract in front of him and, before the ink is dry, says that the first thing he's going to do is buy his mum and dad a house. And I have to tell you it's not unusual.

But then you get the family from hell, who latch onto the player and see him as a way to avoid ever having to work again – or at least, not for so long as their son can scatter his cash their way. I've known players support not just their mums and dads, but also brothers, sisters and their partners as well. The entourage becomes famous (or infamous) at the club concerned and, given that many of these families come from rough and ready backgrounds, you don't get a lot of people (least of all the agents) wanting to cross them. It just takes one little incident for them to explode, and then, even if the dispute is an internal one, anybody in the vicinity runs the risk of personal injury.

There are all sorts of people in the food chain when it comes to the money emanating from a transfer. A fair number of players are still represented by what the FA call 'unlicensed agents'. (Seems like a bit of an oxymoron, but there you go.) The FA brought in a licensing system for agents some years ago. Originally it was fairly easy to get a licence, which meant some fairly dubious individuals were allowed to make a killing within the game without too many questions asked of their pedigree. At least one undischarged bankrupt slipped under the wire; as long as he didn't do anything too awful then he had the licence for life, or as long as he kept his professional indemnity insurance going.

Then FIFA and the FA decided too many agents were coming onto the scene, so they instituted an examination which got progressively harder over the years. There are some individuals out there who have the ears of footballers, but either can't be bothered to take the exam or, if they do take it, have not a snowball's chance in hell of passing. A fair number are ex-professional footballers, and up to now they've managed to get round the regulations – either by working for an agency or finding clubs who were happy to negotiate with them, as long as a licensed agent or a lawyer signed off on the deal.

We as a club have been quite happy to do that. These guys are generally more pleasant to deal with than many of the agents, they understand football and footballers, and the fact that they can't pass an exam doesn't mean they can't do a good job for the one or two clients they have. Because they aren't in a position to run a big organisation, they tend to get much closer to their clients and don't seem to have any huge personal financial ambitions. I know it's against the rules, but we've always been very careful to ensure that anything that goes to the FA makes no mention of anybody who's unlicensed.

The risk for these guys is that they have no security with their clients. Any big agency can come and whisper in their ear, telling them they can get into big trouble for using an unlicensed agent and convincing them they can do a much better job all-round. They can also get the player and the club into a lot of trouble. The FA can't actually touch the unlicensed agent, as he's not subject to their rules, but we can get fined and the player can even get suspended.

Once again, you have to balance the risks against the prospect of losing out on the player. But go explain to a manager that he's going to miss out on a signing because the player is represented by an unlicensed agent; you'll be greeted by a torrent of abuse. Everybody in football bends the rules when it suits them, and that is a fact. I listen to club chairmen mouthing off about rules and regulations and the scandalous amounts they have to pay agents, and I have to smile to myself – knowing that, when it comes to a hot property, they're the first in line to structure the deal in whichever way the player's agent, licensed or otherwise, wants it done.

Some players do get greedy. Notwithstanding all the money they earn, they will sometimes tell the agent he can only act for them if he gives them some of the commission he gets from the club. An agent was in here a few days ago, telling me he got his player a deal worth twenty grand a week, and then had to hand over 200k out of the 250k he received from the club. I tried to point out to him that he still had £50,000 he wouldn't have had if the player had retained another agent, but he wasn't a happy man.

Under these new agents' regulations, the agents are obliged to disclose to the FA the entire money trail as it leaves their account. So, technically, they would have to tell them about all the payments to players' fathers and to the players themselves, but somehow I can't see that happening. Assuming they actually enter the payments in their books, they'll run the risk of an FA audit somewhere along the line. But I can't see the payments being that easy to find, somehow.

So that's where we are in this transfer window. As I've said, it's back to the bad old days, with everybody ducking and diving, looking for ways to make money in an environment where it's become increasingly difficult. Players, agents, players' parents, unlicensed agents, the clubs themselves – they're all out there, looking for the main chance.

Life in football was never easy, but it's now become just that much harder.

JANUARY

*"We have every confidence that we have
the right manager in place to turn the fortunes
of this club around."*

The Chief Executive in an interview with *The Times*, after
The Club's home draw with non-league opposition in the Third
Round of the FA Cup, January 8th

Like most things in football, a whisper of that dreaded word 'confidence' is not what it might appear. In fact it's the very opposite, and usually sounds the death knell for the manager at that particular club. And so, after the dreadful performance against our non-league opponents in the Cup – when we scrambled an equaliser by way of a disputed penalty in the last minute – it was not exactly what The FM wanted to hear. (Assuming he understood what was being said.)

Even with his limited command of the English language, I think he'd have got the general gist of what the home crowd were telling him from the fifth minute of the match, when our opponents took the lead, until the ninety-first minute, when we finally equalised and earned the dubious privilege of going back to their place. It's not a thrilling prospect, as it will all happen under the unrelenting eyes of the media, to be shown live on television. Even worse, it means that for the next ten days I have the dubious pleasure of dealing with their secretary, now so hyped-up and delusional that I think he truly believes disposing of us is just one more step on their triumphant road to Wembley.

Chanting is crude, chanting is brutal, but it's a better barometer of what is really going on at a club than the platitudes of those who speak officially on its behalf. At the end of the match the crowd were chanting for The Manager's return, a few were even calling out for The Chairman as well. The press loved it all. Since the advent of the Premiership, the gap between the elite in that league and the rest of the Football League – let alone the leagues in the pyramid – has grown wider and wider. Consequently, although some of the glamour has gone out of the FA Cup, it's rare for any of the smaller clubs to get past the last sixteen, unless they get the luck of the draw and play clubs of their own level. By the time we get to the last eight, it's rare indeed to find a club from outside the top flight. You may get the odd Championship club struggling through, but by that stage it's just for the big boys.

(The 2008 final was a rarity, with neither team from the top five of the Premiership and one of them coming from the Championship.)

What has really upset the fans is that The FM just didn't take the cup match seriously. He played a team that might have struggled to get into our reserves, and it's his disregard for the traditions of cup football that has incensed the supporters more than the result. I'm not saying English football fans are xenophobic, but there's no doubt they take more easily to British managers than foreigners. Obviously some foreign managers win over the fans by their successes – just look at Arsene Wenger and Jose Mourinho. But neither of them had any popularity outside their own clubs.

Quite the reverse, when you listen to the sort of obscene chanting that has greeted them from opposition crowds over the years. Nobody received more abuse than the unfortunate Avram Grant, who succeeded Mourinho and was dismissed after taking Chelsea to within a penalty of winning The Champions League. His greatest crimes initially were not being Mourinho, having appalling taste in clothes, and the difficulty of translating his dry wit into English.

But words are just words. We've had more trouble with our fans both before and since The Club has come up. After a home game against a rival London club, we had a visit from the police who actually threatened to get our ground closed and force us to play matches behind closed doors. In fact, as the officer pointed out, all they needed to do was say our ground was unpoliceable and then a match just couldn't be played. It's one of the facts of life for a football club that they have to pay extortionate sums for the local constabulary to attend their grounds. The actual amount depends upon the category of the match, but who do you think decides the category? (Got it in one. The police.) You can argue that the fans of certain clubs have never caused trouble when they've visited us till you're blue in the face; if they think there's a high risk of confrontation then that is the level of policing they'll provide, for which we have to pay.

That's not to say there isn't the odd undercurrent of hate and prejudice in the sport, and it's not just aimed at black players. There are a lot of clubs now that have Jewish owners, which has not only brought out the worst in some of the fans (I mentioned their Holocaust 'jokes' earlier), but also a few chairmen and directors, whose views of Jewish ownership wouldn't have been out of place in the Nazi propaganda of the

1930's. Nothing is said to the face, but as a Club Secretary you tend to become invisible, and I've heard some of them having a real tilt at the Jewish money which has suddenly come into the game.

And it's not just anti-Semitism either. Anybody who gets involved in a football club and isn't part of the old boy network is likely to be subject to prejudice. It comes in subtle ways. Deliberately flaunting the dietary requirements of visiting directors and their guests, and then making a big public apology about it just to highlight the differences, is but one. It wasn't always that subtle. One chairman, now deceased but not missed, was so blatantly anti-Semitic that he wouldn't even let a Jewish director from a visiting club into his boardroom. It was really the club's boardroom, but as he felt he owned the club top to tail he wasn't going to acknowledge that. All of this was long before the Race Relations Act, of course, but just introducing laws doesn't make people any less prejudiced.

It's not just directors that I've heard making poisonous comments. The odd manager over the years has also had his 'views'. One visiting manager who'd had a bit too much to drink barged into the boardroom after a match in which his team had been beaten, and made some very unpleasant personal comments about the antecedents of the winning club's foreign owner. He was quickly escorted out. The fact that he hasn't worked in the industry for years at least demonstrates that the great majority of people in control of football clubs don't have a racist bone in their bodies.

Most clubs seem to have got racist chanting under control, though I think our mob were one of the last to stop the monkey chants and the odd throwing of a banana. That was probably because we could never (until recently) afford the better players, and consequently had very few black lads playing for us. Now with foreign players (many of whom are black) and our home-grown black lads making up the majority of our team, if our fans were to abuse every non-white player they'd have nobody left to cheer.

Within the squads themselves, there do seem to be cliques. The black English lads stick together; the foreign imports home in on other players from their country, or those who share a common language; and the younger white boys also hunt in packs. The older players who are married – and whose wives know each other – also tend to be a distinct group within the dressing room, and indeed, off the pitch as well.

Some of those players who have moved around the clubs stick with friends they've made on their travels, and I've never ceased to marvel at how two close friends from different clubs can be at each other's throats on the pitch. There's one particular pair who are best friends, forever on the phone to each other during the week; they even go on holiday together and play golf, whilst their wives and kids sit by the pool. But when they are in opposition each seems hell-bent on getting the other booked or even sent off. Sometimes they actually succeed. Then, come the night of the match, they're off for a meal with their spouses.

Sometimes the women related to football via marriage or partnership can be more trouble than they're worth. We've always encouraged the wives and girlfriends – or WAGs, as they've come to be known – to come to matches. We were one of the first clubs to set up a crèche, so the women could leave the kids for the afternoon and enjoy the match. The fact is, though, that most of them don't really enjoy football at all. It's a social occasion as far as they're concerned, where they can show how their partners have lavished more expensive clothes and jewellery on them than the other members of the team have on their own women. There is a bit of a Mafia element about it, where the women try to outdo each other but without losing sight of their place in the hierarchy. The wife of The Club Captain has seniority over the girlfriend of a young player who's worked his way through the youth team and is making his debut. And the girlfriend had better recognise that, otherwise the other WAGs will simply close ranks, no matter what their personal feelings may be about The Captain's wife.

Inevitably, when a competitive group of women are brought into one social circle, and the other members of that group are testosterone-driven footballers, sex is going to get in the way. I had a player in here this week in tears because he'd discovered another team member had been sleeping with his wife. He felt he had to leave The Club, and now The Chief Executive has had the pair of them in to see if he can at least get them talking, to the point where they can play in the same team without disrupting the side.

That was a fairly sophisticated approach. But I recall us playing a team where a couple of the opposition players looked liked they'd gone ten rounds with Ricky Hatton even before the kick-off. My opposite number told me that one had nicked the other's girlfriend and they'd had the most almighty punch-up at training, which had led to them both being fined. Afterwards they'd both agreed she was a bit of slag and not worth falling out over.

The fact of the matter is that most footballers, however solid or stable they may appear in their relationships, just can't resist the offer of quick, easy sex without ties.

Footballers' wives are pretty clingy and possessive, but are also realistic enough to know they probably have to cut their partners a bit more slack than might be expected in a normal trade. Hence the unspoken understanding about Christmas parties.

We've never had a player at our club with a social disease, but I do know of other clubs that have had that problem with more than one member. Some of their lads thought it a good idea to visit brothels for incognito sex; however, it's a bit difficult to be clandestine when the punter's face is regularly plastered all across the papers. The newspapers have an unerring instinct for digging up this sort of dirt, not to mention the sexual proclivities of Saturday's heroes. Every club has female camp followers who are keen to sleep with footballers and collect notches on their bedposts, just as other youngsters collect football stickers. The principle is the same, I suppose, as both involve licking the players while adding them to the collection. But not that much of the sex takes place in beds. Footballers are happy to have sex wherever they can – be that in the clubs' toilets, changing rooms, or even the treatment room.

So with all this in mind, it's hardly surprising that some of the chants aimed at players suggest the fans have more information about them than they'd care to know. It can't be easy for the women in the stands to have their husbands and loved ones accused of anything from homosexuality to paedophilia, from group sex to dogging, from anal sex to affairs with specific individuals. But then I suppose it gets just that tiny bit easier when they count up the money in the pay packets that accompany the abuse.

LATE JANUARY

"I believe we have turned corners with these results.
I am also above the moon with my new signings."

The FM (speaking without a translator), January 31st

Well, here we are on the last day of the transfer window.
Unbeaten since we managed to win our FA Cup replay,
and actually now in the Fifth Round of the competition after
comfortably beating Championship opposition away during
the last round. The press were gathering at the scent of
blood; the BBC broadcast the match anticipating an upset,
and we disappointed everybody by going a goal up in the
fifth minute and finally winning four-nil. We've drawn the
cup holders at home in the next round, and as they're also
owned by a wealthy foreigner there's going to be a big build-
up to that as well.

Meanwhile we've spent over £50m of The Newcomer's
money strengthening a side which clearly needed strengthening.
We've had our share of interesting deals and I've met some
interesting people, but what has been most challenging of
all, yet again, was trying to operate within the FA's new
agents' regulations.

It all began with the very first transaction, when I had an

Eastern European agent claiming to represent a Slovakian striker in whom we'd shown an interest. I asked him if he had an exclusive contract with the player and, after a slight hesitation, he said he did. So I asked to see it. He said it was in Slovakian and I wouldn't understand it. I had to admit my working knowledge of Slovakian is limited, but I did tell him we actually had a Slovak lady working at The Club who'd be happy to offer her translation services gratis. Suddenly the agreement seemed to have been magically transported back to Prague, where the agent was based, but he would have his office send a fax just as soon as their fax machine was repaired.

"You will understand it is difficult to get workmen in over these holidays," he said.

"I do understand," I replied, "and by the way, have you registered yourself with the FA as a foreign agent conducting business here?"

"Oh, for sure," he said, but I could see at that point his eyes had glazed over. I've found that most agents instinctively say yes to anything that will get them through a deal. I called the FA and, after being kept waiting whilst they tried to provide the information, I learned that he wasn't registered. At which point I told him that we couldn't deal with him on behalf of the player. He was not a happy Slovak, but he went off to the car park and, a few minutes later, I received a call from an English agent with whom we'd had some unfortunate past dealings.

He was the one who tried to get us to pay £2m for a player whose foreign club was prepared to sell him for £1m, as we later discovered, and who tried every trick in the book to stop me (or anybody from The Club) speaking to the selling club in case we discovered the true asking price. Anyway, on this occasion all of that seemed to be forgotten – at least by him. Now he was telling me *he* was acting for the player and always had been, albeit in conjunction with the Eastern European gentleman who'd just left my presence. But he couldn't tell me why his associate had come to see me on his own when he needed to be part of the deal.

After a few pleasantries, emanating from him but not reciprocated by me, he asked if he could come to see me later in the day. I told him that would be fine, and asked him to confirm he had a representation contract with the player which was registered with the FA, and which wasn't in Slovakian. He'd be bringing it along to show me, he told me, and it would be sent off to the FA that very day. An hour or so later, he arrived with the contract (which seemed to be a photocopy of a fax) and asked if we could get on with the negotiations. We could deal with the niceties of the FA requirements once we'd sorted out everything else between us, he insisted. I spoke to The CEO, who said The FM really wanted the player and couldn't see why we shouldn't at least try to reach an agreement.

About four hours later, with my attendance at the meeting constantly interrupted by calls relating to other potential signings, it seemed we'd reached an agreement. At which point the agent dropped his bombshell. It seemed he'd promised the player he wouldn't be picking up the fees, so we had to find a way around the new regulation that said an agent could only be paid by the player, when he'd represented the player in the transaction. The agent then said that as the Eastern European agent hadn't registered his contract with the player anywhere, and as he, the English agent, had clearly told me he hadn't either, why didn't we just say he'd acted for The Club and that would be the end of it?

I have to say I didn't feel comfortable with this, but there were at least three other clubs after the player, including one abroad. Knowing the English clubs as I did, I was confident they were not going to be deterred from closing the deal by the little matter of a few rules. The CEO made a call to The Newcomer, and then simply nodded and told me to do it. I knew I had to put down on the form who'd acted for the player. The CEO actually smiled at the agent, and said he didn't see anybody here representing the player – did I? Well I wasn't going to say so, at least not if I wanted to keep my job. I was told to draw up an agreement between The Club and the agent – and when I was told the figure that was to be included, I knew it was a hell of a lot more than the five percent commission I'd seen in the faxed copy agreement with the player.

So that was it. Just a few days into the new era heralded by the FA, already willing parties had become co-conspirators. As it transpired, when the player actually arrived, and I got to speak to him, he said he'd never met either the Eastern European agent or the English one. He'd just got a call from them out of the blue (presumably after they'd negotiated with me) to ask if he wanted to join The Club and telling him the terms, with which he was delighted. As he'd also been told it wouldn't cost him a penny, he was more than happy to sign off on anything that was placed before him – including, of course, the contract with The Club and the forms to be lodged with the FA, confirming that he'd represented himself. Given that we'd all been conned at The Club, and given that the contract I'd seen was clearly a forgery, I guess we'd actually been telling the truth to the FA when we said that the agent hadn't represented the player. But then in football there are truths and 'truths'. It's just that some are truer than others. At the end of the day though, we got the player we wanted, the player got a good deal and the agent got a good fee. So everybody was happy, including the FA, who hadn't the faintest idea of what had gone on.

And so it went on throughout the window. We were trying to sign the sort of player we could only have dreamed of before The Newcomer's money became available. Consequently, we were in competition with the big boys, and because of who we are we not only had to match them pound for pound, we also had to go that extra mile.

What became clear was that the bigger clubs were obeying the rules when it suited them, and ignoring them when they were desperate to sign a player. Some of the clubs who'd shouted the loudest to rein in the agents were the ones now doing all sorts of deals below the radar to secure the players they wanted. I heard of one club which entered into a substantial scouting deal with a player's father; another which put a club property in trust for the player's parents; and yet another that worked with an agent to set up an offshore company owned through nominees, with which they contracted to source players from various jurisdictions.

Suddenly clubs were finding the need for scouting networks in the farthest corners of the footballing globe. And all the time the players kept signing and the money, by fair means or foul, found its way into the pockets of the agents. Sometimes the players knew all about it, and simply didn't care because they'd got what they wanted. Sometimes they were kept in blissful ignorance, and their own deals could have been greatly improved by the monies that went to their agents.

The CEO and I sat down with The Club's Lawyer and worked out that, when it came to paying fees to secure a player, there was more than one way of skinning a cat.

"This is the way you can do it," The Lawyer said. "This foreign club wants a million for the player. So you give them a million and a half. The agent you want to sort it out has an agreement with the club to be paid the extra 500k for brokering the deal. He gets the player to sign with an agent he trusts, who may need the favour returned a bit further down the road, and your friendly agent tells the other agent what he's agreed with the club on behalf of the player. The other agent has a short-term agreement with the player which he lodges at the FA, gets a small fee for his trouble from the player which your friendly agent has negotiated from the buying club as a grossed-up signing-on fee, and Bob's your uncle. Everybody's happy."

"What about our friends at the FA?" I ask. "Are they happy?"

"Well, given they won't know anything about it they can hardly be unhappy, can they?" The Lawyer says, smiling like the cat who got the cream. He knows he'll be able to charge The Club – or The Newcomer, or whichever company The Newcomer wants to be charged – a juicy fee for the advice, so I guess he can afford to smile.

I heard other clubs were having problems when a player was 'represented' by an unlicensed agent. I've mentioned the ex-footballers, who aren't really a problem, but sometimes they're guys in financial services, who've been asked by the players to act for them after selling them insurance cover . . . and that's another story altogether.

I've had players in tears in my office, asking me to get them out of an obligation to pay monthly insurance premiums they can no longer afford. Before the Financial Services Act came into force, it used to be far worse. All sorts of people were out there selling players life insurance. Some of them were tied into one insurance company because that was how they could maximise their commissions. They'd sell a player an endowment policy for twenty years; the premiums were the same for the whole period, as far as the player was concerned. That was fine whilst he was earning good money, but as his career went on a downward spiral, and then ended completely, he'd find he had nowhere near the income to support or justify the payment of such huge premiums. Then he'd try and surrender the policy, only to find it was worth less than the premiums he'd paid into it – largely because the insurance company had paid their agent a whopping commission upfront.

With new laws and regulations in place it's a bit better, but there are still too many shysters out there trying to gain the confidence of footballers. And then they try to wheedle their way in so they can also do the player's deal for him. Then, knowing the exact size of his signing-on fee and the level of his income, they go for the jugular and persuade him to invest in all sorts of bonds and annuities, which again produce substantial commissions for them.

Until now they were able to hide behind a licensed agent, or even sometimes a lawyer who didn't need to be licensed. Basically most clubs seemed quite happy to deal directly with the unlicensed individual, and then have the front person just come in at the death and sign off on the documentation. They'd pay the front person the commission, and I assume he and the unlicensed agent would have a deal in place to divide up the money.

I'm not quite sure how that worked with the lawyers. I spoke to The Club Lawyer, who told me solicitors are not supposed to share their fees with anybody other than another solicitor. I suspect that particular rule didn't really bother the individual involved, although one or two lawyers we deal with seemed to pay lip service to keeping it legal (at least as far as the Law Society was concerned) by setting themselves up as a limited company operating as a football agency, outside the main body of their practice. That way they were using the fact that they were solicitors to gain exemption from licensing, and the fee to the unlicensed agent was paid out of the company, not out of their practice. Put rules in place and you set the minds of those subject to them whirling and working out ways to avoid them.

These new FA regulations are trying to put an end to all that. They've made lawyers register if they're doing work outside the normal sphere of their practice, including negotiation of the terms for contracts. They've made them subject to their rules, so that now the lawyer can't front for an unlicensed agent and split the fees with him because, just as with licensed agents, the lawyer has to tell the FA who shares his fees. The Club Lawyer told me he thinks that solicitors should be allowed to act for whomsoever they like, including these so-called unlicensed agents, and they aren't really fronting for these people but actually representing them, just like any other client. I've never cared up until now who I dealt with, so long as we got the player on the best terms. Now we'll have to be a bit more cautious, as it seems the FA mean business and the last thing we, as a club, need is a huge fine – though I doubt that would worry The Newcomer – or a deduction of points, which certainly would. Given our position in the league and paucity of points genuinely gained, if they took any number off us we might well find ourselves with negative equity.

Forgetting about the lawyers, the ex-pros and the insurance guys who look after the odd footballer, there are all sorts of fringe players out there in our wonderful pageant of a game. I came across one particular beauty who specialised in getting players to invest their monies in properties he'd found for them. He often recommended new developments with a view to the players buying to let them out. His particular scam was to do a deal with the developer: they upped the prices to the players, and the developer paid the individual a share of the uplift. Then, when the properties were finally rented, he produced two agreements. One was given to the player for a lower rent than was actually being paid. (The fact that it wasn't actually signed by the tenant was a small irrelevance.) The real figure went into the account of the managing agent, who'd also struck a deal with this individual. He paid the lower figure (less his commission) over to the player's bank account, and the balance of the rent (and the commission) was divided between the agent and the individual masterminding the whole plot.

It was only when one or two of the players consulted their accountants about their tax affairs that the scheme began to unravel. When they got valuations on the properties they realised the extent of the fraud. Their professional advisers urged them to go to court, or even to the police – but being footballers, they just wanted a quiet life and, having got their money back, they let it lie. So, this bloke is still out there, as far as I am aware, gaining the trust (and the money) of unsuspecting players.

When players earn as much as some of them do, then the figures take on a degree of unreality. The figures paid out to some of these dodgy characters simply don't mean the same thing as they would to me or you. The players have such low boredom thresholds that they tend not only to pay most attention to the last person they spoke to, but also to sign anything just so they don't have to listen anymore. I've had players in here showing me all sorts of things they've signed without reading. They claim they've not been explained to them either, but who knows? I've seen them putting money into film-development tax-saving schemes, apartments in Dubai that not only aren't built yet but will be worth less than the purchase price even before they fit the front door, and now the latest is properties in Eastern Europe – which may or may not turn out to be great investments, but meanwhile are earning huge commissions for the people selling them. Sometimes it's the players' agents selling them things, sometimes it's any old Tom Dick or Harry who has met them in a pub. I'd love to be a fly on the wall when somebody calls at their homes selling double glazing.

These sorts of investments are relatively small change to the players, but some years ago one particular agent had a more grandiose scheme. He specialised in doing deals abroad where there was far more scope for his machinations. Not only did he lie to players about what they were getting, but he got them to give him a large chunk of their not inconsiderable signing-on fees which he claimed he was investing in property abroad. Well, he *was* sort of doing that, but his methods were dubious to say the least.

He represented some very big names and, consequently, there was big money around. What he did was take all of the money and put it into an offshore company he controlled, even though it was fronted by nominee directors. He put the money on deposit and then actually bought properties with it, but it was very hard to work out which of the players owned which, and how much interest was due to the player on the money that had gone into the fund. The agent solved that problem by keeping all the interest himself, and probably a fair chunk of the rental (presumably by way of management fees), and simply doling money out to players as and when they needed it, like a generous benefactor – which, frankly, he could afford to be. The players loved him and, although many club chairmen knew of his dubious methods, they still came to him when they wanted a player because he was a man with a reputation for getting things done.

The wheels came off the trolley when, having done his usual deal for a particular player, the player's professional advisers then got involved in the legal and taxation side. In fact the agent had manoeuvred them out of the deal, so there was no love lost between them. The foreign club to which the player had been transferred seemed to think it wasn't actually obligated to pay him the vast sums that had been negotiated by the agent. Consequently, the agent and the two erstwhile advisers came to an uneasy truce and went out to the club to sort things out. At some point The Agent got a call to tell him another remunerative deal was about to go down some hundred or so miles away, albeit in the same country, and then took off in search of fresh meat. Somewhere out on the road, it occurred to him that there were some aspects of the transaction best not revealed to people with professional qualifications – and so he telephoned the club.

"Listen," he said, "the advisers don't know about the money you gave to the player off the books when he signed" – he then named a very large sum – "so it's best not to tell them."

By sheer chance, that call was recorded. But when it was played back to the player, it transpired that he didn't know anything about it either. He was so under the agent's spell that he insisted the agent be given the chance to provide an innocent explanation. A breakfast meeting was set up in a hotel with the player listening in on a hidden microphone to the conversation between his lawyer and the agent. The agent insisted that the substantial sum had at one stage been in the deal, but had been taken out. He even illustrated this by writing the figure down on a paper napkin and then crossing it out. The player was now convinced something was amiss.

The player's lawyer wrote a letter before action to the agent's lawyer. The latter protested his client's innocence and, indeed, the outrage he felt at the allegation. The agent did, however, come to a meeting, opening with the words, "I don't know why I'm here. This is a complete waste of time."

He was invited to listen to the tape of the telephone conversation. He continued to bluster until words like 'fraud' and 'squad' came down the line, at which point an urgent appointment was arranged; there was a complete collapse on the part of the agent and a compensatory deal was struck, involving the repayment of all monies plus interest, payment of legal and accountancy fees, and an undertaking never to contact or speak to the player again. But the agent did get the benefit of a confidentiality clause, and was able to carry on making vast fortunes for himself for years – and, to be fair, to ensure his clients made enough to retire. I suppose the lesson is that, if you're going to be a thief, then as long as the victim doesn't really know what he has and is left enough to keep him happy, you're likely to get away scot-free.

I did hear of one really odd deal during the window. A Premiership manager was after a player from a Championship club, and the club agreed a price of £3m to include another player who was thrown in as makeweight. The main purchase target changed his mind but, to everybody's surprise, the manager continued his pursuit of the makeweight. After some negotiation he went back to his chairman and asked him for £4m to buy the latter. The chairman was somewhat in awe of the manager, who'd been lured to the club to get them promoted in the previous season, and had done just that. But he did point out, almost apologetically, that the makeweight could not have been valued at more than a million in the earlier deal.

"Just humour me on this one, chairman," the manager is reputed to have said.

The chairman did humour him, to the extent of four million quid; the player came to the club, played half a dozen games and was jobbed out for a million at the end of the season. The manager left, leaving a club in turmoil behind him, and a lot of unanswered questions as to how the selling club dealt with the £4m they got for a player who was palpably not worth anything like it.

The fact is that, whatever these new FA agents' regulations may say, if an agent (or chairman, unlicensed agent, financial adviser, whoever) decides to rip off a player or a club, or seeks to circumvent the regulations, then the odds are that he's going to succeed. All these complications will do is to take us back to the days when the deals were buried so far underground that nobody really knew what was going on.

All I know is that here we are, at the end of January, we've got the most expensive squad we've ever assembled, a few points in the bag and we're on a cup run. Roll on February, say I – and so, I suspect, do the fans.

FEBRUARY

*"I can afford to hire the best. I have done exactly that.
It is to be regretted that in order to do so I had to
dismiss some people who were not the best."*
The Newcomer, on his appointment of a new Chief Executive Officer
and a new Finance Director, February 14th

There are some people at The Club who think The Newcomer's English has improved all too quickly. I suspect the guys he's just sacked are two of them. One thing you get to learn very quickly in football – and I suspect in most other industries as well – is that money is power, and it's very hard to argue with power backed by serious money. I don't argue, as you'll have already gathered. If I'm directed to do something, then as long as it's not palpably illegal I do it. If I have any concerns, then I try to create a paper trail to demonstrate that I was working under orders – but I do it anyway.

Some wealthy owners of clubs are just power crazy and love to show off their wealth, so long as they have an audience. There are club car parks up and down the country where the chairman's chauffeur sits out the entirety of a match, so that all the visitors to the directors' box know that the most expensive car in the car park is owned by the chairman, who won't have to wait for a moment to make his escape at the end. And sometimes it really is an escape, particularly when a team is doing badly and the crowd are chanting, "sack the board!" (Quite who's going to do the sacking, when it's the board that directs who is hired and fired, I've never understood.)

The Chairman and – in so far as I know him – The Newcomer are almost normal compared to some chairmen I've met. One was utterly paranoid about conspiracies. His team were pressing for promotion when they played another side, which contained the son of the manager of one of their main rivals. After the rival's son and his own team's goalkeeper were sent off, the chairman actually called his opposite number on the Monday after the match and said, "I'm going to sue your fucking manager and his son. That was a deliberate plot to get my keeper sent off."

"But our player was also sent off," replied the other chairman, astonished.

There was much huffing and puffing, but no action was taken.

Chairmen love to threaten proceedings. But then so do managers, I suppose. I watched a television programme about alleged corruption in football, and all the people mentioned subsequently threatened to sue the TV network. As far as I'm aware, the broadcaster is still waiting for the writs to land on its doormat.

It's when chairmen and managers lock horns that the real entertainment starts. In fact it's not really a fair fight. A few managers earn fortunes, but for the most part they just earn a good wage, albeit nothing in comparison to the better paid players. When a chairman takes on a manager, it's usually for one of two reasons: either the chairman has good reason to suspect the manager of villainy, and has sacked him without going through the proper legal procedures; or the manager wants to leave and is trying to walk away from his contract because there's a better proposition in sight. Chairmen can be very vindictive and managers can be very ambitious. Put those two ingredients together and you have a very combustive mix.

The problem is that most managers in the lower divisions see their clubs as a stepping stone to something bigger, and truly believe they're justified in moving on. It's Sod's Law that the timing of such a move is often at a stage in the season when both clubs need them the most. If a club needs a new manager then they want him in place before a transfer window, so that the signings the club makes are *his* signings and the team is *his* team, not just a bunch of blokes he's inherited. But the upwardly mobile manager is truly puzzled by the fact that both the old club and the fans are angry with him for abandoning them.

The other problem is the way our wonderful English legal system deals with the little matter of breaching employment contracts. If we as a club put one foot wrong, then we find ourselves carted off to an industrial tribunal, or, to avoid all that, we have to give the duffest of employees chance after chance, warning after warning, to ensure we comply with all the steps of our disciplinary procedures.

We've had all sorts of problems in that respect. We even had a physio who – after leaving us in the lurch time after time, including some match days – claimed he was too ill to return to work because we'd made him depressed with all the pressure we'd piled on him. Sometimes you just can't make this stuff up. However, if it's a valuable employee like a manager, then the court won't give the club the right to take out an injunction against him taking up his new job. Their view is that there's a perfectly adequate remedy in seeking damages, and you can't enforce a contract for the supply of personal services in this country.

One ex-player I know had begged and pleaded with a club to be given a chance to play a managerial role. He originally offered to work for nothing. They then took him on as an assistant, and even created the position for him when they could ill afford it. The manager left and they appointed him temporarily in charge. He did rather well and was given a proper contract. Trouble was, he did so well that he attracted the attention of a bigger club and, without even bothering to tell the club who'd given him his big chance, agreed to join them. Unfortunately, he only got around to telling his current employer when it was a done deal. So did the club he was joining, who then received a rude shock when they were asked for compensation. War broke out, and it was only settled on the steps of the courts. Still the tanager couldn't see that he'd done anything wrong.

So, taking all that into account, I don't suppose you can blame managers too much for grabbing opportunities where they can. They're pretty much cannon fodder when it comes to job security, and I reckon that any WWI foot-soldier going over the top had as good a chance of long-term survival as most managers. All that's guaranteed for them is a tracksuit bearing their initials and a place on the touchline bench.

The Newcomer has not sacked The FM yet. He'd got to the stage very early on in his tenure at The Club where the press were treating every match as a must-win situation. But a few wins have changed all that, and our focus has shifted from the performances on the pitch to that of the administrators. In one fell swoop The Newcomer has rid himself of The Chief Executive and The Finance Director, although even I don't know what they've done to justify their sudden dismissals.

The Chief Executive, who'd given up a very lucrative job at a high-profile club, is the worst done by of the two. He was summoned, it seems, to a meeting at The Newcomer's main business office and, after hanging around for a couple of hours, was then told The Newcomer had no time to see him but that his lawyer was available. The Lawyer simply told The Chief Executive that The Newcomer was not impressed with his performance, and a pre-prepared resignation was shoved under his nose. It was made clear that, if he signed it without arguing, he'd receive the compensatory amount contained in it. But if he didn't, then he was in for a long and expensive fight, and The Newcomer would spend as much as it took in legal fees to ensure The Chief Executive was ruined both financially and in terms of the game.

It seems The Chief Executive is either very bold or very foolish, because he ripped up the resignation, walked out, and the next day we received a letter before action from his solicitors. I'll follow that one with interest . . . but I've had The Newcomer's lawyers and accountants crawling all over the offices (in particular that of The Chief Executive), trying to uncover some actual wrongdoing as opposed to an imagined sin that caused The Newcomer to get rid of the same man he'd brought in just a few weeks ago. He's certainly not the most patient of men, and I'm doing my best to make myself even more invisible than usual. Most rational men wouldn't have sacked someone who'd been privy to some blatant breaches of the rules and regulations. Mind you, I suppose he can't really blow the whistle without incriminating himself.

The New CEO and The New Finance Director are grey men in suits. One has an American accent, the other talks with the clipped tones of somebody born in Eastern Europe who has travelled the world extensively ever since. They don't look like football people to me. But 'football people' in the football game seem to be getting thinner on the ground. It's all about business, about asset stripping. A secretary of another club I know sat in on a meeting when the current owners were negotiating the sale of the club to some foreigners. The figure quoted seemed absurd, and my friend knew it could only be recouped if the purchaser sold every player on the books as well as the club's ground. What the buyers didn't know was that my friend was able to understand the language in which they were speaking, and it transpired that these were almost exactly their intentions.

Property is the new football. Unless an individual is a cash-rich fan, there almost has to be a property deal in mind for a club to achieve its value on a sale. Obviously there are a few exceptions when the club is also a brand name, but clubs whose family silver has already been pawned are going to the wall without a benefactor to rescue them. I know of another Premiership club where the chairman has been trying to sell it for years, whilst at the same time talking about how much he cares about the club, its traditions and its future. The only thing that's stopped him selling are the local council's somewhat jaundiced view of his planning ambitions, and the fact that he can't find a green-field site to build a stadium within the club's conurbation. Then there's another club which is financed by wealthy individuals who actually support another team – and again, they're willing to sell in the full knowledge that any buyer would have to sell off the club's assets to justify the figure being sought.

Now, I understand that people want a return on their money, but we've come a very long way from the days where individuals invested in clubs for fun, because they knew the club was not allowed to pay dividends on its shares. Now we have the men like our New CEO and New FD, for whom profit and return are everything, who may be building up the value of The Club so that The Newcomer can cash in when the time is right. What I'm now sure of is that, whatever he might say, he's not here for the long ride. He's not here for the good of The Club. Now I understand why, when The Chairman tried to get a clause into the sale agreement ensuring The Club's ground would not be sold unless the proceeds would pay for a suitable alternative, The Newcomer gave all sorts of verbal assurances but wouldn't commit to it in writing.

What's that quote from the movie industry? "A verbal contract is not worth the paper it's written on."

MARCH

"There is no split in my dressing room.
They are all part of my team, whatever their countries
of birth. Whatever language they speak, they all
understand me."

The FM on rumours of warring factions within

The Club, March 2nd

If it's not one thing, it's another. Our results continue to improve, but The FM achieved that by signing some expensive, egotistical players, some of whom have a real attitude problem. At least one of them believes that everything we do here is wrong, and everything done back in his home country is right. I'm not being xenophobic, but I wouldn't mind a return to the old system whereby clubs brought players through their youth system, rather than bringing them in through the cheque book.

There are all sorts of unknowns, all sorts of risks, in buying expensively from abroad. In the first case you never quite know what you're getting in relation to age, temperament or price. Age is a particular problem if you're buying from Africa. In countries where birth registrations are hit and miss, and birth certificates more or less optional, it's not unusual for players (or their agents) to shave a few years off their ages to make them more attractive to English clubs and obtain lucrative deals.

Then there's temperament. Sometimes, settling into an English way of life is very difficult. One South American player, brought up in the countryside, entertained his team mates for Sunday lunch by cooking a huge meal for them in a dustbin. Often, a foreign import is susceptible to the influence of homebred players put in charge of their day-to-day welfare. It's not always the best idea. One young continental, whose grasp of English was particularly poor, thought for the entire duration of his English career that the fourth day of the week was 'Wankday'.

And finally there's the price. The buying club may think they know what the selling club is receiving, but nine times out of ten that's mere wishful thinking. There are all sorts of people taking money out of these transfers. It's common for a foreign club to know the price they want, and to tell an agent that anything he gets on top is his. That's a licence to beef up the price, and obviously the agent does everything in his power to stop the buyer speaking directly to the seller lest the real price slip out – or in case the selling club renege on any deal they have with him, and try to get a slice of the extra money themselves by cutting a new deal with the buyers.

I've heard of situations where even the chairman of the club is on the deal. He'll have sat down with the manager and discussed their target players for the transfer window. The manager will have his own ideas, but the chairman may throw a name into the ring and get some mild interest from the manager on the assumption the price is right. The manager then thinks that, say, £1m is coming out of his budget to buy a player, and is then astonished to read in the papers that the clubs have agreed a fee of £5m.

The way it works is that the club has been told that they

can get a million more than the asking price if they actually push it up by £4m. When the deal is done and the money paid, the chairman's club signs a cheque for the full £5m, the selling club bank it, and promptly transfer £3m to an offshore account designated by the chairman. The £5m has come from the club's coffers, not his personal account, so he's not actually robbing himself.

Still, I suppose as long as everybody's happy then the world keeps spinning round. The only losers are the fans, who think they're getting a £5m player whereas in fact he's only worth a million. And believe me, unless the club are very lucky, that sort of price differential always shows on the pitch. The irony is that, when the club does badly, it's the poor old manager who's blamed for the performances, in particular those of the players he's perceived as having bought.

Some foreign players try to integrate. They take language lessons and attempt to mix with their English counterparts, but others leave knowing as little English as when they arrived. Others find English food very hard to take. A Japanese player put on so much weight, when he moved from his normal domestic diet, that his club had to take drastic action – getting somebody to live in with him to ensure he actually ate the Western food he disliked, while controlling his intake. It's players from Far Eastern and Middle Eastern cultures who seem to be the most alienated and lonely. They come to the club, they're polite and respectful, they train hard, and then they go home. They rarely mix socially, and even more rarely make any real effort to learn the language. That's all going to change, now that immigration laws are making knowledge of the English language conditional to a work permit. I'm not sure how anybody thinks they're going to get around that one.

There are some very odd things that go on with foreign players. Apart from the question of their ages there are all sorts of shenanigans over work permits as well. At first sight there appear to be some very strict rules about non-EU players coming into England. (I was going to say the UK, but the Scottish FA seems to be a law unto itself.) As far as England is concerned, a non-EU player needs a work permit just like any other foreign worker. He's practically guaranteed to get one if he's played at least seventy-five percent of internationals for his own country in the period before he wants to enter the UK, and if his country is among the upper echelons of the footballing nations. The PFA are very protective of English footballers, and I'm told they'll object to players of lower status coming into the country and taking the bread out of the mouths of their members. Very commendable, say I, when there are so many players looking for jobs at the end of every season. But then there's the situation where a club wants a player who doesn't fit the criteria, and they try to buck the system by looking for ways around it.

Some clubs on the continent seem to be able to secure EU passports for the most unlikely immigrant footballers. Parents and grandparents with EU-eligible nationality are conveniently found, or a passport is legally (or in some cases illegally) acquired for a player from fringe EU countries. Not many people seem to realise that a non-EU national can come here and work for six months if he's living with an EU national. He comes in under a special permit and, whilst it's time-specific and depends upon him continuing to cohabit with the EU resident, it does give him the chance to get his foot in the door.

Some agent tried to pull the wool over our eyes during the

last transfer window, by selling us an African player who was living with a Danish girl whilst playing in Scandinavia. The price seemed to be a bargain, we had a look at the lad and he seemed really good. He didn't fit the established international criteria, but the agent gave us a heavily edited summary of the entry rules which seemed to suggest he would get a work permit because he'd been with his Danish girlfriend for a couple of years. It was only when I looked into it myself that I realised there'd be a review after six months and, in any event, if he split from the lady then his permission to stay and work would automatically be terminated. So here we were, being asked to pay over a million for his services and to give him a six-figure signing-on fee. But if he and the girl had a tiff, then we were minus a player and severely out of pocket. Thanks, but no thanks. We said we might consider a loan, but all of a sudden he was no longer available – at which point we realised that the Scandinavian club had been spun a yarn as well.

I'm not sure how much of this is down to the players being economical with the truth, or the agents. Or I suppose that the clubs who hold the players' registrations might want to cash in as well. When we have odd rules such as relatives qualifying a player to work here, or when it's dependant on who he's married to or how easily a dodgy passport can be obtained, it's no wonder the system gets abused.

Mind you, the players get abused themselves. One foreign player we were very keen on in the last window didn't have anything like the number of international caps his skills deserved. Whilst we were working on the deal, and trying to see if there was any way we could get him special dispensation, he told me the manager of his national team had told him that he wouldn't pick him unless he changed to an agent of the manager's choice.

Presumably, the new agent would have split any commissions he received with the international manager, and they would have been much higher given that the player would have been a regular international. I found it hard to believe at the time, but I've since spoken to a few other club officials who said they heard similar stories. I suppose that, provided the players an international manager picks are all much of a muchness, and he gets enough results to keep him in a job, then he'll get away with it. I can't see it happening here though – you have to look at a few one-cap wonders who've pulled on an England shirt and wonder just how they ever became internationals. Maybe they were related to whoever the manager was at the time, or had enough information to blackmail him into selecting them.

Anyway, The FM has had a huge clear-the-air meeting where there seemed to be more interpreters than players, and everybody agreed to settle their differences. All sorts of pledges for team bonding were made. One of our players had to shave his hair off for an operation, and they've all agreed to do the same thing for Saturday's game. They're also spending as much time on rehearsing goal celebrations as they are on the moves that give them the goals in the first place. Still, at least the goals are coming now – although we're still in the bottom three, it's only on goal difference.

Goal celebrations of an orchestrated kind are a relatively new phenomenon. We used to have a player score, get patted on the back by his nearest team-mate, and then run back to the halfway line in readiness for the kick-off. After we got past the hugging and kissing stage, things began to get totally out of hand. Shirts were whipped off to reveal all sorts of messages, players leapt (or threw their shirts) into the crowd, shorts were dropped to the knees, there were somersaults, back-flips, it was like a circus.

Then the referees got tough, and when players got booked just for being happy – or even risked a red card if they'd been booked already – some of the joy went out of it. An uneasy truce now seems to have acknowledged that a short dance in unison, a quick whirl around a corner flag or a piece of solo gymnastics are acceptable – as long as they don't seem to be deliberate time-wasting tactics. What I don't like is the sheer viciousness of some of the players, when they score in front of rival fans: the finger-waving; the hand to the ear as they taunt them; the clenched fist of triumph. Sooner or later, the fans will get so wound up by it that the anger and violence will implode. We'll have some real problems then, either in the stadium or after the match. But tell that to a nineteen-year-old who's just scored his first goal for a team he's supported since he was a kid, against the club's deadly rivals in a local derby.

We are all geared up for our Sixth Round Cup-Tie. The African players we lost to the African Nations Cup are all back with us, although one or two were delayed en route. That didn't really help the unity in the dressing room either. They had some interesting excuses, but then footballers do have vivid imaginations when it comes to avoiding fines. And that doesn't just apply to those returning late from international duty. One player was allegedly at a family funeral when spotted in a London nightclub. (Funerals are footballers' stock in trade for alibis, as you may have gathered by now.) Called into the club and faced with photographic evidence, he still tried to bluff it out by claiming the photos weren't of him – and that, even if they were, he wasn't there at the time so they must have been old photos. At which point he ran out of steam, confessed all, and did what many professional sportsmen and women do at the moment of truth: burst into tears.

That, in my experience, has often been the problem with players. They just panic when they've been found out, but don't think of the repercussions whilst they're in the process of the act itself. During the last transfer window we were extending a contract for a player. An agent we knew told us he was acting for him, and also confirmed that he'd lodged his contract with the FA. We started talking to him, and the player was well aware that negotiations were taking place.

We then got a call from another agent who claimed to represent the player. He also said he had a contract, and had lodged it at the FA within five days of it being signed. It was, supposedly, signed two days before the contract we were already dealing with. I was a bit suspicious of that, and wondered if the second agent had been holding onto a signed but undated contract in case he might have been able to persuade us to agree to put down on the FA form that he'd been acting for us. But there we were, faced with two claimants saying they acted for the player. So I called the player in

"Who do you think is acting for you?" I asked.

"The first bloke you mentioned," he replied.

"Do you know so-and-so?" I asked, giving him the name of the second agent.

There was a pause. I could almost see his brain going into gear, searching for an answer that would stop this line of questioning.

"Yeah, I do know him. From around."

"Have you signed a contract with him?" I persisted.

"No fucking way." There was no hesitation this time.

"So what do you make of this?" I asked, showing him a copy of the contract.

"It's a forgery."

"I'm not sure this chap would submit a forged document to the FA. Anyway, your signature looks identical on both contracts."

There was a pause.

"I think I may have signed both of them. But the second bloke said he'd tear his up if I changed my mind, and now the cunt has gone and sent it off to the fucking FA."

So in the parallel universe the player inhabited, this was all the fault of the second agent.

I decided we'd let them all battle it out, and wasn't surprised to learn that the FA had hauled the player up for signing contracts with two agents. The agents agreed to split the fee (which was coming from the player anyway), and I suppose that justice in this instance was just about served. In the crazy world of football that's about as good as it gets.

The opposition fans homed in on the internal troubles at The Club. They always love that, as they feel it gives their team an edge. Only this time, our players of all nationalities got their heads down and actually played. We won three-nil, with one of our African players scoring one of the best goals we've ever seen here, celebrating with a triple somersault that hurt his neck in the process. Mind you, as they carried him off on a stretcher he was pulling his shirt out in front of him and kissing the badge.

Footballers, don't you just love 'em?

LATE MARCH

"I now begin to understand the magic of the FA Cup."
The FM, March 20th

For a club like ours, an FA Cup run is both a surprise and a lifeline. Here we are at the end of March, looking forward to a semi-final against the holders which is going to be played at Villa Park in Birmingham. At the same time we've clawed our way up the table and have five clubs below us, whilst we're six points clear of relegation. The Newcomer is happy, The FM is happy and The New CEO is even happier, because he has all sorts of bonuses written into his contract based upon the profitability of The Club.

Right now we're making money hand-over-fist from ticket sales, replica shirts and the promise of television money for our match. But I don't know where all these fans have come from. All of a sudden we have 'lifelong' supporters from all over the country, most of whom seem to have a perfectly plausible excuse as to why they've not come to see a league match here for over twenty years. The thing they all have in common is they want a ticket for the semi-final and, in anticipation of us pulling off a major surprise and winning, also want to book their tickets (note that they always request pairs) for Wembley.

Meanwhile, I had to carry out a sad task this morning. As a season progresses it becomes quite clear that certain players have no future with The Club. It's actually cheaper to pay them up than to keep them hanging around in the vague hope we might call on their services. Disaffected, they can even become disruptive influences in the dressing room.

When I say pay their contract up, I don't mean that we calculate everything that would have been due and pay every penny. We're a football club, not a registered charity. We work out what the player would have had after tax; we then calculate what it would have cost us to pay him gross plus our employer's National Insurance contribution. We can pay him £30,000 *ex-gratia* and that's tax free, so it becomes worth about 50k as far as he's concerned. Our friends at the Inland Revenue always seem to accept it, so we have some room to manoeuvre where payment is concerned. The advantage to him is that he's getting an accelerated payment and can make immediate plans for the future. As far as we're concerned, we've cut our losses and drawn a line under that particular player's career.

Obviously, some players come back to haunt you. But, generally speaking, when a player is regarded as being so disposable that he can be paid off, you can be fairly sure the manager has made the right decision. Like most clubs, we also do the same when we're stuck with a player with a long-term injury. If it's career-ending, then the situation is much clearer and we can take advantage of the standard termination clause in the Premier League contract. Yes, we have to get a doctor's opinion, yes, he has the right to a second opinion, yes, there may have to be a third opinion if the two doctors disagree. But, at the end of the day (and it can be quite a long day), it's done and dusted. It used to be much simpler: you got somebody to certify that the player's career had ended, and gave him six months' notice; if you were nice, you also gave him a testimonial. Life just keeps getting more and more complicated.

This player we are paying up actually broke down and cried in my office – even though he hadn't been playing for us, and would be walking away with a fat cheque as soon as he signed off on the compromise agreement we always insist upon. We even pay an independent lawyer the massive sum of £250 (plus VAT of course!) to give the player some advice on the document. Some of the lawyers try to earn their fee, and get clever by asking us to indemnify the player in case the taxman ever comes knocking at his door – but of course we always say no. I've never had a problem, and generally, once the amount has been agreed – which obviously depends on how greedy the player or his agent gets – these things tend to run quite smoothly.

Mind you, I have heard some real horror stories concerning a player's departure from a club. During the last transfer window, one club wanted to sell one of their players to another which was offering around £400,000. The selling club had appointed one particular agent to handle all their sales. But the player didn't fancy the new club, and told his current club that if they wanted him out they would have to make it worth his while to go. The chairman asked him how much he wanted and he said £100,000. That was probably a bit optimistic, but it was somewhere to start. Eventually the chairman said he'd give him £50,000, and the player agreed.

Another club then came after him. The chairman told them the price would be close to a million because he had to give the player 100k of it. The second club agreed the deal, and the player began to talk to them about terms.

To his amazement, he discovered that the agent who'd been appointed by his club to sell him had popped up at the buying club, claiming to be acting for him. He disabused them of their error and agreed terms, assuming he was going to get the agreed £50,000 from his old club. The chairman then told him he was only going to get £30,000. He seemed to be under the misapprehension that the 30k would be tax-free in the player's hands and would equate with 50k. But that sort of concession only works when the player has his contract terminated, and if it had been terminated the club wouldn't have been getting a transfer fee. And it actually got worse, because it appeared the chairman had not consulted the manager before selling the player. So, to placate the manager (who was a friend of the agent who was supposed to be acting for the club), the chairman told the player he wasn't even going to pay the £30,000 unless the player got the agent who'd acted for the buying club to pay over some of his commission to the selling club's agent, who'd been supposedly 'squeezed out' of a deal he hadn't been involved with in the first place.

It's not just players, agents, clubs and their officials who cause problems. Match officials can give you grief as well. We groaned a bit when we saw the name of the referee who's going to be in charge of the most important game of our season. He's already sent off two of our defenders this season, and I've just made a quick tally-up that shows how, when he's been in charge of any of our matches over the past three seasons, he's booked fifteen players and sent off five. Now, I'm not saying that none of them deserved it, but he certainly seems to have a down on us.

That's part of the problem when a team or a player gets a reputation for playing the game hard. There's a very fine line between sheer determination and a deliberate attempt to put an opponent out of the game. In the past we've had Jack Charlton's 'little black book', allegedly containing the names of players to whom he intended to show no mercy. We've had ex-players admitting in their autobiographies that they've gone on the pitch with the prime objective of conducting a vendetta. Although I know for sure that a bit of that still goes on, today, for the most part, players want to win games fairly. I've known footballers actually traumatised when they injured an opponent, and I don't think many home-grown players try to get fellow professionals booked deliberately or to feign injuries. But I'm not so sure the same can be said for some of our recent imports; to get the balance right though, at least one former England manager used to spend part of his team's training sessions getting them to dive into the penalty area, when they'd been fouled just outside of it.

I'm not suggesting there's any real corruption amongst English referees, but some certainly do have a mindset that's hard to explain. Neither do we have the match-fixing problems that some of my contacts suggest have reached epidemic proportions on the continent. One top-level referee told me that, before one match, the chairman of a competing club introduced him to his three 'daughters', none of whom looked remotely alike, asking him which one (or which two) he wanted to keep him company that evening.

The same referee (who obviously enjoyed an interesting life) also told me of a European match for which he and another English ref had been commissioned to officiate. When he got there, the home chairman told him he'd be paying for their hotel and other expenses. The Englishmen told them their expenses were always paid for anyway, but the chairman wouldn't have it and insisted on thrusting a fairly substantial amount of cash on them (in the local currency). They had no idea what to do, and then came up with the idea of asking the chairman to put it in his safe for them until after the match. The home team won one-nil and the money never resurfaced, as the chairman obviously considered that, having got the result fair and square, there was no need for a retrospective bribe.

Mind you, some referees can be fun. One of our players recently turned to one after he'd made two or three poor decisions, and said, "Ref, you're having a fucking nightmare game."

The referee smiled and said, "You should know, because you're having one too," before running off after the ball.

Although we do now have a Press Officer firmly in place, journalists that I know are trying to circumvent her and come to me. They know she'll say no and they think there's a possibility I may say yes. I listen politely to them, have a chat and enquire after their families' wellbeing. Then I say no.

I suspect it's dawned on them that, if we actually win the cup, then we'll be in Europe, and the one thing that journalists love is a European jolly. Once out of England and away from their wives and sweethearts – and in a few cases their male partners – they're like kids in a sweetshop. In the old days they had virtually open expense accounts and access to the players. Now interviews are strictly rationed and orchestrated, so they settle for dinner with agents and sundry hangers-on who can usefully be described as 'insiders' in their articles. Then after dinner it's drinks, and more drinks, and finally there is usually a visit to some welcoming ladies. They might be a bit hard to put down on the expenses, but sometimes the agents are happy to foot the bill – particularly when the journalist has already been or is about to become helpful in publicising a player's unhappiness at a club, in order to kick-start a transfer.

There's not quite so much opportunity for those sorts of shenanigans in Birmingham. We're playing lunchtime on a Sunday, so – although most journalists are pretty inventive, especially when it comes to stories about players – even they might be hard-pushed to come up with an excuse for staying in the Midlands, when the match will be over by three-ish and they're just about a hundred miles from home.

But I can't be too worried about referees and journalists at the moment. There are a hundred and one things to do before we play: tickets, programmes, sponsors, transportation, hotels, kit, all being dealt with by somebody at The Club, but all finally coming to rest on my desk. And now The New FD has asked me to look at all the players' contracts to see how much it'll cost us in bonuses. Everybody thinks that clubs make a fortune from a cup run, but it really depends on who you play and where, and whether or not the match is televised. If you're drawn away to a small team in the early rounds, and only get forty-five percent of the gate, it doesn't cut any ice with the players who have bonuses in their contract for progressing in the cup. What it does mean is that, although you win, you may well lose money on the day, particularly if you have to pay out the win bonus. At that point you're left waiting with bated breath for that Monday lunchtime draw, to see if you have a plum tie against Manchester United or the like.

Now, with a semi-final against the holders, a match that is going to be televised worldwide, whatever we may be paying out to the players we're still going to make money. But, not unreasonably, The New FD wants to know exactly what we are in for. We do have a squad bonus which applies to everybody, but we also have one or two players whose agents inserted extra success bonuses for if we win the cup – although, having checked, nobody is on anything extra for this semi-final. However, even without that, the bonus is really generous. I suspect this will be because The Chairman, who negotiated it before the season started, did not think we had a chance of getting this far. Thus he was quite happy to throw it in, so that the players' representatives compromised on something else that, at the time, seemed far more attainable.

There's nothing we can do about the bonuses right now. Even if we wanted to offer our players a greater incentive, we couldn't. That would be a contractual renegotiation and, if we did that during the season, we'd also have to offer them a minimum one-year extension. Unless a term forms part of the contract that is lodged with and approved by the FA, then it just doesn't count. I heard of a club recently who reckoned they had a player hooked, because he'd signed a side-letter granting them an option to extend the contract. But when they tried to exercise it, the player's agent told them to get stuffed, as it didn't form part of the contract sent to the FA at the time they'd signed him. The club tried to argue that it was a perfectly enforceable agreement in law, but when the player threatened to take the whole matter to the FA they backed down. Presumably there were some other skeletons in their cupboard that they didn't want exposed to light of day.

On a smaller scale, I have heard of a couple of £50 notes

being tucked into envelopes and distributed to players in the lower leagues if they won an important match. I also knew of a director with a car dealership who'd happily hand out brand new cars if the club gained promotion. I'm quite sure that in neither case did the Inland Revenue find out about it – although they do have a dedicated tax office in Birmingham, tracking footballers to see what benefit in kind may come their way without actually trickling through to their tax returns

That's my phone ringing again. Somebody wants tickets for his ninety-year-old dad and, as he's a bit doddery and the caller needs to take him to the match, they obviously need two. I note his name and number, and wonder just what would happen to the tickets if I did find them a couple. It's hard to sort the wheat from the chaff when it comes to hard luck stories.

I learned a long time ago that, when it comes to football, there is only one maxim to follow: Believe nobody and trust even fewer.

APRIL

*"At the end of the season nobody remembers the losing
semi-finalists or the teams who get relegated."*

Columnist in the *London Evening Standard,* on the eve of the
FA Cup Semi-Final, April 7th

We've travelled up to the Midlands three days before the
match, and we're giving the players a taste of luxury
that few of them have experienced before with this club. The
recent high earners we've signed just take all this for granted.
They've seen it all before at their previous clubs, and would be
surprised to be treated in any other way. A few problems have
still surfaced since we've been here. One of the chambermaids
complained that one of our players touched her breasts when
she came in to clean his room. He's only one of the reserves
and a mere kid. Of course, he denied it, but when The
Manager and I cross-examined him he owned up. We just
made him write the girl a letter of apology. But later I found
out he'd been put up to it by one of the senior pros, who'd had
the rest of the squad in hysterics, telling them how he'd
convinced the youngster it was some kind of initiation rite.

You'd think that the older footballers get, the better they'd
behave, but then logic never seems to apply in football. They
just get a little more devious, a little more sophisticated, a little

more wary of being found out. They now know the media takes more delight in a piece of misbehaviour or scandal involving a 'name' than in that involving a kid, so they tend to tread more carefully. Except sometimes, when they're fuelled by alcohol and testosterone, and caution truly gets thrown to the wind.

One England international was always regarded as whiter than white, but his team-mates knew better. He was often to be found encouraging the young players to do all the things he'd thought up, but wasn't going to risk doing himself. Dropping an autograph book given to him by a young female fan was a favourite. As the book hit the floor and the girl bent down to retrieve it, he'd nod or wink at his dupe, who'd either pinch or slap the girl's bottom, or even shove her over. The senior player then looked appalled as he helped her to her feet, apologised, and then shot a look of disapproval at whichever hapless youngster he'd set up to do the evil deed. On occasions the press got a shot of him lending a helping hand, but never a picture of the little glance that set the whole thing up.

Big-name senior players can be an asset as well as a problem. One player who joined a club for a huge fee began to believe his own reputation. Nothing was ever right. Either the club trained too long or for not long enough. The ball was too hard or too soft. The pitch was too wet or too dry. The food at the training ground was awful. The club's preparation for matches was amateurish. He even complained about the design of the kit. But nothing that ever happened, on or off the pitch, was his fault. The crosses from the wingers were too high or too low; the long balls forward that he lacked the pace to reach were misdirected. Eventually, nobody at the club was talking to him, and when the manager decided to discipline him by fining him two weeks' wages, the chairman was too cowardly to face up to him and reversed the decision. Fortunately, at the moment we have nobody like that on our staff. For once we're all pulling in the same direction.

This is a big night for us. The FM wants everybody tucked up in bed by ten. I'm not sure any of our lads are going to try anything on, although stories about players in hotels on the night before an important match are legendary. Some are so bizarre that it's hard to believe they're true. One team was in Spain on tour, and the manager looked out of his window to see one of his players giving hand relief to a very satisfied donkey. Then there was the time that a couple of well-known hardened drinkers actually bullied two of the kids to commute from their own rooms to the drinkers' beds as soon as they'd been checked up on themselves, to ensure the management would see warm bodies occupying the sheets. Meanwhile, the two senior pros were out enjoying the local bars.

That was risky because it depended on timing; more recently, another pair of players bribed two of the hotel staff to sleep in their beds whilst they went out on the town. It only took a very small percentage of their considerable salaries to keep everybody happy. Both players took to the field the next day with massive hangovers, yet by some miracle still managed to finish on the winning side.

There was even one player who specialised in jumping over cars after a night on the tiles, when his team was on tour. I don't think anybody here is going to be risking that before tomorrow's match.

The FM has decided the whole squad are going to sit together and watch a film after supper. Players have this amazing ability to obtain bootleg videos of current films, sometimes before they even cross the Atlantic to officially hit the screens here. One player from a Midlands club really put his foot in it when he was asked what film the players had watched on the coach; he told him they'd viewed the fourth in a series of action-adventures when only the third was released to the cinemas over here, let alone out on DVD. Team-mates had to cover for him by explaining that arithmetic wasn't his strong point, and that they'd really watched the second film in the series, which was readily and legally available.

The FM chose *Reservoir Dogs* for the team to watch – which, I suppose, as a basis for team building isn't a bad selection. I just hope we have more survivors on the pitch tomorrow than Tarantino permitted to last until the end of his film. The boys, even though most of them have seen it before, seemed to enjoy it and went off to bed quite happy, calling each other Mr Pink or Mr White and suchlike. It's at times like these, when they're acting like overgrown, excited school kids, that you feel rather fond of them. It's the lull before the storm. I can almost imagine The FM (if he were able to understand all that was being said) putting his ear to their keyholes to gauge the mood of his troops, just like *Henry V* before Agincourt.

I doubt whether any of our players have ever seen a Shakespeare play or would get the analogy. Mind you, at least one very experienced striker is a regular at Royal Shakespeare Company performances in Stratford-on-Avon, and, as he's rather big, I can't believe any of his team-mates would mock him for that. Generally though, players get given a hard time if they read a broadsheet paper rather than a tabloid. Taking the *Daily Mail* on a regular basis makes them an intellectual.

I remember a Premiership player, who's now a regular newspaper columnist, saying that some of the players he'd lined up alongside were convinced he was gay because he read *The Guardian*.

We had a gay player at The Club a couple of seasons ago. There'd been a few rumours about him before he joined us, but he was a decent player, we didn't have a lot of money at the time, and his price was very competitive. I have no problem with any individual's sexual preferences, as long as he doesn't cause problems for anybody else. (I'd like to say that some of my best friends are gay, but in truth I just don't mix in those particular circles.) It does, however, seem to trouble your average footballer, who may have grown up on a council estate where anybody who didn't fit a particular profile, or seemed a bit different, became fair game for abuse, or even violence.

I've listened to some of the dressing-room conversations and know that, if a few of these lads didn't have a particular talent in their feet, they may very well have ended up doing time. I've listened to the stories of taunts, the abuse that's been thrown at gays, blacks, Asians and Jews alike – it's all said in such a matter-of-fact way that you soon realise it's not even pure racism. It's just ignorance, linked to a contagious way of life. But the minute they saw our gay player wasn't chatting up girls or joining in the crude banter with the rest of them, then, as you might imagine, it was open season on him.

It was low-profile to start with – a tampon left in his locker – and then it heated up a bit. Wolf-whistles when he came into the dressing room; a refusal to room with him in hotels; crude slogans on his kit-bag. It built up to such a pitch that the poor guy couldn't even face turning up for work. Eventually he had a nervous breakdown, never played again, and ended by committing suicide in his garage. The team wore black armbands that week, and we had a minute's silence before the game. Even that was broken by a few idiots in the crowd.

Our fans have never been particularly bigoted, though the opponents we face tomorrow have supporters with some track record in that respect. Certainly, complaints were made after one final against Spurs, when the chant, "Gassed in the morning, you'll be gassed in the morning!" was heard, followed by a series of Nazi salutes. Charming people, some football fans. I was going to say charming fellows, but the odd female fan can be just as vicious as her male counterparts. In the heyday of gang warfare there was never a lack of girls to egg on the lads. To have a scar from fighting fans of a rival club was a good way to get a girl into bed. (Though they probably didn't use beds, just the nearest available alleyway. It's not just rock bands that have groupies – nor, indeed, is it only football players.)

It's an odd culture really. The gangs of fans have their own camp followers, and then the players have their private female fan club too. There's no doubt it's a feather in the cap to sleep with a footballer, and some of these girls have collected enough for a full Indian headdress. I'm told there's an active market for footballers' phone numbers amongst this bunch of admirers, who are happy to send out texts inviting the players for NSA sex (no strings attached). However, there's always a chance that they may catch something, and a few clubs have had to invent injuries for players not up to performing on the pitch due to the STD they caught whilst playing off of it. It's not just one-way traffic either, because the players also have the numbers of girls regarded as safe bets. You have to ask yourself why some players are still prepared to pay for sex when it's offered to them on a plate for free. Maybe they think prostitutes are less likely to sell their stories to the papers?

Wandering around this hotel at night, seeing some of the single girls propping up the bars with one thought on their mind, it's hard not to turn to the subject of sex and the footballer. Some of the girls are more inventive than others. At one of the smaller London clubs, a football groupie managed to wangle her way into the dressing room after halftime, and waited patiently for the first player to be substituted to return for his early bath. In fact, she was able to meet a player who'd been red-carded and, although he was unhappy to be sent off, his humour was partly restored by being jerked off.

Another girl booked into the same hotel as the team of her choice, discovered the room number of her target player, somehow or other conned her way into the empty room, and then hid in a wardrobe to await her gladiator's entry. The fact that he was accompanied by a team-mate in no way put her off, and, having serviced her original choice, she then extended the favour to the other player before making her exit. That particular girl tried to sell her story to the Sunday papers, and it took all the expertise of a publicity guy to persuade the paper that they had no proof and were risking a libel action.

I've not really mentioned the way some of these PR people exploit the industry. There are quite a few famous footballers (and managers), not to mention one or two of the higher profile directors, who pay a publicist a retainer to ensure the real dirt doesn't hit the front pages. Or if it does, then they have to try to ensure it doesn't refer to them. It's almost a barter system: "Leave my client alone, and in return I'll feed you a better story about somebody I don't represent." Sometimes they really do act as publicists, and the rest of the time they're covering up potentially damaging dirt.

People in football say they hate publicity, but they hate it more when they're ignored. "You have to respect my privacy," they say, but that's only *when* they want it to be respected. As you'll have gathered by now, I'm not the sort of person to go clubbing, but I did hear of one famous player who went to a club wearing dark glasses, so as not to be recognised, and then, when he was refused admission, got very upset.

"Don't you know who I am?"

"Not with those shades on, I don't," replied the large and threatening doorman.

Tomorrow everybody will know who our lads are. There'll be nowhere to hide, with or without dark glasses. They'll be under the microscope long before kick-off, their strengths and weaknesses analysed by the so-called experts. They'll be asked the usual inane questions:

"What does winning this match mean to you?"

"Just how important is it going to be out there tomorrow?"

"Is this the high-point of your life so far?"

"Do you think you can win?"

I long for one player to have the guts to answer as follows:

"Not a lot."

"Not very, in the greater scheme of things."

"Well, my wedding day wasn't bad either."

"We haven't a prayer, I'm just showing up for the money."

It's not going to happen, but it would be a whole load more entertaining. There's one particular interviewer who is very serious, and I know for a fact that, unbeknownst to him,

236

many of the lads just send him up with their monosyllabic answers to his lengthy, 'probing' questions.

When you listen to these experts in the studios, sometimes you can hear the envy in their voices. They don't want to be sitting in a television studio, they want to be out there kicking a football. Some of them kick every ball anyway. Others just give a verbal kicking to players and managers against whom they've harboured a grudge for years. It's not exactly fair. The recipients of the criticism hardly get the right to reply. It's strange really, how individuals you knew as perfectly decent folk when they were players develop a mean streak when they go over to the dark side of the media. I suppose it's such a cutthroat business that maybe you need that mean streak to survive.

One of our players got so riled by what one particular pundit was saying about him that he told one of his team-mates he intended going round to the bloke's house, to sort him out. The team-mate, sensibly, told The New Assistant Manager, who calmed him down by telling him that if he went to jail for GBH, there was no way The Club was going to carry on paying his wages. That's always a problem when a club has a player facing a custodial sentence. Do they cut him loose and lose any future transfer value, or do they stand by him and pay out a load of money for him to do nothing – except to grow increasingly unfit on a prison diet? One club took the high moral ground, and refused to pay when their player got banged up for a fairly serious crime – but, incredibly, as they'd not followed the rules to the letter, the FA told them that if they didn't pay the wages of their erstwhile player they were going to kick them out of the league.

Players are not even always honest about what's going on

in their lives. One club knew that their player had a court case pending, but he told them it was just a motoring offence. In fact it turned out to be an armed robbery where he'd not only been an accomplice, but a victim had also been killed by another defendant. Not surprisingly (at least to everybody except the club, who just expected him to lose his licence), the player was put away for several years. It still amazes me how some of these guys can sleep easy in their beds, when you look at the kind of scams they try to pull.

I'm finding I can't sleep tonight, either. I go downstairs and join some of our administrative staff in the late-night coffee club. We've all had our roles to play in the build-up to this week, but tomorrow we will all be helpless as we just stand and watch. Tomorrow, for once, as far as The Club is concerned, it's all about the players and what happens on the pitch.

MID-APRIL

"We don't want to be the club who wins the cup and gets relegated in the same season. If you have to play away at Scunthorpe, nobody is going to be too impressed that you're the FA Cup holders."

The New CEO, April 15th

The thing about great events is that you don't realise they're going to be great until they finish, and you don't enjoy them whilst you're waiting for them to end. And then you look back, and suddenly it's all over. It was that way with the semi-final. For once I actually got to watch the game. When we play at home, as I've said, I'm forever troubleshooting, wandering around the ground, liaising with our security officials, gate-men, programme sellers, even the catering staff. All I hear is a roar, and then I turn around to wait for the action replay that never comes because we don't have that facility. But this was at a neutral ground, and the organisation was largely out of my hands – although that didn't stop the police asking me to come to their security camera vantage point, to see if I recognised any of our known troublemakers in the crowd. (I did, but I didn't say so. I just wanted to get back to my seat.)

Just when it was looking like a replay that nobody really wanted, The Club Captain came up for a corner and sent a rocket of a header into the top left-hand corner of the net. He looks back at our bench, stares straight at The FM and gives him a two-fingered sign. The fans think it's V for victory and go wild, but both The Club Captain and The FM know exactly what he meant. Notwithstanding it's the goal that will take us into the final, the relationship between them just went from bad to worse.

We've got to April, and the FA Cup Final is a good five weeks away. Before that we've some vital league games to play and win, in order to guarantee our survival in the top flight. Not that anybody seems to be much fussed about it, except for The Newcomer, The CEO, The New FD and The FM. The players seem to love the glory of being in the limelight, and don't seem averse to the extra cash that's going to be coming their way either. But, players being players, they haven't reread their playing contracts – if they had, then they would have discovered that, if they get relegated, there's a twenty-five percent reduction in their basic salaries. That's a bit unfair on them, because we'll get the 'parachute' money after relegation from the Premier League – so that for at least one season, we'll be better off playing in a lower division.

The players have all met to vote on which agent is going to be running the Cup Final pool. Surprise, surprise, they've appointed an agent who represents five of the players in the squad. This hasn't much impressed the rest of the team, who'd all been encouraged by their own agents to argue the case for their particular man. Half a dozen of them, including some of the leading players, have threatened not to co-operate, saying they don't like or trust The Pool Agent.

One of them claims The Pool Agent ripped him off in the past: The Pool Agent had found him a commercial opportunity, even though he didn't actually act for him; the player had agreed to do it and pay a commission of ten percent, even though he thought the fee was on the low side for what he was required to do. He spoke to some of the other players who were involved in this particular promotion, and discovered that they were getting more than him. So he decided to speak to the company directly. They told him they thought they were paying him exactly what the others were earning; in fact, what had happened was that The Pool Agent had creamed money off of both ends. He'd lied to the player about the fee and simply pocketed the difference, and then had the gall to charge him the commission on what he'd magnanimously left him.

The player who'd been wronged tried to explain that to the squad, but to no avail. The Pool Agent had his own players in his pocket. They all owed him money that he'd loaned to help pay off gambling debts, hire-purchase arrears, the odd pregnant girl, legal fees, etc, and he knew they were his forever, whatever he might do. He also knew that he could choose clubs for them when a transfer was in the offing, sending them wherever he would earn the biggest commission.

Meanwhile, there is nothing in the playing contracts of any of the dissenting players to say they have to co-operate with the pool. I've never heard anything like this before, in all my years in the game. The way a pool works is that nobody gives any interviews or accepts any commercial opportunities (other than from their own contracted sponsors) without the money going into the pool and being divided up according to the number of games players appear in on their way to Wembley. Eventually, the doomsday scenario of fragmentation was avoided by some last-minute diplomacy brokered by The New CEO. The players have now agreed to appoint a group of three agents to deal with all the income, and the original Pool Agent is acting as a spokesman but finalising nothing without the approval of the other two. So at least – unless they all go rogue – the players will get their proper entitlement. Oh, and they all need to sign the cheques. Nothing like a bit of mutual trust.

That's all going to hot up as we get nearer and nearer to Wembley. I know already that there are going to be problems, because I've heard what they're planning to charge for interviews and photo opportunities. The journos won't like that at all. They're a bit like some of the agents, in as far as they truly believe the players are their property to do with as they please. A few years ago, a Cup Final pool manager struck an exclusive deal with one of the leading tabloids which left the other papers, in particular its main rival, stranded and excluded. The rival tabloid was so incensed that it spent a sum exceeding that paid to the pool to dig up dirt about the team's players, and ran a series of stories in parallel with the exclusives, just to ruin the impact of the positive publicity. It's not for nothing that articles like that are called 'spoilers'.

I've been asked by The New CEO to monitor any potential conflicts with our own sponsors. It's always a problem when a player joins a club, particularly one that's high-profile, when he already has a sponsorship deal with the main competitor of his new club's kit sponsor. Obviously, we ensure all players wear official kit when they're on official duty, but that doesn't stop attempts at 'ambush marketing'. Players are allowed to wear boots of their own choice, and goalkeepers can use any gloves they like as these are clearly 'tools of the trade'. But if they want to promote any *other* company they have to be a bit inventive. You'll see a player roll down his socks as he comes off the pitch to reveal the make of his shin-guards. You'll see them wearing baseball caps of rival brands the minute they leave the dressing room and make their way towards their cars. As soon as they're a metre beyond the restrictive boundaries of the stadium, you'll see them holding a bottle of a particular drink brand.

What a player's sponsor really hates to see is the player on the front page of the club's brochure, promoting a brand for which he has not been paid a penny. (Although, if you were being uncharitable, you might argue that within his not insubstantial salary there's considerably more than a penny provided by the sponsor he's doing his damnedest to avoid promoting.) It's a little game within a game, although there are big bucks at stake. The standard Premier League contract has clauses inserted to protect the integrity of a club's main sponsor, but, as the final of a major trophy approaches, it gets harder and harder.

It's also hard to protect the tickets for the match. Each club has an allocation of thirty thousand. Our opponents have been to Wembley innumerable times, but the secretary there still tells me he could have sold five times that number. Even with our limited support, I'm inundated with ticket requests. Although we've enough to ensure all our regulars get at least one ticket, the real problem is what happens once the tickets get into the hands of the fans. I know I may have seemed a bit unkind to agents, players, directors and journalists, but the fans are no angels either – certainly not where a profit is concerned. The temptation to get up to a grand for a top-price ticket may just prove too much for them. Even an offer of five hundred quid from a tout who's going to make a hundred percent mark-up may be too hard to resist, when they know they can still see the match from the comfort of their homes.

The FA, the government, the police and the clubs themselves have all done their best to clamp down on the activities of ticket touts, but still they survive and make more than a decent living. Their tickets come from all different sources. Players are their main targets, but they also come club officials, other clubs, county authorities and, dare I say it, a few individuals at the FA, no doubt. Tickets are supposed to be used only by the individual they're issued to, and whoever goes through the turnstiles on the day must retain the stub to return to the FA, should they so request. But in practice it's an event that's almost impossible to police, and if there wasn't still a profit and a living in it, touts would long since have ceased to exist.

The thing about touts is that nobody I've ever met in football has a good word to say about them, yet everybody seems to have the numbers of the leading touts and is willing to use them when they're desperate. Just like agents and journalists, touts have one or two players at all the bigger clubs who 'belong' to them – by which I mean that, as their contacts, they not only supply tickets to them, but also source them from other players, particularly younger squad members who don't want to do anything that might upset the senior professionals.

Meanwhile, there's a huge difference between the well-known touts who have a regular clientele and regular suppliers, and the amateurs who may simply get a ticket or two and offer it for resale on the internet. Sell to one of the latter, and anyone in the game is likely to find himself in big trouble. Sell to one of the pros and, incredibly enough, you're pretty safe, as vested interests always keep them going. They know that their customers either want the tickets for themselves or an important client, and the odds of *them* selling them on for profit are pretty remote.

Some of the touts from the past were huge, legendary characters: Johnny-the-Stick, or Stan 'the Man' Flashman, for example. Johnny was a huge Spurs fan who'd been struck down with polio when very young, and only walked with the aid of a stick. If you wanted a ticket for anything from the Cup Final and the Derby to Wimbledon, or even garden parties at Buckingham Palace, then Johnny was your man. His greatest wish was to be buried in the Spurs shirt of his hero, Jimmy Greaves, but his death came to pass rather earlier than anticipated. A rival tout was told by a Sunday newspaper that they were going to write an exposé of him. The rival then cut a deal with the paper to dish the dirt on Johnny, provided they left him alone. Not too long after the article was published, Johnny had a fatal heart attack. The rival had the gall to visit the house of mourning, and was promptly thrown out on the pavement. Satisfying perhaps, but it didn't bring Johnny back to his loved ones. Stan Flashman also died a tragic death from cancer, his wealth and his clients all gone after the tax man bullied him to the grave.

Today's touts are far more sophisticated, often acting behind the façade of a seemingly respectable ticket agency, or as a parallel business to something far more reputable. The fact is, any player, club or association official revealed to have sold their ticket allocations in whole or part to a tout do run a serious risk nowadays. There are random checks on who is actually using the ticket and, if caught, the culprits face substantial fines, bans from receiving future tickets and, for more serious cases, even a suspension or ban from the game.

Yet, as far as the players are concerned, all the money they earn is not likely to stop them selling their allocation, if they think they can make a sizeable profit. Not all of them, of course. Many of the good guys ensure that parents, wives, brothers, sisters, grandparents and close friends get to see the match, and bear all the costs of it themselves. They'll even buy extra tickets from their team-mates, just to ensure that all those close to them can share their big day.

But for us, two more league defeats have thrown a damper over the event. We've still five matches to play, which includes games in hand against everybody else down at the foot of the table. We've sat around and run through all the mathematical permutations, leading to a conviction that we must get nine points to be safe. Three wins, or two wins and three draws. All looks easy on paper, but when the opposition players we've analysed and found wanting suddenly take on flesh and blood and leap off The FM's flip-charts, onto the pitch, it's a totally different proposition. Football is played in the head just as much as with the feet, and the media is making a big fuss about the possibility of us winning the cup and being relegated in the same season. We've not won since the semi-final, and The FM has almost got to the stage of banning newspapers from the team coach and dressing rooms; it's as if the players are starting to believe everything negative being written about them.

There's one particular journalist who has a real down on The Club. He seems to hate The FM, The Newcomer and The CEO with an equal amount of bile. In fact, I know he was a close friend of The Chairman and was always given a seat in the directors' box, with a free meal and wine beforehand. With the arrival of The Newcomer all this stopped, and the change in the tone of his articles was extraordinary. Unsurprisingly, I was ordered to pronounce him *persona non grata* at the stadium, which was a signal for even more poison to flow from his pen.

Fair criticism is acceptable. Everybody in football has to accept that (with the possible exception of one dinosaur manager who simply refuses to speak to anybody who dares disagree with him), but this bloke went beyond the pale. He was always careful to stay just on the safe side of defamatory, but most people who read his articles were in no doubt as to exactly how he felt, what he really meant and wanted to say. I don't see why people should expect to be treated with respect in football if they're clearly not football people themselves. And as for journalists who use their column inches just to wage private vendettas – well, least said, soonest mended.

There's another cloud on the horizon too. An investigative journalist from the so-called quality papers has been sniffing around. He's a bit more intelligent than many of the others, and it seems he's got wind of some problems brewing for The Newcomer back in his homeland. There are all sorts of rumours around as to how he made his money. Whatever the truth of it, there's no doubting he's had some powerful past benefactors and patrons. One of those has just died in somewhat mysterious circumstances and it seems that his replacement may well have another agenda. Nothing as yet has brought it all out into the open, but in my position you get to sense where the weathercock is pointing, even before the wind begins to blow.

MAY

"We may have the FA Cup Final to look forward to, but today's match really IS our cup final."

The Club Captain on the eve of the last Premiership game of the season, which The Club has to win in order to have a chance of staying up, May 3rd

This is it. The big one. It's a phrase we use all the time in football, but this time it really does apply. It's all down to the last game. Unbelievable, as one TV pundit says when he means 'mildly exciting'. After everything that's gone on since last August, it's now down to just ninety minutes of football. Ninety minutes to decide whether we stay up or fall back down to the Championship, with the prospect of trips to places like Plymouth, Burnley and Barnsley.

Everybody has been making brave speeches (except The Newcomer, who rarely reveals his frankly scary command of English unless absolutely necessary). Even The FM seems to have learned enough English to give interviews without the help of an interpreter, as he knows that his whole reputation, and maybe his future in English football, will be judged on the result of this one match. Yes, we have the FA Cup Final to look forward to, but if we lose today and get relegated then our Wembley appearance will just become a footnote in this season's history.

It's not helped our situation that we have to travel away – but then, we are playing a team who, though absolutely safe, are only six points and two places above us. The situation from our perspective is this: if we win, we stay up; if we draw, and the team below us either draws or loses, we still stay up; if they win and we either draw or lose, then we're down and out.

Our friends in the press have gone as far as suggesting that, as our opponents have nothing to play for, they may go easy on us. There's also a *hint* of a suggestion, no more, from our most hostile critic that The Newcomer's money has made absolutely sure that the result goes our way. I very much doubt that. In theory, I suppose one or two of the opposition could have been got at, but that still leaves the rest of the team doing their best, and unless their manager is also in The Newcomer's pocket he's likely to substitute any of his players who are playing like a nightmare, whether purposely or not.

I'm not saying it's impossible to fix a match in England, and I'm not saying that matches haven't been fixed in the past. Players have all sorts of problems, and sometimes the only way out when a player is in heavy debt to a bookmaker or loan shark is to take a bung and rig a result. But it's still difficult to guarantee the desired result. If the keeper has been paid to make a mistake, then what happens if his team-mate the striker plays a blinder and gets a hat-trick? Or vice-versa? A striker can miss all the chances he wants, but he can't score for the opposition if his goalkeeper is playing out of his skin. Well, I suppose he can put it through his own net, but it just might be a bit obvious. A goalless draw is unlikely to be a result upon which big money has been wagered. A bought-off combination of a striker, central defender and keeper may just about work, but it's likely to prove expensive and also relies upon all three keeping their mouths shut forever. No guarantee of that when a career is over, and an ex-player is looking for one more payday by selling his exclusive story to a tabloid.

We've heard this year about one player in England in rehab, who seems to have admitted to taking 50k to fix a match and pay off a couple of team-mates. But as I say, it's not endemic over here. Overseas it's an entirely different matter. A couple of English players ending their careers in a small European country were told before a match against local rivals that they shouldn't be trying too hard, as an 'understanding' had been reached with the opposition. They couldn't believe what they'd just heard, deciding it was either a joke or, if it wasn't, then they were going to ignore the instructions and do their best. They each scored a goal to put the team two-up within the first half-hour, and both were avoiding any eye contact with the bench, where the coach had a face as black as thunder. Suddenly, one of them felt a sharp blow to the back of his head and realised he'd been head-butted – by a member of his own team. They then saw an extraordinary penalty given away by a deliberate handball from one of their own defenders, and off they went at halftime, two-one up, with the fans chanting their names, as they'd clearly been the stars of the first half.

They began to walk along the corridor that led to their dressing room, when they suddenly found themselves blindfolded from behind and pushed into a side-room little bigger than a broom cupboard. Each received a series of punches to their bodies, with a warning in English:

"Now, maybe you don't play so well in the second half.

And if you do then at fulltime, instead of a fist in your stomach, it will be a knife."

The English lads were tough guys from the North of England, and still had their pride.

"Are we going to let these foreign cunts tell us what to do?" one said to the other.

The reply was instantaneous. "No fucking way."

They came out and one immediately laid on a pass for the other, to make the score three-one. The crowd went crazy, and then went even crazier when they were both substituted. The team eventually lost four-three, but the two Englishmen were not there to see it. They had left the stadium without changing, going back to their hotel and packing for the first plane back home. They never got paid, because the club claimed they'd broken their contracts, but at least no part of their respective anatomies was broken.

Stories like that, though maybe not so extreme, are not unusual when English players go to less sophisticated foreign countries. I know of one player who went out to the Far East with all sorts of promises of a huge salary and a great lifestyle. When he arrived, he found he'd be living in a grey, communist-style, high-rise block of flats, and the financial package that induced him to go was, in reality, less than half that amount. He decided very quickly this was not for him, and asked for his return ticket – only to be told that, unless he stayed a week to give the club a chance to persuade him to sign, then not only would he have to pay his own fare home, but the club would expect him to reimburse them for his outward fare too.

Faced with that prospect he reluctantly decided to stay for the week, during which he was subject to constant pressure to sign, to a point where it became a cross between water-torture and brainwashing. At all times of the night they'd phone him at his hotel, and even threatened to tell his wife he'd been regularly entertaining hookers. He stood up to them and saw the week out. But when they repeated their demand that he pay to get himself back home, he actually threatened them with physical violence. The people of that country are not huge in stature, and this player was pretty large. So taken aback were they that they helped him pack, took him to the airport and virtually escorted him onto the plane.

Yet another player sneaked out of his Mediterranean hotel, got into his car and drove like mad for the border, just to escape the persistent efforts of officials to make him sign for a team for which he really didn't want to play.

These horror stories are endless. A dream move to a Middle Eastern state with promises of a huge, tax-free salary crumbled into the sands of the desert when the player wasn't paid anything at all. Mind you, neither was his agent nor, astonishingly, the club which had sold him. The club and the player went to FIFA, the world governing body of football, and, under threat of international bans for the club, they eventually did receive their monies. The agent, on the other hand, was left to bring a claim through the FIFA arbitration system, which they somehow managed to lose for him on a technicality. No more sympathy for agents at FIFA than anywhere else in the footballing world, I fear. And now they've just told them they have to re-qualify with fresh exams every five years. Can you imagine that happening to lawyers or doctors?

I'm not xenophobic and, believe me, at this time I'm not even thinking of what might be happening in the transfer market before the start of next season. But, somehow, transfers that just involve English players moving from one English club to another, with only English agents representing the clubs or the players, are much simpler and more transparent. Wherever there's a foreign element there's always a middleman who doesn't have a contract with anybody, yet inevitably seems to earn more money out of the deal than any of the other negotiating parties. I heard of one deal at the end of the last transfer window that involved five agents; the player had never met any of them before they all descended on his Premier League club. So much for the new FA agents' regulations.

As you can see, my mind has been wandering out to football's furthest reaches, all to avoid the awful thought that we might lose this game and go back out into the wilderness. The FM has made some difficult decisions over selection. He's decided that one of our African midfielders (the one who came back late from the African Nations) is going to be on the bench. Apart from his international absences and suspensions, this player has still started every match. He's so unhappy with the decision that he's left the team hotel in a huff, without telling anybody where he's gone. The FM now has a problem: does he present the team sheet to the referee with the African's name on it, and risk starting the match with only four substitutes – or does he promote one of the youngsters and hope he's not needed? Inevitably, the press have got hold of the story, presumably via a tip-off from one of the hotel staff, and I'm told they're looking for our missing midfielder as hard as our management. If they find him in bed with some young lady then their day will be made, but for us, before a match of this magnitude, it's hardly the ideal build-up.

The FM decided to have everybody eat breakfast together, but a few of the lads have decided to have a lie-in, or have maybe just overslept. It never ceases to amaze me how unfazed some players can be. But then I've also known some who have to visit the loo half a dozen times before a match, and others who actually make themselves physically sick. At least one player took diuretics before a game because he thought they made him lighter and speedier, whereas, in reality, by the middle of the second half his strength was fading fast.

Then there are the superstitious. Some of them will only come out of the tunnel in a certain order, and problems can arise when more than one player has the same superstition. Two players in the same team were in such a dispute about their personal superstitions that they held up the team's entry onto the pitch, until the referee had to sort it out. They'd both wanted to run out of the tunnel last, and neither would give way. Eventually, out they came, sheepishly side by side, and as their team lost both were convinced it was all because they'd not been able to follow their normal custom.

Some players always put one boot on before the other. Others have lucky boots which they have repaired until they're falling to pieces and beyond repair. One player had to wait until all the rest of the team had finished their preparations. Then they'd say as a chorus, "We're not doing anything more. We're all ready," at which point he'd remove his false teeth.

It's not just players who have their foibles in this respect. Managers wear the same suit for the whole of a cup run, and seem surprised when the magic wears off and they lose in the final. A chairman refused to cut his hair for an entire season, until his team were finally promoted. Another chairman regarded one particular fan as a lucky mascot, and kept a thank-you note she'd sent him on the office window ledge all by itself, until the club he chaired had finally achieved promotion. Even when the fan couldn't get to games he was insistent she watched them on television, convinced she had some magical powers.

Fans are equally superstitious. They have the same pre-match routines. Same cup for tea in the morning. Same stop-off on the way to a match. Same scarf they wore at a particular match where their team won a memorable victory. They know it's impossible for their side to win every game, but somehow they find an excuse as to why the magic doesn't work on every particular occasion.

Halftime and it's nil-nil. The only other team who can overtake us are a goal down. It's all going well. Then there's a rumbling amongst our fans, nearly all of whom have radios tuned to commentaries on the other match. Our rivals have equalised. Now a goal at either game can mean the difference between triumph and disaster. Twenty minutes to go, and we're still staying up. That's what our travelling fans are singing, at least. Then they stop singing. I can see from a television monitor showing Sky that our rivals have a penalty. There's a great sound of anguish from thousands of our fans, and taunting from the home supporters which suggests we'll never play there again. There's a surreal atmosphere in the stadium as our players pass the ball around with all the urgency of a pre-season friendly. We wait. There's a huge groan as we hear the penalty has been converted. They are winning, we are drawing, and if it stays that way then we're going down. The FM makes some frantic gestures to his players. They look at him as if he's lost his mind, and then The Club Captain cups his hand to his ear and gets the message loud and clear from The Assistant Manager. Unless we score, then we're out of the Premiership.

The home fans are driving the message home, not realising it's spurring our players on. "Going down, going down!" they're chanting, accompanied by much hand waving and shouts of "Cheerio!" The Newcomer has a face like thunder. I sense that in his country he'd have his own way of dealing with this sort of failure.

Before the seconds were dragging along, now they're flying by. Five minutes, four minutes . . . the home team penalty area is like the Alamo, as our players throw themselves forward in wave after wave of attack. Three minutes, two minutes . . . a scramble off the line, a breakaway attack for them rebuffed and turned into another onslaught from us. One minute . . . the third official is lifting up his sign to indicate the number of added minutes. We hold our breath. How long have we got? We are dying men, grasping at the last moments of life. I've been involved in football for many years, but I've never experienced anything like this before. It only takes a couple of seconds to score a goal, I keep telling myself. And then there is a goal. But not from us. And certainly not what we expected . . .

MID-MAY

*"If this Club were to win today then we'll
have achieved a double this season beyond our
wildest dreams."*

The FM in a BBC interview on the morning of the
Cup Final, May 17th

Even I, who regard myself as the most cynical of individuals, can't believe that we're here at Wembley. And not only here, but with our Premiership future assured for next season. That last-minute own-goal by our rivals was a dramatic end to a dramatic season. Our critics have called us lucky, have said it's a disgrace that we've stayed up, whilst a club which allegedly plays 'nice' football and has a long tradition in the top flight has gone down. But you know what? That's football.

Nobody thought Wimbledon would win the FA Cup, or stay so long in the upper echelons of the league. The same applied to Wigan. Yet eventually they got used to it – just as we got used (for a few seasons at least) to seeing Nottingham Forest struggling to get out of League One, or so-called 'big clubs' like Sheffield Wednesday without a prayer of an early return to the Premiership. That was always our big fear, that once we got relegated we'd never get back. It would have been hard to envisage The Newcomer sticking with The Club at that level, and without his money and backing I could see us sliding right back to where we started, or even going out of business. Instead, we have all the income from the FA Cup, win or lose, guaranteed Premiership income from TV etc for next year, and a not insubstantial sum just for staying up. And all of this without the benefit of however many millions The Newcomer will toss into the pot in the close season.

I've heard no more about potential exposure of The Newcomer's domestic problems, so maybe the threat will go away. Over the years I've learned there's no point worrying about things you can do nothing about. There have also been a few issues over bonuses for the final as, despite what's in the players' contracts, they've banded together and suggested it's not enough. I've had to tell them that the FA won't let us change their contracts at this late stage of the season. That's a fact. We can give them all new contracts – but if we did that, they'd have to be for at least a year longer than the current versions. It's only in the close season that you can renegotiate a contract without extending it by that minimum period. The New CEO had them all in, one by one, and gave them various promises as to what they can expect next year. They seem to have gone away reasonably happy. Unlike me, they don't know that there's no such thing as a promise in football.

It's nice to know we're not the only club who has to deal with undesirables. I told you about questionable deals between directors and agents right at the start of this season, and now I'm hearing more of the same. The club secretary of our opponents and I had a long meeting over all the arrangements for the match. Afterwards, we shared a well-earned drink and he told me an amazing story of what happened at his club in last summer's transfer window.

One of their players was strapped for cash and his agent was renegotiating his contract. The club had offered him a huge rise, from about 6k a week to nearly 40k because, as far as they were concerned, he'd become a really hot property and they wanted to keep him. His agent had thought he was doing the lad a favour, and hadn't yet told him just what a great deal was on the table in case he spent it before he actually got it. Meanwhile, the club director who dealt with new contracts telephoned an agent with whom he was in cahoots and tipped him off about the deal, to enable him to muscle in.

This agent then phoned the player and turned his head completely, by telling him he had three huge clubs interested and that he shouldn't sign anything. He even produced some faxes (forged!) from all of the clubs. The player dumped his old agent, telling the club that he was looking after himself and he wasn't signing. Things dragged along until 31st August, the last day of the transfer window, when the player was becoming increasingly desperate.

At that point his 'new agent', with whom he'd never signed, told him at the last minute that the three clubs had cooled off, and that he ought to re-sign with his existing club. He also told him the offer on the table was in the region of 20k per week – exactly half of what had been on offer to his old agent, of which he'd never been aware. Being on only 6k a week, with nothing else in the offing, he took the chance to more than double his money and signed again with his present club. At that point, the director told the board how many millions he'd saved the club over the period of the contract, and convinced them it justified paying the 'new agent' a cool million-pound fee for *acting for the club*. He'd technically never acted for the player, skating along the parameters of the new FA regulations. But, having happily banked the money at the expense of the player, he promptly shared his ill-gotten gains with the director who'd brought him into the deal in the first place. The secretary shook his head. He knew all about it, yet had no proof. Just like me he wanted to keep his job, so he'd do nothing about it. The world would continue to turn.

That's not the only time I've heard of a director working the system with an agent. One player's new agent worked very hard to find him a new club. He came up with some half a dozen options, and then the current club came up with an improved offer which was very attractive. The agent was flying back from abroad to do the deal; having changed planes in Europe, he called his player to make arrangements to meet him at the club, only to be told that he'd been advised by a director that the offer was only on the table if he used one particular agent – in fact, the same agent he'd previously left to join his new agent. Everybody knew the old agent would be sharing his commission with the director, but nobody could prove it. That's the way of things in this beautiful game of ours. There's never any proof positive. Only rumour. But these rumours are so prevalent, and you hear the same stories from so many different sources, that you can't help but believe sometimes.

Whatever the failings of The Newcomer, there's no way he or any other board member would be pulling such strokes at The Club. The directors would be too scared, and as for any senior members of staff, well, they'd be terrified. I hate to think what he might do if he found out anybody had been trying to cheat him.

Now that we're staying up, I suppose we'll have the usual merry-go-round of players coming and going in the close season. But right now our only focus is the FA Cup. It's a nice, bright day for the final, which puts me in mind of the cup tie that never was: A London team had to fly up to the Northwest for a replay. The weather in London was appalling, but it hadn't travelled north so it was perfectly clear and playable up there. The coach driver took the team to the airport in a blizzard, and a few of the players, mindful of the Munich disaster, said there was no way they were flying. The manager told the driver to slow down and go around the block a few times, until he was satisfied they'd missed their flight. The television cameras showed a clear pitch at the northern ground, with their commentators asking the obvious question, "Where's the team?"

For my part in the cup final, I'd been instructed to do all the things that might be deemed lucky. Book into the hotel where last year's winners had stayed; ensure they got the same breakfasts they ate before the semi-final; even arrange for the same players to room together. And I did all that, not because I believe in luck, or share their superstition, but because it's easier to do what I'm told than to argue the illogicality of it all.

As it transpired, it was all pretty much a waste of time. Our players just froze on the day. It happens.

The occasion got to them from the first minute, when our striker went clean through and blazed one over the bar. Their fans (who somehow wildly outnumbered ours) loved that. From that moment on, they jeered him every time he touched the ball. Maybe they'd have done that anyway, but the fact was that, because of that miss, he actually heard them. He heard them because he was listening for it, and they weren't about to disappoint him. Fans can be not only cruel but irrational. I've been at matches where a home player has been sent off after committing the most terrible foul, nothing but a red card could possibly have been the outcome. Yet, when the visiting player he's fouled has limped back onto the field, he's been subjected to wholesale abuse for the rest of the match, just because he hadn't had his leg broken. That, presumably, might have justified the sending off.

They scored just before halftime, got another in ten minutes into the second half, and, when they scored their third fifteen minutes before the end, we were into damage limitation. The FM rang the changes, brought on all three subs, but to no avail. In ninety minutes we didn't have a shot on target, and the best we achieved was to get two corners. You could see that the players just wanted to get off the pitch, wanted the season to end, and didn't even want to go up for their losers' medals. The FM made them run to the fans, all of whom did their best to lift them up, though I think quite a few of them had left before the end. They, at least, had the option.

Losing didn't mean that we missed out on a post-match party. Everybody was booked into the same hotel for the weekend. It was a wild night, though still not as wild as a few of which I'd heard. One club had an army training camp nearby, and the lads always invited some of the fellows in with their partners. One player was legless and kept asking to be taken to the toilet. The other players wound him up and told him he *was* in the toilet, at which point he unzipped his flies and urinated all over the dress of a soldier's wife. After revenge had been exacted, as you can well imagine, he wasn't able to train for a good few days.

Our boys carried on 'celebrating' – in so far as you celebrate losing a cup final – until the small hours of the

FOOTBALL BABYLON

morning. That was when two of them set fire to the curtains, and another put out a cigar on the lid of an expensive piano by pouring a whole jug of water over it. We decided enough was enough, and put them to bed. They'd done their best. Only their best wasn't good enough on the day. And, in football, it's always what happens on the day that counts, because you don't often get the same chance tomorrow.

Now all that was left was the open-top tour of the town that had been arranged, win, lose or draw. And then it really was the end of the season. In an odd way I was sorry it was over. I'd been to clubs I'd never dreamed I'd visit in an official capacity. I'd met people who'd just been legendary names to me, and all too often I'd found them wanting in every way imaginable. We'd stayed up against all the odds, and played in a Wembley final. If you'd told me that would happen to Thamesmead City all those years ago, when I started here, I'd have laughed in your face. Now I realise that, in football, nothing is impossible if you dream the dream.

Only sometimes that dream can so easily become a nightmare, as we were to discover all too soon.

JUNE

*"My client is entirely innocent of these charges,
which he has instructed me to defend most strenuously
on his behalf. There have been no financial
improprieties in his life, nor at The Club which has
become so very close to his heart."*

The Newcomer's solicitor, after the arrest of his client
in a dawn raid, June 2nd

L ike most disasters, it happened when you least expected it.
June is always a quiet time at a football club. Players and
staff alike try to grab their holidays then, between the season's
end and the start of pre-season training and friendly matches.
The gap seems to get shorter and shorter every year, what with
play-offs and the like, but if you go to the usual spots you're
fairly certain to meet up with footballers in one shape or
another. Places like Dubai, the better parts of Spain, the
Caribbean and Florida attract the player with a family, or
those who have got married at the end of a season and are
taking their opportunity for a honeymoon. The older, more
settled players tend to go anywhere there is guaranteed sun,
good hotels and a nice beach for the kids. They are not the
types to be wandering around ancient monuments with guide
books. Tenerife and Magaluf are magnets for the gangs of
single players who go away as a group to have a good time,
and forget the discipline they've endured for the last ten or
eleven months. Occasionally you might get the player with a

wife (or more likely just a girlfriend) being allowed to join his single team-mates.

It's people like me, as The Club Secretary, who tend to stick around. There's so much tidying up to do at season's end. I have to ensure we get in all our income from the Cup Final; oversee the season ticket sales; liaise with our sponsors for the forthcoming season; and ensure we've got all our new playing contracts ready for players to sign, effective from the beginning of July. It's amazing to think that, when we were coming up through the lower leagues, I did most of that myself, but even though we now have different departments dealing with different aspects, at the end of the day it still seems to fall to me to be the person who knows what's going on, and to report back to The New CEO.

I just wasn't ready for the police invasion when they turned up with their warrants. They'd already arrested The Newcomer in a dawn raid, with the accompaniment of a lot of press photographers who always seem to get tipped off about this sort of thing. I'd got in early to my office, the habit of an early start during the season being a hard one to break. I find that if I don't do what I need to do before nine in the morning, I get no peace or quiet after that.

They were very polite to me, the police, just wanted to know where we kept all the files on our player transactions and carried out box-load after box-load – as well as the computers that were used by The Newcomer, The New CEO and The New FD.

At exactly the same time, the investigative journalist who'd been sniffing around months ago arrived, and clearly knew exactly what was going on. He seemed annoyed that he'd not been able to break his exclusive before all this blew up, and even more annoyed that he might have to wait until the police investigation was over to write his full story. But that didn't stop him asking me question after question. Even when I knew the answers I said very little, just using the exchange to try to find out exactly what was going on.

It seems the police had arrested The Newcomer on suspicion of money laundering and various tax offences, and there were a few agents in custody as well, not to mention a few others who wouldn't be sleeping easy until investigations were complete. It also seems The Newcomer is likely to be charged, and the police will be opposing bail as they see him as a flight risk. It also seems there are those back in his own country who would be very keen to meet his plane, should he actually be deported.

(Not that the police are whiter than white when it comes to football. One match between rival police teams ended in a twenty-man brawl, with several officers facing charges ranging from causing an affray to ABH and GBH. The trial left the streets of the town clear for villains for weeks.)

Eventually the police left, the press decamped as they realised they were unlikely to get photos of anyone interesting, and just a few fans came to ask how this would affect The Club. I told them I thought we'd be around for a while to come, and that seemed to satisfy them.

But the fans' notice board and their blogs make interesting reading. They never liked The Newcomer – unlike The Chairman, he never spoke to them, never consulted them, never arranged meetings to let them know what was going on. It all comes spilling out, all the xenophobic poison that was there all the time. We've stayed up because of his money, we've actually qualified for Europe because the cup winners were already in the Champions League, but none of that is good enough for them. None of it makes up for neither The FM nor The Newcomer being English. It's amazing. So many leading clubs with foreign owners and managers, so many teams that contain not one English player, and you realise that, at the first hint of failure, their fans are going to react exactly the same way as our bunch. Mind you, we've always had a pretty rightwing fan base here.

I just sit down quietly. I've first professional contracts to do for three of our youngsters who are coming up to eighteen. They signed off on the terms ages ago, but we've not been able to register them until they come of age. Technically they could have changed their minds, as a player can't sign professionally till he's actually eighteen, but once they sign something, even though they're underage, they tend to feel committed. I'm not quite sure what sort of club they'll be playing for though. In fact, if it all goes pear-shaped and we can no longer afford our highly-paid foreigners, then the kids may get a big surprise and find themselves playing first-team football.

Of course I've been asked to make a statement. The police seem satisfied that I've just been doing my job, that I neither saw nor heard anything that I should have reported, and that any nefarious dealings would occur outside the ambit of my particular world. Everybody else seems to be pointing fingers at each other, dishing as much dirt as they can in the hope it will get them out of trouble – or maybe earn them a reduced sentence. Loyalty in football is a rare commodity.

I remember from years ago a story about a rabble-rousing manager and one of his players, who was so close to him as to be described as a friend. The club, which was based up north, played a Saturday game in London. The manager decided to stay on for some R&R, and told the player he'd be back by Monday. But when the players assembled for training after the weekend there was no sign of him. His wife, who'd just had a baby, was frantic as she had heard nothing from him either. She called the player.

"Can you come over and try to track him down? You know where he's most likely to be."

The player certainly had a good idea, and made a round of phone calls to the manager's favourite London watering holes. He called them one by one and asked if the manager was there. The answer was always a firm, "No," often followed by the phone being slammed down.

The wife asked the player to stay over, and to pretend it was a semi-permanent arrangement. The player went off to training on Tuesday, where he was asked, "Where's the gaffer?"

"Bad dose of flu," he replied.

The assistant manager asked when his boss was likely to reappear.

"I've no idea. He's really ill."

On Tuesday night the player started calling again. He even called a model who'd secretly been the manager's girlfriend, but she denied all knowledge of his whereabouts. On the Wednesday the player dutifully went into training again to attend what was the normal practice match. Club officials suggested they should send in the club doctor to look at the manager, at which point the player had to think quickly.

"I don't think that's a very good idea. It's really catching and he doesn't want it spreading to the rest of the squad."

"But you've not caught it," somebody pointed out.

"Yeah, but I've been around him for so long that I reckon I'm immune," said the player, his lies becoming ever wilder.

On Thursday they asked what the manager's team selection was going to be for the weekend's forthcoming match. By now, the player was so into the role of accomplished liar that he just said, "Oh, he says the same as last week."

"What, the team we started with or the team we finished with?" the assistant manager asked.

"The one we started with," the player replied, by now living in a parallel universe.

The chairman was becoming increasingly suspicious, and said that he intended visiting the manager that afternoon. The player raced back to get there first, and he and the wife decided to bring the baby into play. When the chairman rang the doorbell they opened the door a fraction on a chain. The wife got the baby screaming to the point that the chairman left, but insisted on speaking to the manager's doctor, who had allegedly been treating him. Panic set in again for the player and the manager's wife but they called the doctor, who'd actually seen the manager and given him antibiotics, albeit six months earlier.

"Look," the player said, "you did see him six months ago, you did visit the house and you did give him antibiotics. All you need to do is to avoid any questions as to when it all took place."

When the chairman called, the doctor told him that doctor-patient confidentiality meant he couldn't tell him too much, but he did confirm he'd visited the manager's home, had found him to be ill and prescribed some drugs. The chairman didn't think to ask as to when all those events had taken place.

Finally, on Thursday night, the player realised he was going about tracing the missing manager the wrong way. So, instead of calling nightclubs and asking if he was there, he called and asked to speak to him, pretending he'd been told to call. He struck lucky on the second call.

"Look, it's fucking chaos here. I feel like the little Dutch boy with his finger in the dyke. You need to get back."

"All right," the manager said, "I've had my fingers in a few birds but not any dykes. I'll be back tomorrow. Can you meet me off the train with some fresh clothes and my wash things?"

The player obliged, and was shocked to see the manager still wearing the clothes he'd left him in on the previous Saturday, with a six-day growth of beard. The manager hugged the player in gratitude and told him he'd saved his life. The player took the manager to the training ground, where he showered, shaved, changed and emerged looking like a million dollars.

Everybody was in training, at which point the chairman issued an instruction saying that nobody was to leave the training ground. The manager then posted up the first team and the reserve team for the next day's game. To his astonishment, the player saw that not only was his name missing from the first team sheet, but he was fifth stand-by for the reserves. He was just about to argue with the manager when the chairman loomed up behind him, told him he was barred from the ground, the club would be giving him a free transfer and he'd never play for them again. The manager had given the chairman his version of events, and the player had not come out at all well. So much for gratitude and loyalty.

As it was then, so it is now. Every man for himself. And that includes me.

EPILOGUE

"The first rule of administration is never to make a loss. So the fact that we have so many parties interested in buying The Club is very encouraging. Whoever finally takes over will be starting with a clean sheet. Only The Club Secretary has been retained from the old regime."

The Administrator, after The Club had been deducted ten points for entering into administration and relegated, July 1st

So, after all that, it still ended in tears. And with us back in the Championship. I'm not even sure they're going to let us play in Europe.

They've charged The Newcomer with all sorts of things, and he's still on remand despite the efforts of his lawyers to get him bail. Almost the first thing he did from his prison cell was to demand repayment of all the monies he put into The Club, which, it appears, have been treated in our books as loans payable on demand. Actually I'm not sure which set of books contained them in that way, as it emerges that he and The New FD were running parallel sets of accounts. Different people saw different versions, depending on what was being asked of them.

At least he didn't do what the president of a European club did when things went pear-shaped, and run off to South America. That guy would sit on the beach in his swimming trunks, surrounded by a bevy of suntanned bimbos in bikinis, giving interviews which always contained a message to his son along the lines of, "Be strong my son, in what are difficult times for yourself and the club."

They were indeed difficult times for the son because, unlike his father, he'd stayed behind, been arrested and was watching Papa on a television in his prison cell.

The Newcomer's actions have been far more damaging than long-distance video broadcasts. Immediately, his loan repayment demand has made The Club insolvent. I've always thought that the FA should insist that money that goes into a club from a wealthy patron should be tied down within the club, and this pretty much proves me right. We were deducted ten points for going into administration, and that was enough to send us down.

A fire sale of our better players has been organised by The Administrator, and all we're going to be left with at the start of the season are the players nobody wants – and the kids. The players had to agree to postpone their wages for a couple of months at least, and the PFA is doing its best to negotiate on their behalf with The Administrator to get them paid by September. It's very hard for them, what with their families and mortgages, but this is not the first time The Administrator has been in charge of the rundown of a club. He's immune to any of their personal hard luck stories; he just wants to get in and out, take his fee and move on to the next disaster area.

A lot of the older players, most of who weren't playing under The FM, have decided to stick it out, as there's no guarantee of signing to a new club when there's up to a thousand players released from other clubs also trying to strike deals. At least, if they wait, there's a good chance they'll get all their wage arrears and maybe a new contract –

although it won't be anything like what they've been used to. Unless the club does pay all its players eventually, and all its other creditors, it won't be allowed to stay in the league. The Revenue are not happy about that, and are saying that, if the creditors do get paid, then they for their part are going to push The Club into liquidation. That would mean us having to start all over again, if we were lucky, from somewhere like the Ryman League.

Mind you, The Administrator thinks he's got somebody interested. Amazingly, it's The Chairman – wanting to come back for round two, and sensing a bargain. He reckons he can pick The Club up for about a tenth of what he got from The Newcomer, and still have the same assets he was always planning to maximise. He's been on the phone to me, asking if I'll stay on in my old role if he does go ahead. Of course, I've said yes.

The Administrator has also confirmed that I have a job as long as The Club is in administration under him. So, either way, it looks like I'll be here for the foreseeable future. You see, although I don't run this club – never have and never wanted to – nobody else knows exactly how it *does* run. Nobody else knows the nuts and bolts of the machinery, or even what machinery is there.

I look at my desk and tidy the papers on it. I like a nice clean desk. I look at my watch: eleven in the morning. It's time for coffee. I always have a coffee at this time. It's part of my schedule. I'm a creature of habit.

But then the phone rings. They're asking about season ticket sales for next season. They ask me who they're speaking to.

"Me? I'm nobody," I reply. "Just The Club Secretary."

Pennant Books

Titles That Pack A Punch

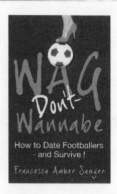

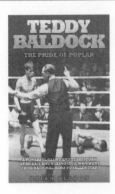

TEDDY BALDOCK

The Pride of Poplar

By Brian Belton

*The tears-and-glory story of an East End boxing idol
who went from national hero to fallen star. Includes many
previously unseen photographs.*

The name Teddy Baldock is enshrined in the record books as Britain's youngest ever world champion. Born in Poplar on May 20 1908, Baldock's brilliant boxing skills and colourful style saw him fight in world-famous venues like Madison Square Gardens, on the same card as James J. Braddock (the 'Cinderella Man').

Baldock's story is the stuff of legend; when he retired after a distinguished career of over 80 fights, he remained a hero both to the East End and to the British aristocracy. But in 1971, when he died penniless in an Essex infirmary, he didn't even have his own pyjamas. The man who thrilled packed boxing arenas with his noble art was completely forgotten . . . until now.

BIOGRAPHY/SPORT – HARDBACK – £16.99.
Available in all good bookshops. To order your copy direct send a cheque or postal order to: Pennant Books, PO Box 5675, London W1A 3FB. Postage is free within the UK.